It was late for June to be getting her first cup of coffee at Fuller's Café across the street; she usually stopped there on her way to the clinic at about seven. And it's possible that this delay of caffeine and sugar had had an effect on her disposition, for June was typically even-tempered.

"Full morning, huh, June?" George Fuller wanted to know. "Daniel Culley gets his rump full of shot and Chris Forrest is coming home, all divorced and everything. You still have a shine for him, June?"

"George, that was high school. Don't be silly."

"Why else would he come back to Grace Valley?"

"Well, George, gee… Why indeed? Could it be because he has family here? Or could it be because it's a good town in which to raise teenagers? Or maybe he just likes the place where he grew up?"

George grinned stupidly. "And what if he wants to get back together with you?"

"George, that was *high school!*" June said, exasperated.

"I wonder, does he know how cranky you've gotten over the years?"

"Robyn Carr provides readers [with] a powerful, thought-provoking work of contemporary fiction."
—*Midwest Book Review* on *Deep in the Valley*

ROBYN CARR

JUST OVER THE MOUNTAIN

MIRA®

ISBN 1-55166-940-4

JUST OVER THE MOUNTAIN

Visit us at www.mirabooks.com

Printed in U.S.A.

For Carla Neggers, with affection.

One

June Hudson had nerves of steel. She was thirty-seven years old, had been the town doctor in Grace Valley, California, for over ten years and the things she'd been called upon to do were not for the faint of heart. June had delivered a baby in the back of a pickup truck, kept a logger's severed limb on ice waiting for the emergency helicopter and had given calm, intelligent medical advice while looking down the barrel of a marijuana farmer's gun. Oh, she was feminine enough, but tough. Strong. Fearless.

Maybe not fearless, but she had certainly learned how to *appear* fearless. She had learned this in Omnipotent Physician 101.

Then came an early morning phone call bearing portentous news that caused her heart to race and her brow and upper lip to bead with sweat. All the strength bled out of her legs as she sank helplessly to the kitchen stool.

The conversation started out innocently enough with her friend Birdie reporting, "Chris is coming home with the boys." Chris was Birdie's son, the boys her twin fourteen-year-old grandsons.

"For a visit?" June half asked, half assumed.

"For good, he says. He and Nancy are divorcing."

June was silent. Shocked. Dismayed. *Divorcing?*

"He asked if you were still single," Birdie went on, a lilt to her chipper voice. A hopeful little lilt.

That was when June the Fearless began to tremble and quake. Chris was an old boyfriend. In fact, her first love. Also her first and most terrible broken heart. Chris Forrest was the man June always vowed she would tie up and torture for the agony he had brought to her youth.

The only son of Birdie and Judge Forrest, Chris had lived in southern California for eighteen or so years, married to another high-school friend—or rival—Nancy Cruise. He had only returned to Grace Valley for visits a few times; his parents enjoyed their trips to his home in San Diego. During his rare appearances, June did her best to avoid him. When she did happen upon him, she was as cool as a cucumber, aloof and detached. Her posture and expression said that bygones were bygones, that she rarely even thought about him.

It was partly true. She didn't spend a great deal of time mooning over a twenty-year-old romance gone awry. On the other hand, whenever she saw him, she was instantly reminded of two things: right after high school he had dumped her for Nancy without explanation or apology, and his boyish good looks had not deserted him. She hated him on both counts.

And now, divorced, he wondered if she was available? Hah! In your dreams, Chris Forrest, she thought with the long-lasting venom of a lover scorned.

She made a little small talk with Birdie, who was quite naturally excited by this turn of events. After hanging up the phone June remained on the kitchen stool, dazed, her thoughts concentrated mainly on planning Chris's slow death. Then the phone rang again.

"Chris Forrest is moving back to Grace Valley," her father, Elmer, reported.

"Really?" she faked. "Birdie and Judge must be delighted."

"Seems he split with Nancy and has custody of his kids, which I suppose makes sense, them being boys and all."

"How nice."

"Divorced," Elmer clarified.

"I didn't mean that part was nice," June said. "Him coming back here with sons. That's nice. Especially for Birdie and Judge."

"Does that put a little flush in your cheeks?" Elmer wanted to know. "Him being single again?"

She felt her cheeks, which were aflame, but not with the heat of passion. Could her father actually imagine she'd welcome the lout back into her arms? "Certainly not. That was a childhood thing. I've been over that for a couple of decades now."

"That so?" Elmer wanted to know. "Meat loaf tonight at your place?"

"Dad? Did you happen to hear when they're coming back?"

"I believe Judge said right away, as Chris wants

to get his boys signed up for school. So...meat loaf?
It's Tuesday again already."

"Right away?" She absently touched her hair, still
damp from the shower. She'd never been good at
things like hair. She could get an inflamed appendix
out in no time and leave a scar that would be the
envy of a plastic surgeon, but her dark blond, shoul-
der-length hair—or dishwater blond, as her mother
used to call it—was beyond her understanding.

Nancy had always had great hair: thick, richly
brown, long, shiny.

June looked at her hands. Doctor's hands. Short
nails, pink knuckles from scrubbing them dozens of
times a day, and...what was that? An *age* spot?

She had heard that Chris, Nancy and their boys
belonged to a country club.

"I'll see you here at about six, Dad."

"You okay, June? You sound awfully tired. You
go out on calls last night?"

She heard a familiar alarm from her bedroom when
her pager, set to vibrate, began dancing around on top
of the bedside stand. Grrrr. With the cordless phone
at her ear, she dashed to get it. "No, I wasn't called
out at all. It was a quiet night. Oops, gotta go, Dad.
I've got a page. See you later?"

"Later," he agreed.

The pager revealed the number for the police department, with a 911 attached to indicate an emergency. Chris Forrest disappeared as June went into a
different mind-set and dialed. "June here," she said.

Deputy Ricky Rios had paged her. "Chief Toopeek

responded to a call about a shooting at the Culley stables, June. Said he needs you out there as soon as possible.''

''Is Tom calling for the paramedics or a helicopter?'' she asked while slipping on her shoes.

''He just asked for you,'' Ricky said.

June grabbed her bag and a clip for her damp hair, whistled for her collie, Sadie, and was out the door in under fifteen seconds. She was on call, a service she shared with John Stone, the other Grace Valley physician, and therefore drove the town's new ambulance. It was so new that it still intimidated her, and though she turned on the lights and siren, she didn't drive any faster than usual. It was early morning; she didn't want to hit an animal or round a curve in the road and slam into slow-moving farm equipment.

Even though June now had a radio at her disposal, she didn't use it to contact Tom Toopeek to ask about the shooting, because many of the citizens in Grace Valley also had radios. It was like a big party line. Of course, with the way everyone minded everyone else's business in the town, she might as well get on the radio and give them a heads up. They'd have all the details by lunchtime anyway.

Daniel and Blythe Culley lived in a medium-size, ordinary ranch house on acreage large enough to support two stables that were by no means ordinary, five corrals, and still provide plentiful grazing land at the foothills of the Coast Ranges mountains. Horse people from Kentucky, they had started out small but a

decade or so back they'd had great success with a
stallion racing in San Francisco and San Diego, and
the reputation of the stable had soared. Boarders,
breeders, trainers and sometimes racers, they employed as many as twenty hands, depending on how
many horses they had in residence. Clients came from
everywhere and the Culleys were kept busy year-
round.

June didn't speculate much on what might have
happened. Nearly everyone in the valley had guns,
especially if they lived in the country and had to contend with wildlife. One of the hands might have had
a mishap or, less likely, a disagreement that led to a
showdown. Rushing to the stables, she thought ab-
stractedly about the Culleys and the kind of people
they were—salt of the earth. It came to mind how
happy and devoted a couple they had always been.
Quiet, but friendly and helpful. They kept to themselves, since building up a stable of some repute required backbreaking commitment. Farmers, ranchers,
vintners, loggers and the like worked from dawn to
dusk, slept hard and worked more. A strong partner-
ship, a strong marriage, like what the Culleys had,
was required. June thought it such a pity that they
hadn't had children to raise on their land. They'd have
made admirable parents.

Although it was now 7:00 a.m., the tall trees caused
the sun to slant weakly into the yard and an eerie
cloud of fog lingered in front of the house. Tom's
Range Rover was parked about a hundred yards from
the house and he stood beside it, his rifle balanced in

a nonthreatening way upon his right shoulder. A barrel had been tipped onto its side and Daniel lay over it, his pants pulled unceremoniously down to his thighs, his buttocks, freckled with buckshot, catching the cool morning breeze.

"Daniel, what the heck…?" she began, getting out of the ambulance with her bag in hand.

"That old woman's lost her mind," he said.

"*Blythe* did this to you?"

"You know any other crazy old woman out here?" he wanted to know.

"Well, I—" First of all, she thought, they're not old. Blythe was around fifty-five, Daniel maybe a little bit older. It was hard to tell. They were a young couple when they'd moved to Grace Valley, and June hadn't had occasion to treat either one of them. That in itself had never been curious to her until that moment. Why would they travel to another town for their medical needs? Had they not trusted her father, Elmer, the town doctor before her? They were quite friendly with Elmer. Perhaps, unlike most of the townsfolk, they didn't *want* a doctor with whom they were well acquainted.

"Where is Blythe?" she finally asked.

Tom, not uttering a word, tipped his rifle slightly in the direction of the house. There, through the morning mist, June could see Blythe sitting in a rocking chair on the porch, the gun lying comfortably across her lap.

"Have you talked to her?" she asked Tom.

"Just from a safe distance. It appears she needs a little time to think about things."

"You let that woman think much longer," Daniel said, "she's likely to stomp down here and put the muzzle to my head, which I should have had examined about thirty years ago for getting into this bargain."

June looked at his pocked, inflamed backside. "I'm going to have to take you to the clinic, Daniel. We'll need some antiseptic and bandages…and nice, fine tweezers. But you'll be all right." She coughed lightly and behind her hand she said, "Perhaps scarred."

"There's only one way I'm going to that clinic, Doc. And that's lyin' facedown."

"I can understand that. If I pull the stretcher out of the back of the ambulance, you think you can get yourself on it?"

"I can give it a try."

"Meanwhile, I do think someone needs to see if there's anything we can do for Blythe."

"*Do* for Blythe?" he asked, incredulous.

"You think I ought to lock her up?" Tom inquired.

"What do you usually do when someone shoots someone?" Daniel said. "Throw a little jamboree?"

"Come on, Daniel," June said patiently. "Let's see if we can stand you up and get you to the ambulance. I can't imagine what you must have done to upset Blythe to this degree, as sweet-natured as I've always known her to be."

"Shows what you know," he grumbled, easing

himself off the barrel, grabbing his pants in the front
so they wouldn't drift any lower, and finally taking
tiny, painful steps toward the back of the vehicle
while leaning on June.

"I do know her to be softhearted and sweet," June
said. "Try not to bleed all over my new ambulance,
Daniel. I'm just breaking it in." He stopped in his
tracks, turned his head and glowered at her.
"Well..." She shrugged, apologetic. They moved on,
tenderly.

Although the driver's door stood open, Sadie continued to sit rather majestically in the passenger seat.
She never presumed. She thought of herself as a
working dog. "Sadie, come on, girl. Have a grass
break. That's my girl." The dog appeared to smile as
she made her way elegantly over the console and out
the door.

"I can't imagine what you must have done," June
said again.

"That's right, you can't," he snapped back.

The butt of Tom's rifle was pointed forward as he
walked slowly toward the porch. With Daniel and
June behind the ambulance, he felt a little more con-
fident about approaching Blythe. As he drew in on
her, he could see that she looked exhausted and ag-
grieved. He knew one or two things about domestic
discord. They'd probably been up arguing late, maybe
even all night. This could've been heating up for
days, or even weeks.

Blythe Culley wasn't exactly pretty, though she had

a round face and rosy cheeks that lit up like Christmas when she smiled. But it sure wasn't Christmas now. Middle age had put a few pounds on her and her once-pitch hair was now lightened by gray streaks. Usually, when she didn't have dark circles under red eyes, Tom thought of her as handsome.

"You've had yourself a stressful morning," he said to her.

"I might've been a bit testy."

He lifted his dark eyebrows. Tom Toopeek was of the Cherokee Nation, transplanted from Oklahoma as a small boy. He hadn't been raised on the reservation, but he *was* raised in Native ways by his parents, Philana and Lincoln, who lived with Tom's family still. It was natural for Tom to listen more than speak, to watch rather than act. The time to act and speak always seemed to come a little sooner than he expected.

"I think we've got it all straightened out now," she said, and a large tear spilled over and ran down her cheek.

Tom slowly lowered his rifle and leaned it against the porch railing. Then he took two slow steps up to the porch, helped himself to the gun that lay across her lap and made sure there was no more shot in the chamber. He leaned the rifle against the railing beside his. "No, Blythe, it isn't straightened out. I spoke to Daniel."

"What did he tell you?" Her eyes looked a little startled, as if she feared having all the secrets of their quarrel aired in public.

"He thinks you're crazy. To put it simply."

The fear drained quickly away and was replaced by a look of anger. "Hmm. He would."

"You going to tell me what possessed you to shoot your husband in the butt?"

"He said some things to me he shouldn't ever have said."

"Like?"

"I don't believe we have to get into all that."

"Maybe we should," Tom said. "I'd like to know what a man could say to a woman that would make her shoot him. Now, Daniel, he's not a drinking man, so I know he didn't go out and get drunk and break up the furniture. He's not a violent man. In fact, I'd call him gentle, though he's strong enough to hold back a stallion at breeding. If I had to guess, I'd say he's one of the better husbands in the valley...and I'd say you're lucky to have him."

Blythe began to quietly cry. Her chin dropped, her face took on a pained expression, her shoulders began to shake and tears fell onto her heavy bosom. "Well, there you have it. I've been lucky to have him. And now someone else is about to have him instead of me."

That said, she got up from the rocker, went into the house and slammed the front door.

Tom wasn't able to leave Blythe alone, he was that uncertain of her frame of mind. She might hurt herself. But when he stretched his mind to which friend of hers he might call to talk to her, sit with her, get her the help she needed, he was stumped for a name. That was probably the first time he considered how isolated Daniel and Blythe had been from the town. How could they be both well known and well liked in a town as small as Grace Valley, yet have no close friends? Hands who'd been lying low since the trouble started slowly came into evidence around the corrals and stables. Tom asked a trio of them, "You know who I might call to come and tend to Blythe?" The men shrugged and shook their heads.

Tom knew if he called a neighbor, one would come. But this wasn't a barn fire or illness; it was a serious domestic dispute. It required the presence of an intimate friend. Or a professional.

In the end he called Jerry Powell, the only private therapist in town.

"Does she want to talk to me?" Jerry asked.

"It doesn't matter, Jerry. She can either talk to you or go to the police station. Come on over."

All this transpired at the stable while, in town at the clinic, June had been plucking shot out of Daniel's behind, asking repeatedly what he might have done to drive Blythe to such ends. "Woman's just plain crazy" was all he would say on the matter.

One of Daniel's hired men came for him in a pickup with a couple of bales of hay in the back, which he was happy to lie over on the ride home.

Then there were patients to be seen, an uncomfortable number of them asking questions about Daniel's condition. It was midmorning before June took the clip out of her hair and plied it with a brush. It was perfectly hopeless. After being twisted into a clip while damp, it had a mind of its own. She'd always assumed her natural wave would come in handy if she had any talent with hair, but alas, none. She pulled it back and reclipped it.

It was late for her to be getting her first cup of coffee at Fuller's Café across the street; she usually stopped there on her way in to the clinic at about seven. It's possible this delay of caffeine and sugar had had an effect on her disposition, though June was typically even-tempered.

"Full morning, huh, June?" George Fuller wanted to know. "Daniel Culley gets a rumpful of shot and Chris Forrest is coming home, all divorced and everything. You still have a shine for him, June?"

"George, that was high school. Don't be silly."

"Why else would he come back to Grace Valley?"

"Well, George, gee... Why indeed? Could it be because he has family here? Or could it be it's a good little town in which to raise teenagers? Or maybe he just likes the place where he grew up?"

George grinned stupidly. "And what if he wants to get back together with you?"

"George, it was *high school!*"

"I wonder, does he know how cranky you've gotten over the years?"

"If you'd just shut up and give me my coffee and a bear claw, I could mellow out. But every morning you have something to give me grief over."

"I've been giving you bear claws and sticky buns for ten years now, June, and you're still as thin as you were in junior high. You reckon you have an overactive metabolism?''

"Probably."

George slapped a hand on his belly, which was straining the buttons on his shirt. He looked about seven months along. "You reckon mine's broken?" he asked with a huge grin.

"That, and a few other of your mechanisms," she said, taking the coffee and bun.

She turned away and behind her, he said, "I don't take no offense. I'd be crabby if I'd spent all morning pickin' shot out of some old rancher's butt."

It had made for an interesting morning so far, she thought. She would have taken her coffee and bear claw back to the clinic, but she spotted Tom down the counter with a couple of the locals, so she went in that direction.

"We got a little bet going, Doc," Ray Gilmore said. "I say Blythe put about thirty pellets in Dan'l's arse, but Sam says he sold Dan that old gun and it'll only give about nine pellets per round and isn't steady enough for anyone to put four rounds in a target as small as Daniel's skinny butt. Sam says a dozen pellets, tops. Who buys the coffee?"

"Don't you boys have anything better to do?" she asked.

Sam and Ray looked at each other, shrugged and said, "Nope. You?"

"This town," she said, shaking her head. She looked at Tom. "What did you do with Blythe?"

"She seems all calmed down now," he said, which

was neither accurate nor did he disclose any information.

"Wouldn't they be about the last couple in town you'd expect to have a row like that?" she said. "With a firearm involved?"

"About the last," he agreed.

"Marriage," she said. "Delicate thing, isn't it?"

Tom, Sam Cussler and Ray, all married to willful women, just shook their heads. One whistled, one laughed ruefully and one muttered, "Yer damn skippy," under his breath. That last was Sam, a very fit and energetic seventy-year-old who had recently married Justine, aged twenty-six.

"So, June," Ray said, "you must be tickled your old flame is coming home. And he's a bachelor again."

It was going to be a very long day.

Two

June, Tom Toopeek, Chris Forrest and Greg Silva had grown up together. They were best pals, confidants, equals. The boys didn't seem to even notice that June was a girl until puberty hit, at which point she became somewhat aloof, having to contend with private matters. Instead of being sensitive, they'd climbed the big tree outside her bedroom window and tried to catch a glimpse of something female. Chris fell and broke his arm. Elmer applied a heavier than necessary cast and Chris walked with a starboard list for six weeks.

By the end of junior high, Chris and June were an item. Steadies. They were a couple all through high school—she the cheerleader, he the quarterback. There was another cheerleader, Nancy Cruise, who chased Chris relentlessly, despite the fact that he already *had* a girlfriend. Chris, only a boy really, proved susceptible. There were times he questioned whether he should be tied down while so young. When he strayed, it was always in the same direction—to Nancy Cruise. And during those brief periods of victory, Nancy would gloat. Then Chris would beg June to take him back promising never to wander again, and Nancy would plot ways to break them up. It was a four-year tug-of-war. June scored more time on the quarterback's dance card, but Nancy was a constant and very real threat.

If Nancy was hard to take, her mother was unbearable. She was a domineering, bossy woman and a fearful presence in the town, the chair of every committee and president of the PTA for three straight years. She was a bully, to boot. What damage Nancy endeavored to inflict on poor June, Mrs. Cruise would attempt to double.

As June remembered it, the romantic triangle Nancy and Chris presented caused the only flaw in an otherwise happy high-school experience. In retrospect, she should have dumped him after the first cheat. But, like most girls, she didn't want to be alone, and there was no one she wanted besides Chris. Then, after much negotiation—his begging, June's waffling—she yielded her virginity. From that point until graduation, Chris did not stray again. That June knew about, anyway.

There was one area in which Chris and June weren't at all compatible and that was the importance they put on performance in school. June enjoyed studying, which made her high grades appear effortless. Chris was restless, easily bored, and he struggled to stay focused. She was valedictorian; he barely graduated. When it was time for college, that difference played a major role in breaking them up. June got scholarships and went off to Berkeley while

Chris's parents were lucky to get him to enroll in the local junior college.

For a while they wrote each other long love letters, enjoyed passionate weekend visits, made plans for school breaks and fantasized about marriage. Just after Christmas of her freshman year, June decided to change her major from nursing to premed. The new program was even more difficult and she found her studies exhausting. She didn't go home as many weekends, the love letters became love notes. The change happened overnight. June's mother, Marilyn, phoned her at school to tell her that Chris had dropped out of school, run off to join the navy, and had taken Nancy Cruise with him. They had eloped.

He never explained, never said goodbye, never said he was sorry.

Six months later, when Chris had his first real leave from the navy, Mrs. Cruise threw a huge reception for the couple and invited the whole town—even June. It had all the flavor of a victory lap.

June's devastation knew no bounds. She was wrecked. But fortunately she was also angry. She realized, too late, that Chris had zigzagged between her and Nancy for the better part of four years, and the fact that she had him in her camp more often was little consolation. If the three of them had lived in the same town, it would probably have continued. He was just a two-timing lout with a short attention span. She was better off without him and was relieved that Chris and Nancy had moved away. June got herself ready to be a doctor. Berkeley looked a damn site better than Grace Valley at that point in her life, and she welcomed the opportunity to lose herself in study. She rarely thought about Chris, and when she did think about him, she hoped he wasn't happy.

Now June sat at her desk, in her clinic, staring at a patient's chart but not seeing it. This only happened to her when she heard Chris was going to be home, when she thought about the prospect of actually seeing him. The curse that lay on her was that they'd never had any closure. Shoot, he hadn't even bothered to break up with me before he got married, she thought.

But things were different this time. Chris was single.

Once she had survived the pain of a broken heart, she hadn't had any regrets about the way her life had gone, sans Chris. There had been a relationship or two along the way; she was hardly a nun. And at thirty-seven, there was still time for a long and even fruitful union.

Remembering that phone call from her mother...

Being teased by the men in town about having her old flame come back to reclaim her...

Thinking about never knowing *why*...

"I need a distraction," she said aloud. "I can't be dwelling on things past. Stupid things." She flipped the pages of the chart, glanced at her watch, wondered what her aunt Myrna was doing for lunch.

Then the door to her office burst open and there stood her nurse, Charlotte, a strong whiff of Benson & Hedges wafting in with her. June jumped in surprise as she did several times a day, every day, because Charlotte simply would *not* knock.

"Sorry," Charlotte said. "Dr. Hudson called to ask if you're still doing meat loaf tonight."

June made a face and chewed on the end of her pen, looking up at Charlotte from a lowered brow. That was another thing. She always referred to Elmer as Dr. Hudson and June as June. Charlotte had been Elmer's nurse first, and seemed to still hold his retirement against June.

"Charlotte, who cooks at your house?" June asked.

"You know Bud's cooked since he got laid off last time," she said crossly.

"Doesn't it seem kind of funny that I make Elmer meat loaf every Tuesday night, and he's retired?"

Charlotte crossed her arms over her heavy bosom and looked sternly at June. "I think he's earned that meat loaf," she said.

"Well, that figures," June said, looking back at the chart, pen poised over the paper. "I've already told him I'll see him at six. Remind him for me, will you?" She scribbled a note in the margin of some blood test results. There was no movement or sound from the doorway. She looked up. Charlotte appeared to have frozen there, her eyes wide open, her mouth agog, her coloring fading quickly to pallor. One arm began to rise trembling toward her chest when she went down fast with a huge thud.

"Charlotte!"

June got to her first, but John Stone and the receptionist, Jessie, were beside her in a flash. June pressed the stethoscope to Charlotte's chest. Nothing. She placed her fingertips on her carotid arteries on each side of her fleshy neck.

"Jessie," John instructed, "get the crash cart right now. We'll set up the EKG and defibrillator here in the hallway. Then call the police department. We're going to want a driver and an escort to Valley Hospital. June, start compressions. I'll get the intubation set up and bag her."

June started compressing her nurse's chest, counting aloud as she did so. "One, two, three, four..."

The sound of squeaking wheels announced the arrival of the cart. It held the EKG machine, emergency drugs, paddles, everything necessary to treat cardiac arrest. John, with great speed, knelt at Charlotte's shoulders, tilted her head back, got the intubator down her throat and began squeezing the bag.

June stopped her compressions long enough to quickly open Charlotte's white uniform and begin attaching electrodes to her chest. "Jessie, after you call the police, call my dad and Bud Burnham." The girl was running down the hall again. "Those goddamn cigarettes," June muttered.

"Hurry up," John said. "Do we have sinus rhythm?"

The EKG machine was old. Slow. June was in agony waiting for the first strip of wet graph to feed out. "She's flat," June said, reaching for the paddles. She squirted them liberally with gel, pressed them against Charlotte's chest and yelled, "Clear!" John lifted his hands free of the bag. The jolt lifted Charlotte's heavy body off the floor. There was no change. June increased the voltage, pressed the paddles again to the woman's chest and said, "Come on, old girl! Clear!" She watched the tape. Flat.

"I've got lidocaine ready," John said.

June moved aside while John made the injection directly into Charlotte's chest. The second he finished, June increased the voltage and pressed the paddles to Charlotte's chest again. "Sinus rhythm," she said with huge relief.

"That's our girl," John said. "Stubborn. Start an IV of Ringers TKO. I'll dose Lasix and beta-blockers. She have a chart?"

"Jessie'll find it. John, this is going to upset my dad. Charlotte was his nurse for thirty years. At least."

"It's going to upset all of us, June," he said. Though John had been with the clinic for only a few months, he was already attached to the gruff but extremely skilled old nurse. "I'll back the ambulance up to the door and get the gurney out, if you think you can handle this now."

"Go. The sooner we get her to Valley's cardiac unit, the better her chances."

John ran down the clinic hall to the back door. June, kneeling beside her nurse, gently stroked the woman's forehead. "When I said I needed a distraction, I didn't mean anything as dramatic as this."

June and Elmer spent the evening at Valley Hospital with the Burnham family. Charlotte was conscious and holding her own, but this heart event had not been a warning. It was the real McCoy—a myocardial infarction. The only question was the extent of damage. The best-case scenario was that Charlotte would recover, but she could not go back to her old ways. And that included nursing.

"She always said that was the best part of her life," her son, Archie, told June and Elmer.

June took his hand. "She always told us that raising you kids was the best part."

"She'll have more time for the grandkids now," Elmer said. "Within reason."

"She's going to make it, isn't she, Doc?" Bud wanted to know. "I mean, I know she'll have to watch it, but she's going to make it, right?" He looked back and forth between June and Elmer, not specifying which doctor he was asking.

"Bud, we don't know too much right now," June said. "Her heart took a bad whack. But medical science is amazing, and what might've killed her ten years ago is just a setback now. The good thing is, it hit at work. We were on her right away. She was resuscitated and medicated immediately. That helps in the recovery."

"I don't know how we'll ever thank you," he said.

"Perish the thought!" June said. "Wouldn't Charlotte have been there for either of us? And hasn't she been, a hundred times?"

As Elmer and June left the hospital, she said to her father, "What are we going to do for a nurse?"

"Call the registry. They'll send someone out."

"I know that. I mean in the long term. We both know Charlotte is done nursing."

"I wouldn't write her off that fast. She's always been a feisty pain in the butt," Elmer said.

June thought it might take a bit more than feistiness this time.

John was on call and had the ambulance for the night, so Elmer gave June a lift back to Grace Valley in his truck. As they rode, June called John on her cell phone and gave him an update on Charlotte's condition. Then, instead of meat loaf at June's, they availed themselves of roast beef at the Café. Sadie, who had waited patiently at the clinic, joined them. George always had a supply of dog food on hand.

Charlotte was, as much as Elmer, a fixture at the center of the town. She'd been a nurse for forty years, all of them in Grace Valley. She had barely taken the time off to have her own children, and there were six of them. Nearly every citizen in the valley had crossed Charlotte's path at one time or other. News of her cardiac arrest had spread through town and almost everyone who happened to be at George Fuller's café wanted to know how she was doing.

By the time June and Sadie got home, it was after ten…and her porch light was on.

June knew she hadn't left the light on. There was also a light on inside, and this made her smile.

It was sometime last spring that she'd met him— her secret man. Jim Post was a DEA operative and he'd been working undercover in the Trinity Alps, the inside man at a marijuana farm. One of the growers had gotten shot and Jim brought him to June's clinic where, at the point of his gun, he demanded she remove the bullet and tend the injury. The romance began shortly thereafter, and no weapon was necessary. June fell for the strong, handsome agent instantly.

The only downside was that Jim was still at work for the DEA, undercover. For his safety, and June's, no one could know about him. Having a secret lover was at once filling…and lonely.

She let herself into the house quietly. She tiptoed through the living room and kitchen, toward the light, toward the bedroom. He reclined in the armchair in the corner, his feet up on the ottoman, the throw from the foot of her bed pulled over him and a book facedown on his chest.

He'd grown a beard since the last time she'd seen him. A very handsome beard of light brown. His hair was shorter, though. It was almost a buzz cut. And he was not quite as tan, but then he'd been working in an office for the past couple of months, and summer was drawing to an end. There was a definite fall chill in the late-night air.

Some secret agent, she thought with a smile. He didn't so much as stir while she and Sadie studied him. She crept closer, knelt beside the chair, stealthily pulled the book off his chest and lay her head there. His arms came slowly and predictably around her.

"What are you doing here?" she said. "You know it's meat loaf night."

"Meat loaf didn't appear to be happening. I waited

till about nine, then decided if Elmer came home with you, you'd know by the porch light that I was inside.''

"It's the middle of the week. This isn't a vacation, is it?"

"No, it's good news and bad news.''

"I hate those,'' she said, not asking for either.

"I have a couple of days.''

"Is that the bad news?'' she asked, knowing better.

"I'm being sent to the Ozarks...because I have such a lot of good goddamn mountain experience.''

She was quiet for a moment. "That's too far away.''

"Don't I know it.''

"Why didn't you just wait till morning to tell me that?''

"I couldn't do that to you,'' he said. "There aren't too many perks in this relationship. You're entitled to the truth, at least.''

She smiled against his chest but didn't let him see. To tell the truth, she needed him right now. And he'd been the last person she'd expected to come along and give comfort of any kind, much less the best kind.

"Why isn't there meat loaf tonight?'' he asked. "Patients?''

"We had an emergency. My nurse. Our nurse, Charlotte. She had a coronary on the job today. A real bad one. We almost lost her.''

"'Almost' means you saved her?''

"John and I, by the hair on our chinny-chin-chins. She's not in good shape.''

"I guess this means you can't get away for a couple of days...on short notice."

"If we'd met when we were much younger," she began, "would you have chosen another line of work?"

"Would you?" he countered.

"You'd have made a terrible husband."

"You'd have made a dynamite wife."

"Flattery has never worked on me," she insisted, wondering if he could feel her smile against his chest. Hell, her whole body was smiling.

"If you can't get away for a couple of days, will you at least take all your clothes off?"

"Well," she said, sighing heavily, "I suppose since you're going off to war again, it's the least I could do."

His arms tightened around her. "I have one more piece of news. This one probably should wait until morning, but I don't like holding things back from you."

This made her shiver, thinking sexual things instead of practical ones. "What is it?"

"I don't know if it's good or bad. You'll have to decide."

"Well. What *is* it?"

"After this next job I'm going to be offered a chance to retire early, with full benefits."

She lifted her head and looked into his eyes. Her mouth hung open slightly. Did this mean the next job was really dangerous? Would take a long time? Did it mean she wouldn't see him for months? He'd said "offered." Did that mean he might say no? Would he say yes…and show up at her door, planning to stay for good? There were a lot of issues inside that simple statement, though she had no intention of staying up all night talking. She was not at all opposed to staying up all night…but not talking.

"Let's not discuss it anymore right now," she said. She bit his lower lip, but lightly. "I don't want to waste any more precious time."

Three

In the middle of the night June got out of bed, plucked an article of clothing off the floor in the dark and crept out of the bedroom. How could a man who was so strong yet gentle a lover, so considerate of her every desire, *snore?*

It turned out she'd picked up Jim's T-shirt, which she put on. It came to her knees and slipped off her shoulder, but she pulled it around her in a hug and smelled the scent of him. She would only have him for one more day, then he would be gone again. But at some point in the not-too-distant future, he would be back. For good. For good?

She heard an objectionable snort come from the direction of her bedroom, but instead of grimacing, she smiled a secret smile. Adenoids. They'd have to come out.

Sadie so liked having a man in the house, she hadn't even left the bedroom with June, and Sadie usually clung to June's side, following her everywhere unless she was instructed to *stay*. But even with that god-awful snoring, Sadie was content on the floor beside the bed.

Jim was forty and had never married; she was

thirty-seven and hadn't either. Their time together had been so brief, there were a hundred things they hadn't discussed. What if he took that early retirement, came to Grace Valley to start a new life, and they found they were totally incompatible?

She sat on the floor, legs crossed, in front of her twenty-year-old record player. She leafed through old records in their dusty jackets. Her taste in music had always been odd; she liked things that would be more natural for her father. She put on a Perry Como record, the volume very low, and listened to his voice, like velvet, sing to her that she should make someone happy, just one someone happy...

Perry Como, Andy Williams, Nat King Cole, Mel Torme, Johnny Mathis. All were like drifting across a lake in a lolling rowboat.

She heard the jingle of Sadie's collar and the click of her nails against the kitchen floor. Sadie flopped down beside her, but Jim came on silent feet and sat behind her on the floor, his long legs on either side of hers. His arms encircled her and he kissed the back of her neck.

"There's something I've been wanting to tell you," she said. "But only if you think you want a future with me. Not that I accept, I just want to know what your expectations are."

"I want you forever," he said.

"You think so?"

"So far. But I'm sure you could do better if you applied yourself."

"Applied myself to getting a man?"

"Never mind. What was I thinking."

"Okay, what I've been meaning to tell you is, I'm pretty sure I can't have children. How do you feel about that?"

She felt him sit up a bit straighter, withdraw slightly.

"Ah," she said. "You weren't planning to have children?"

"June, we're not kids. I didn't think *you'd* be interested. You're pretty busy, after all. You take care of the whole damn town."

"I am interested," she said. "But I don't think I can."

"Why is that?"

"The last couple of times you were here, I forgot the diaphragm. But nothing happened. And if I'm honest with myself, I've always been a little sloppy about birth control." She turned and looked over her shoulder at him. "Funny thing for a doctor to admit, huh? It's the thing I absolutely harangue my patients about."

"If you think that, why'd you remember the diaphragm last night?"

"On the off chance I'm wrong. Though I have been wanting a baby."

"If you're wanting a—"

"Oh, I wouldn't do that to you! I wouldn't do that to any unsuspecting man. If I decided, seriously, to try to have a baby, I'd use an anonymous donor."

Frank Sinatra began to sing "New York, New York."

"Women are very strange," he observed. "Right down to their taste in music."

"Would you be wanting children?" she asked.

He laughed softly. "I'm very flexible."

"Well, then would you be willing to have your adenoids removed?"

In the morning, without the benefit of much sleep, June showered, dressed and kissed the sleepy agent goodbye. "I like this, kissing you goodbye in the morning."

"Oh, it won't be long before you're complaining that I don't have your breakfast ready on time."

"I have to go to the hospital at least twice today, since Charlotte's there, but I have an idea. After you've had a leisurely morning, why not drive over to Westport. There's a small inn near the sea. It's connected to a mediocre steak house and you can hear the surf. We could spend the night there. It's pretty close to the hospital."

"Are you allowed to do that?" he asked.

"Uh-huh. If I lie."

"Oh, I see."

"Well, that's your doing. Your job thing."

"Not for too much longer."

He hadn't said yet how much longer, nor had he given her other details about this next mission or early retirement. She'd had her wish, they'd done things other than talk. "Maybe we can talk about all that tonight, while we listen to the surf. That way you won't have to stay invisible here at the house."

"Good idea. Just ask for Dr. Stump."

"Can you come up with a new alias? It sounds so…I don't know…awful…"

"I'll specify that I'm an orthopedist. How's that?"

She stroked his beard, ignoring his crudity. "It's interesting, this beard. Are you keeping it for a while?"

"I'm taking it to the Ozarks. I'll probably have to shave it then. Why?"

"It hides your face. Makes you so mysterious."

"It hides the scars. Remember?"

"Too well," she said.

After his mission in the Trinity Alps had been completed and the marijuana camp busted up, Jim had had to run for his life. He'd slid down a steep, rocky hill and was stopped once by a tree with fiercely sharp bark and once by the asphalt of the road. He'd been scuffed up all over and one side of his face had been skinned raw.

Without knowing whether he was safe, June had been in the clinic all that night, tending both law enforcement personnel and criminals who had been arrested, all injured in the raid. She had come home to find Jim waiting for her in her house, bruised and bloody.

Now she'd like to see how he had healed.

June wasn't at all surprised to see Elmer's truck in the hospital parking lot. She had to pass through a clot of four of the six Burnham offspring circled around one of the few outdoor ashtrays. Sadie went

with her as far as the information desk where an elderly woman in a volunteer's pink coat offered to
dog-sit. June found the other two Burnham kids waiting in a special room off the Intensive Care area.
Small town and country hospitals were used to whole
families practically moving in and refusing to leave
until their loved one did.

June took one look at Charlotte and thought it quite
possible they would leave without her. She was gray,
the color of death, and though her eyes were open,
there was very little life in them. She had a plethora
of tubes coming out of her.

Elmer sat at her bedside, Bud stood on the other
side. June went to the nurses' station and asked to see
Charlotte's chart. She reviewed the last EKG tape, the
meds that had been prescribed by the cardiologist, the
doctors' orders for the day. The one thing she wished
she could read here was not going to appear. Would
Charlotte survive this?

While June read the chart, the nurse urged Bud and
Elmer away. "Okay, gentlemen, time's up. Charlotte
needs her beauty sleep, you know. Someone can see
her again in an hour."

Intensive care personnel were very strict about lim-
iting the visitors and the time spent at a patient's bedside during these critical hours. But June was not hus-
tled out. With the chart in hand, she went to the
bedside. She touched Charlotte's hand, which was
clammy. She gave the hand a squeeze. Charlotte had
a tracheotomy and oxygen, so couldn't speak, but she

looked into June's eyes and mouthed, "Thank you, Doctor."

Doctor. June felt a swell of tears. "You'll be okay, Charlotte. You're tough."

Charlotte nodded, but there was no conviction in it. She closed her eyes.

June found her dad in the waiting room, chatting with one of the Burnhams. "Dad, got a second?" He excused himself and went to June. "Are you needed here? Or can you escape for a few moments?"

"What for?"

"I have another patient here. You might enjoy seeing her."

"Who?"

"Jurea Mull. There's going to be an unveiling."

"This morning? I wouldn't miss it!"

June had become acquainted with the Mull family for the first time several months ago. One early morning she'd run for the kitchen phone wearing only a towel and found the four of them seated, nice as you please, in her living room. Clarence, a Vietnam vet, Jurea, his wife, and teenagers Clinton and Wanda. Although the Mulls had come in search of treatment for Clinton's injured foot, the first and most obvious thing June saw had been Jurea Mull's morbidly scarred face. One whole side was crushed, leaving a cheekbone caved in and her eye sealed closed by scar tissue. The accident had happened when she was a little girl and her family, mountain people, hadn't had medical treatment available. The injury had healed, her cranium and facial bones grew, and the result was freakish.

June was able to convince Jurea to have a consultation with a visiting plastic surgeon who, with his team of traveling volunteers, did surgery for the poor and uninsured. Jurea not only qualified in both categories, but her face presented the doctor with a challenge he could get excited about. Doubtless the case would appear in a medical book, or at least a periodical. In fact, Dr. Cohen was excited enough about the potential for Jurea's facial reconstruction that he had decided to come to her, to Valley Hospital, and do the first surgery right away.

"The first surgery was the most taxing for Jurea," June told her father as they walked toward her room. "Dr. Cohen sheared away some bone, inserted a plastic prosthetic piece under the cheek, reshaped part of her chin and removed considerable scar tissue. It was the most invasive. The consecutive surgeries will probably be concentrated on eliminating surface scaring and dermabrasion."

"Will the whole family be there?" Elmer wondered.

"School hasn't started yet, so I expect they will."

The surprise was finding John Stone present. "Who's running the shop?" June asked her partner.

"You didn't think I'd miss this, did you? Jessie can handle things for a little while. Besides, I want to stop in and see Charlotte after."

Jurea sat upright in the hospital bed, half of her head covered with a thick, bulky bandage. What showed of her face and arms looked tanned against the stark white of the sheets and hospital gown. June went first to her, asked her if she was nervous, then greeted each one of her family individually. If Jurea looked nervous, Clarence looked terrified. Sixteen-year-old Clinton and fourteen-year-old Wanda, however, appeared excited. For these two, their odd little family was only beginning to take on some semblance of normalcy.

When June had first met them they were isolated in a small backwoods shack, Jurea hiding her morbidly scarred face and Clarence sheltering himself against the paranoia and post-traumatic stress disorder he'd brought back from Vietnam. With the introduction of counseling, a good antidepressant and a visit with a plastic surgeon, there was hope for this family. And they'd come out of the woods to rent a little house in town so the kids could finally attend classes in a public school.

"If there's one thing I've learned," Dr. Cohen said, flying into the room with a dressing tray he carried himself, "it's show up early on the day you say the bandages will come off! Hello, everyone. Are we all ready?"

No one answered. They all held their collective breath.

Dr. Cohen was practiced at even this. He didn't waste their time, but applied his scissors to the surgical dressings. He cut straight up from the chin to the scalp and the bandage broke away. An eye patch was all that remained in place, for Jurea's eye, perfectly normal they'd discovered, had been closed by the scar and would be hypersensitive to light.

There were many imperfections and even some thick and heavy stitching, but this was the first time since Jurea was five years old that her face had a normal shape. First time she had a cheekbone, an even chin, bone where her eyebrow should be and a cranium shape that formed a temple. Her face was almost symmetrical. And even though there was stitched incisions, harsh redness and some swelling, the improvement was almost too dramatic to believe.

The silence in the room said it all. The quiet was reverent.

"Mama," Wanda finally said. "You're beautiful."

Dr. Cohen produced a hand mirror immediately. Jurea took it tentatively. It shook as she held it unsteadily. "My heavens," she said in a breath. Her trembling fingers rose to her cheek, touching carefully.

"It's a small, plastic disc, inserted under the skin to give you the shape you need," Dr. Cohen explained. "We're going to let the doctor of ophthalmology remove the eye patch and test you for vision impairment but, Jurea, underneath all that scar tissue, the eye appears to be normal. A few more surgeries, far more minor than this one was, will smooth out all the rough edges and give you a better finished product. A more beautiful face."

She looked up at him, her fingers lightly touching her new cheek. "More beautiful than this?" she asked, stunned.

He laughed softly. "Much better than this, Jurea. This is just the first step. It's the toughest surgery, so the worst is over now."

"Never…" she began. A tear spilled down her cheek. "I never would have believed…"

June looked at Clarence and saw that his face was wet with tears, but just as she met his eyes, he bolted.

"Dad?" Clinton called out. "I'll go after him, Ma."

"Poor Clarence… He just wasn't ready for it, I don't think," Jurea said. "When can I go home, Doctor?"

"After you see the ophthalmologist and the nurse gives you some instructions on how I'd like you to take care of the surgical site. This afternoon?"

"Really?"

"Sure. The hard part is over."

A little while later, on the way back to the Intensive Care Unit, June tugged on her dad's arm, pulling him to a stop in the hallway. "Dad, Charlotte looks bad."

"I know it," he said, shaking his head sadly.

"You should tell her, Dad."

He knew exactly what she meant, for he hung his head. But he didn't speak. He was going to make her put it into words.

"Do it with Bud. Tell her if she wants to fight it out, you'll be there for her. But she doesn't have to fight for your sake. Tell her that it's okay. When she's had enough—"

"I know," he said, and lifted his head. He was just a little guy and worry made him appear smaller. "I've been losing a lot of old friends lately,'' he said. ''Wears on me.''

''Think about Charlotte, Dad. You know she won't let go till she hears it from you. Even Bud doesn't have the kind of hold on her that you do.''

''She's a good old girl. I'll do the right thing, June. But I have to work up to it.''

She kissed him on the cheek. ''Are you planning to be here this evening?''

''Probably. Unless you want to try again for meat loaf.''

''Actually, I heard from a friend I haven't seen in ages. He's going to be up this way and asked if I'd like to meet him for dinner.''

Elmer squinted and looked at her over the top of his glasses. ''June? You blushing?''

She ignored his question. ''If you think you'll need me, or Charlotte will, I'll take a rain check. But if I can be spared...''

''You *are* blushing. He must be quite a guy. I haven't seen you blush since high school.'' He cackled a little. ''It would do my heart good to see you give that Chris Forrest some competition.''

That killed the blush. ''Now don't *you* start,'' she warned.

''Go ahead, June. Enjoy yourself. I'll keep watch here and call you on your cell phone if there's any change.''

The day seemed to drag slowly toward evening, despite the fact that June stayed very busy and a great deal was accomplished. For one thing, Susan Stone came into the clinic and took over Charlotte's duties. Susan had been a practicing RN when John met and married her, but even so, June hadn't thought of the possibility of Susan helping out. It changed the whole culture of the clinic, for Susan was Charlotte's opposite. Where Charlotte was grouchy, Susan was cheerful. While Charlotte was hardworking, Susan was brisk and efficient. And while Charlotte had trouble getting along with twenty-year-old Jessie, Susan acted like her older sister and the two got on famously.

Still, it seemed altogether wrong that Charlotte was not present.

It was nearly five and June was getting ready to leave the clinic when her cell phone twittered in her pocket. She went into her office to answer.

"It's me," Jim said. "I've been cursed."

"What is it?"

"I'm already here. Can you hear the ocean in the background?"

"It sounds like static. I'll be along shortly, right after I..."

"June, wait. I'm being called in. It's an emergency. I have to go right away."

"No!"

"I may not be in touch for a while. I'll try. I'll do the best I can."

"Please, please be careful! Please be so careful!"

"Will you remember something? Will you remember that I said I love you? And that I want you forever?"

"I'll remember." She felt the sting of tears threaten, but she didn't know if it was disappointment, fear for him or just the usual pain of saying goodbye.

"I have an important question to ask you, but not on the phone."

"I'll die waiting. Ask me. Please."

"No. I'll be back before you know it and then we'll sort everything out."

"What if we're not right for each other? What if we just think we are because we never *see* each other?"

"June, listen to me. I've never asked a person to wait for me. Never in my whole life. Never in my career as an agent. But I'm asking you. Wait for me, June. I'll be right back."

"You better not get hurt!"

He laughed, that deep, amused chuckle. "With all I have to look forward to? You think I'm crazy? I'll be fine. And I'm so sorry. About tonight."

"You owe me."

"Big time," he said. "Say goodbye, June. I have to go."

"I can't."

"Okay. Keep a good thought."

The line went dead.

June sat at her desk, holding the phone. Once again, nothing had been resolved. He moved in and out of her life so stealthily that sometimes she wondered if he was real.

There was a light rapping at her office door.

"Yes?"

John poked his head in. "We just had a call from Clinton Mull. He can't find his father anywhere. When he ran out of the hospital room this morning, he took off and hasn't been back since."

Four

June was feeling a little sorry for herself, to tell the truth. Charlotte was still barely holding on a few days after her heart attack, with Elmer sitting a painful vigil at her side. June was unable to spend much time comforting her father or her nurse because the clinic was full of kids whose parents had waited till the last minute to get them school and sports' physicals and catch up on immunizations. Clarence Mull hadn't come home yet, leaving Jurea wringing her hands in that stoic but distraught manner of hers. And June hadn't heard a word from Jim.

She'd dreamed about Jim the night before, a dream so real and voluptuous, she woke short of breath and with his scent on her. It took long moments for her to realize that it was only the pillow he'd used. That, combined with her longing, made the whole nocturnal event so real. Then she turned over and said a prayer that he'd be safe, and a second prayer that he'd still love her as passionately when this next assignment was past.

There was a definite bright spot in the chaos, and that was Susan, who kept things moving with such efficient pacing that they were able to keep up with the heavy load without imposing on Elmer for help. It was difficult to believe she'd never been an office nurse, impossible to imagine that in the past seven years she hadn't worked as a nurse at all. She was assisting in OB-GYN exams, removing stitches, helping Jessie schedule appointments, taking patient histories, giving shots and, most importantly, keeping the doctors moving if they started to get behind. Although it felt like a sacrilege, June thought she was even more capable than Charlotte, and that was saying something.

She caught John in the clinic hall, between patients. "I don't know how we managed before we had Susan in here," she whispered to him.

"Now you know how I felt when I met her. She was a surgical nurse. My life was a mess and she straightened me right out."

"At least you know how lucky you are."

"And if I don't, she'll be happy to remind me," he teased.

"Seriously, John, she's a fantastic nurse. Do you think there's any possibility she'd stay on? Full-time? With Sydney in first grade this year…"

"Sorry, she'd never even consider it. Susan is completely devoted to being a full-time wife and mother."

"That's too bad," June said with disappointment. "I mean, not too bad that she wants to be a full-time wife and mother, but too bad that she can't squeeze one more career into her day. You know what I mean."

"Sydney is already starting to complain, and she's been in here less than a week."

She was just about to ask him if he was complaining as well, but she was distracted by the sight of two teenage boys—twins—who were replicas of her first boyfriend. Tall for their fourteen years, lanky, freckled, with unruly, curling brown hair. They wore identical sulks typical of their age, and long baggy shorts that hung low on their skinny frames. It was like stepping into the past. They had to be Chris's boys.

"Right this way, gentlemen," Susan was commanding. She followed them into an examining room and closed the door. June shook her head with silent laughter. She considered what a handful those two must have been and felt a pang of momentary envy.

A few moments later she and Susan were exiting their examining rooms at the same time. Susan put two folders into the slot outside the door and said, "I'm giving the Forrest twins to John because he's a male doctor and they're at 'that age,' you know."

"Good move. Physicals? For sports?"

"Football. And they're behind on immunizations, like everyone else."

"Football," she said, perhaps wistfully. Of course. "Did their father bring them in?"

"No, actually. Birdie did. She's in the waiting room. Would you like to see her?"

"No need," June said, but she was thinking, Sooner or later we're going to come face-to-face, Chris and I. She had no idea what to expect.

* * *

Tom went alone back into the woods of Shell
Mountain, in Trinity County. He drove his Range
Rover along an old, abandoned logging road, and he
had second thoughts now that he had come this far.
He should've called Jerry, the shrink. Or maybe his
Veterans Administration counterpart, Charlie Mac-
Neil. And it would have been appropriate to call in
some law enforcement with jurisdiction, since he was
beyond his territory. But he wasn't here on legal business, he rationalized. He just wanted to talk to a
friend.

When the Mulls first visited June months ago, it
was because their sixteen-year-old, Clinton, had been
stepped on by their jenny, and his foot had begun
showing symptoms of gangrene. She had instructed
them to go immediately to the hospital, lest Clinton
die. But Clarence, who had suffered from paranoia
and delusions since the war, took the boy straight
back home, to their little shanty in the woods. This
was where Tom found him the first time, and where
he suspected Clarence might have fled now.

But why was the question. Since they'd rescued
him, Clarence had been doing great on antidepressant
and psychotropic drugs. Things had been going well
for the family. Added to that, there was the miracle
of Jurea's plastic surgery, an event no one could have
predicted. Well, no one but June, he thought with a
smile. Anyone who looked at Jurea's morbid scars
would have thought her condition hopeless. Why,
when things were so good, would Clarence flee?

Tom parked the Range Rover out of sight of the

shanty and went the rest of the way on foot. As it came into sight, it became clear Clarence was there. The jenny was back in the small, crudely fenced corral and smoke curled from the makeshift chimney. Relief was still a ways off, though. The first time Tom had approached this place, back when Clinton's foot was injured and before Clarence was on medication, all that greeted him was a shotgun blast.

He stood behind a good-size tree. "Hey, Clarence!" he yelled.

It was a little while before there was any sign of life. The rag pulled back from the hole in the door that served as a glassless window. "What you want, Chief?"

He sounded sane. But then...

"I was just wondering where you went off to," Tom yelled. "Jurea...she's worried."

"She'd know where to find me," he yelled back.

True. It was Jurea who'd mentioned the house in the forest about the same time the idea had popped into Tom's head. She couldn't herself go after him; she was postsurgical. Plus, she didn't drive. And she didn't want the kids to go fetch him. She wanted him back, that was all.

"You gonna let me come in?" Tom wanted to know.

"What for?"

"Come on, Clarence! You know what for! We have to at least *talk!*"

There was no sound or movement for a long moment, then the door slowly creaked open. Tom took a deep breath as he walked toward the porch. He had his rifle, but it wasn't at the ready. He was clearly at a disadvantage. If he shoots me, Tom thought, I'm going to be so pissed.

When he got inside the shanty, he found it unchanged from the last time he'd seen it. The lantern on the table was turned up to light the place, there were a couple of small, uncomfortable-looking cots, a table and two chairs, stacks and piles of books, newspapers, magazines and supplies. There was a crude stove with a corroded pipe that stretched through the roof, and a hanging blanket that served as a back door for the jenny to come in and out. The place had a faint smell of dung and wood smoke.

Clarence sat at the table, looking down.

"Lucky some squatter didn't come in here and take over your place, Clarence. I didn't realize you left it like it was."

"Make your point and leave," he said.

"Jesus, Clarence, when did you get so unfriendly? Last time we talked, we were like old friends. You upset about something?"

"That your point? That was hardly worth the drive, now, was it?"

Clarence still hadn't raised his eyes and Tom really wanted a look at his pupils. Tom pulled out the other chair and took a seat opposite.

"Here's my point, Clarence. Your wife just had a meaningful operation. She's still a little under the weather, though she's healthy enough. But weak as a kitten. The kids are looking after her, but everyone is

put out that you took off like you did. They'd be
grateful to know why, at least."

Clarence didn't take any time at all to answer. "It
was a little too much for me."

"What? The operation?"

"That, and everything else."

"Being?"

"You know."

"If I knew, I wouldn't have troubled myself to
drive up here."

"Why did you then?"

"I thought I explained that! Jurea and the kids are
upset that you ran off."

"I just need some time to get used to the idea!"

"What idea?"

Clarence hit the table, causing the lantern to rock.
"The idea that her face is gonna be all right!"

"Well, for God's sake, Clarence..."

"What they gonna need me for? Jurea and the kids,
they got everything they need now. They don't need
me."

"Now, Clarence, that's just plain ridiculous."

Clarence looked into Tom's eyes. "Is it?"

He was serious. It *was* ridiculous, but Clarence obviously felt this deeply. Tom tried to think of it from
Clarence's perspective. He'd been an isolated, dropout vet when he stumbled upon Jurea's family. There
she was, a fragile young woman whose parents and
brothers had kept hidden because they found her hid-
eous. Clarence took her, married her, built an insub-
stantial little place in the woods. He fed her from the

woods, taught her to read, even delivered his own two babies, who he also schooled and fed and sheltered.

All the while, Clarence treated his own mental illness by staying hidden, isolated, paranoid and falsely safe in the dark and quiet of the forest. Medication had changed his life completely, changed the family's existence totally. They came out of the woods into the town where they'd taken up residence in a small, run-down house that was like a palace to them. The kids proved well educated enough to go to public school and Clarence took up some janitorial jobs around town for rent and grocery money. Charlie MacNeil at the VA office had gotten Clarence involved in a group of vets suffering from Post-Traumatic Stress Disorder.

"Are you taking your medicine, Clarence?" Tom asked.

"If it's any of your business, yes."

"Good. What do you want me to tell Jurea?"

He shrugged. "They'd be better off without me."

"I'm not telling them that! That's just plain cruel!"

"Well, ain't it just the plain truth?"

"I don't think so. I can see how you might think so, after all the years none of 'em could have survived the day without you to take care of them. Did it never occur to you that, in addition to depending on you, they love you?"

He didn't answer, but had a look in his eyes that bespoke of tragedy and longing. So, he had never presumed on more than his family's dependence, but if he were honest, Clarence would probably say he *hoped* they loved him. He was a sick old vet though, and his self-esteem wouldn't allow for him to even ask.

"What should I tell them, Clarence? They want you home."

"Tell them... Tell them after a while they won't hardly notice I'm not there."

Tom sighed deeply. "Clarence, you're some load, you know that? I'm not telling them anything like that. It would scare 'em to death and break their hearts. And I know you don't mean to hurt anyone. Do you?"

"'Course not."

"Nor yourself?"

"'Course not."

"Seems like you just need a little time to think about things. Seems like you might benefit from having someone come out and talk to you about things."

"I'd sooner be left alone," he said.

"So here's what I'm going to do," Tom said. "I'm going to tell Jurea and the kids that it was too much too fast and you're taking a breather. You need some time to get adjusted."

"That'd work."

"Meanwhile, I'm going to tell Charlie MacNeil you're having some trouble adjusting to the changes in your family..."

"He that redheaded freckled fella from the VA?"

Tom frowned. He didn't like that Clarence couldn't place Charlie any faster than that. He'd spent quite a bit of time with Charlie. "The same. And you keep taking your pills. Remember, Clarence, without the pills, things get dark and confusing. The first time I came out here to your house, you thought I was Vietcong.''

"That so?''

"You don't remember?''

He shrugged. "The nicest part about the medicine is I don't have to remember how crazy I was. Don't worry, Chief. I'm taking the pills.''

"Good.''

"That why you came all the way out here? To tell me Jurea's worried and to ask if I'm taking my pills?''

Tom reached across the table and grabbed Clarence's fist in a rough grip. "Well, Clarence, I consider you my friend. Friends look out for each other.''

That made Clarence almost smile. "You were good in country, too.''

That's when he knew for sure. Tom had never been to Vietnam. Clarence was delusional. If he was taking his drugs, he wasn't taking them as prescribed. He was missing enough medication to let the craziness creep back in. Or the medicine wasn't working anymore and should be adjusted. Whatever the case, it was not good. Tom would hate telling Jurea that.

The clinic was open beyond the usual 5:00 p.m. to accommodate the rush of school-age patients. June was doing the last of her paperwork a little after six, hurrying through it. She had received a note from Tom earlier asking her to meet him for coffee at the café after work and she was curious about what he wanted. Susan tapped at the door and waited for June to invite her in.

She carried a few charts and a tablet upon which she'd made notes. "Here's what you have scheduled for tomorrow, and if you have time I'd like you to review the notes I've made in these charts to be sure I'm doing it the way you want it done."

"I'm sure you are, Susan. I can't tell you what a difference you've made around here. I can't believe you haven't worked in a family practice before."

She shrugged. "When John did his second residency in family medicine, I filled in a few times for one of the nurses at a neighborhood office. I was kind of surprised by how much I liked it."

"It would appear you're much more experienced than that." June took the charts. "I'm sorry you had to stay so late. It isn't usually this wild."

"At least it's only schoolchildren and not an epidemic. Um, June? You have a few extra minutes? I have something on my mind."

June braced herself. Susan was going to tell her she couldn't come in anymore, she just knew it. "Sure, have a seat," June said, laying down her pen and giving the nurse her complete attention.

Susan sat on the edge of her chair, a bit nervously, it seemed. "I know you've run ads in local papers and contacted the nurses' registry for a full-time nurse-practitioner, and I know I'm only an old operating-room RN with no special postgraduate training, but is there any way you could be persuaded to keep me on? Maybe even part-time?''

June's mouth fell open in shock. ''Susan?'' she said, afraid to believe what she'd just heard.

''I'm sure if there are other duties you'd require a nurse-practitioner's skill for, like prenatal exams and that sort of thing, I could learn...''

''Susan, I only advertised for a nurse-practitioner so I'd be sure to get at least RN applicants. When you run ads like this in small-town papers, every nurse's aide in a sixty-mile radius wants an interview. You'd be amazed at how many people who have worked two weeks in a nursing home think they're registered nurses. I would die to have you!''

''Seriously?'' Susan edged farther back into her chair, confidence melting her features into her usual smile.

''But John told me you'd never consider it.''

''That's what he thinks...because he doesn't listen. But I've never had so much fun in my life.''

''What about Sydney? Can you find day care or a baby-sitter?''

''My best friend, Julianna Dickson, has a first-grader also. As long as I can get Sydney to school in the morning, Julianna will take her home in the afternoon. She's been doing that all this week, having the time of her life.''

June frowned. It didn't sound as if Sydney was complaining. ''As far as I'm concerned, it's a deal. But I'm worried about John. He obviously doesn't realize you'd like to do this full-time. How are we going to handle that?''

Susan put up a finger, signaling "just a minute." She left the office, but was back in a flash. June accepted the piece of paper she was being handed. "Show him my résumé, June. Tell him I applied for the job. The rest is between the two of you."

"But Susan, I don't want to get into the middle of some marital—"

"Would you hire any nurse without getting John's opinion?"

"Of course not."

"Then that's how you should do it. I've been telling John for a long time now that I'd like to work again, but when you move to a place like Grace Valley, where surgeries aren't abundant and there's a long list of qualified surgical techs and nurses waiting for an opening at Valley Hospital, the discussion is pretty short. And then there's Charlotte. I thought she'd probably work to the last day of her life, but I honestly didn't think it would threaten so soon or I would have talked to you before now. I would have let you know you didn't have to worry about having a nurse available in the event of an emergency." She lifted a blond eyebrow. "There was no point in offering to substitute for Charlotte. She wasn't about to let anyone else into her sacred space."

"Well, I'll be." June shook her head, trying to grasp her good luck. "Should we talk about salary?"

"Why bother? I know you'll pay me what you can."

June stretched a hand across her desk. "You have a deal. If I can convince your husband."

"I'm sure he'll be convinced," she said, smiling. "John would like to have sex again in his life." She stood to leave but stopped and turned as she got to the office door. "Those Forrest twins? Are they the kids of the old boyfriend I've been hearing about?"

"I don't know. What are you hearing?" June asked cagily.

"Just that you dated Birdie and Judge's son in high school and he's moved back with his sons."

Sounded pretty harmless. "Yeah. The same."

"Pistols," Susan said. "Better not turn your back on them."

"Really?"

"Oh, really. I left them in the examining room for maybe ten minutes and they were into everything. I had to reclaim a speculum from one's pocket."

"Seriously?"

"Uh-huh. If they were mine, I'd frisk them every day when they came home."

It was almost seven by the time June was able to call Tom and tell him she could finally have that cup of coffee. Since it was so late, she ordered a hamburger for herself and a bowl of chow outside the back door for Sadie. Tom arrived just as June was taking her first bite.

"I'm sorry, Tom. Have you eaten?"

"I took a dinner break at home a couple of hours

ago. What's going on at the clinic? I think I saw every car I know over there today."

"Back-to-school physicals. Nothing earthshaking. What's on your mind?"

"You should have a heads up. I found Clarence. He's back in that hovel in the forest. And he's either not taking his drugs or they're not working."

"Oh no!"

"He's not real bad yet—"

"He was never real bad, Tom, as long as he had his environment under control."

Tom scratched his chin. "That's right," he said facetiously. "I really shouldn't misinterpret him shooting me as evidence that he was in a bad way."

June leaned forward. "We agreed, if he had wanted to hit you, you'd be dead."

"June, he mistook me for someone he served with in Vietnam."

"Poor Clarence," she said. "Did you get him out of there? Get him to the hospital? Or at least home?"

Tom shook his head. "He won't budge. He told me to tell his family that they were better off without him."

June put her hamburger down. "Oh God. Is he suicidal?"

"I'm not sure. I told Jurea and the kids that he was upset by the changes they've gone through in the past few months. It *has* been quite a lot, if you think about it. And I have a call in to Charlie at the VA. You might want to check on Jurea, see how she's doing."

"I might want to check on Clarence…"

"Let's be careful not to bombard him with attention. I just wanted you to know that the Mulls are in trouble again."

"I am so, so disappointed to hear that. I'll give social services a call tomorrow, see if Corsica Rios or some other caseworker can drop by and see if Jurea and the kids need anything. But I can't think of much more we can do."

Tom shook his head in exasperation. "I've thought of every possibility, including tranquilizer darts."

"Tom!" June scolded. She tried again with her burger, taking a big bite. Mustard, ketchup and the grease George Fuller was famous for squished out and a big splotch of it landed right between her breasts on her pale blue knit top. It was not a small splotch.

"Nice," Tom said.

Before she could even put the burger down and grab a napkin, Judge Forrest and Chris came sauntering into the café. They were immediately greeted by someone at the counter who hadn't seen Chris since he'd been back.

"Great timing," Tom observed.

She began to scrub the spot with her napkin and while chewing, muttered, "He keeps giving me reasons to hate him."

"You might as well get this over with," Tom said.

"Why? I'll just make a run for it and you can apologize for me. Say my beeper went off or something."

"Don't be a coward. Cowards die painfully in the end."

"God," she said, scrubbing. "Cherokee wisdom, as if I don't suffer enough."

"Hi, June."

She looked up and there he was, looking down at her as she scrubbed her shirt.

"Well," she said, mortified.

"Looks like you got a little on you," he said, and winked. *Winked.*

She heard a sound that she knew was Tom stifling a laugh and she contemplated many punishments for him also. "Well, hi there! I wondered when I'd run into you. Welcome back."

"Thanks. It's nice to—"

"Oh nuts," she said, reaching for the pager attached to her belt. She pressed a button on it which lit up the last number phoned in. But he wouldn't know that, right? "I'm sorry, Chris. We're going to have to continue this later." She reached out to shake his hand. "Good to see you, though." Then to Tom, "I'll talk to you about that other matter tomorrow," she said. She grabbed her plate and headed to the counter where George met her with a cardboard to-go box; he was a very well-trained café owner. She dropped her hamburger in and zipped out the door.

Five minutes later she was again at her desk, this time finishing her dinner, when she looked up to see Tom leaning in the door frame. Her mouth was full, but at least the food was all in her mouth. She chewed, swallowed and lifted the napkin to her lips to blot them. All the while Tom just watched, a slight curve to his lips. He was so damn patient! And his quiet appraisal seemed accusatory.

"Well, I didn't want to talk to him. And definitely not right after I'd spilled my dinner on my shirt, okay?"

"You're not a good liar," he said. "He knows you bolted."

"He does not! He *thinks* I bolted, but he'll never be sure."

"Eventually, you'll have to talk to him, because he's going to be living here now. And he's been asking if you're seeing anyone."

She seethed. What nerve! Two angry red patches grew on her cheeks. "Did you see what he did? He *winked* at me!"

"He'll learn," Tom said. But what he thought was, This is going to be good!

Five

Part of Tom's routine was cruising Grace Valley, both the town and the outlying rural community. In town, a mere ten blocks held one hundred small homes and a half dozen businesses, including the police department and the clinic. Grace Valley was mostly rural and didn't even have its own grocery store. The schools were located west of town, and the high school was shared with the town of Rockport. Beyond the town, Tom had to be familiar with all the back roads, the dirt paths, the abandoned roads from the logging and mining days, the trails between farms, the cow and horse paths. He regularly inventoried the outbuildings on farms, abandoned storage sheds on the edges of property as well as those in use. If he ever had the need to chase someone, he should know where they might find a route away from him and where they might hide.

Tourism was on the rise in all of northern California. People came to hunt, fish, camp and just enjoy the beauty. They had been spared the insult of big resorts, but quaint bed-and-breakfasts had sprung up all over the place. That meant a lot of the cars, trucks and campers on the roads did not belong to locals. It was hard enough to take care of a town as spread out as Grace Valley, but with strangers continually passing through, it increased the load tenfold. The police department was still just three men—Tom and deputies Ricky and Lee.

Tom thought it wise to be a visible presence, and his two young deputies also toured the roads with regularity, especially the roads that connected major thoroughfares and highways to the town. To strangers, it might look as if there were a lot more than three of them.

The time Tom spent at the café was more for the benefit of contact with the people than for the food, though he thought George Fuller's cooking at least passable. Tom liked to take his meals at home whenever possible, and on his way to and from he would take different routes so he could have a look around. He covered a lot of territory just getting himself fed every day.

On this particular day he came across a covered pickup with California plates parked by the side of a well-traveled road. He pulled up behind it, got out of his Range Rover and looked the pickup over. It was in pretty good shape for its age, but dirty. The owner had probably spent lots of time on back roads and hadn't visited a car wash in a long time.

He shined his flashlight into the windows. The seats were covered with towels and there were clothes, a bedroll and camping gear in the back. It was important to talk to campers from out of the area whenever possible; a lot of people didn't realize the dangers hidden behind the great beauty of the mountains. There were fire hazards, wildlife that could be dangerous if misunderstood and the human element. Clarence Mull was not the only squatter hidden in the forest. And there were marijuana farms hidden back there with very territorial landlords. A camper or hiker could easily stumble into unfriendly territory.

"Ho there," a voice called.

Tom saw a tall redheaded man lumbering through the brush toward his truck. He had a shaggy and unkempt look about him, but he was dressed in the sort of clothing an old-fashioned college professor might wear—khaki pants, brown, laced shoes, sweater vest and tweedy jacket with patches on the elbows. Around his neck dangled binoculars and a camera; over his shoulder a large canvas bag.

"Hello, Officer, is there a problem with my vehicle?"

"I was going to ask you the same question, sir," Tom said. "I thought it might be abandoned."

"No chance of that, Officer." He came around the truck to stand in front of Tom. "I haven't broken any laws, have I?" he asked. His accent was either British or Australian, Tom wasn't sure. Formal, in any case. And perhaps a tad effeminate as well.

"Depends on what your business is."

"Bird-watching, as a matter of fact. I've been chasing a ruby-crowned kinglet, a rare sight for this part of the country, particularly in the late summer and early fall. It's a tiny little beauty and I suspect there's a nest around here." He chortled as if he'd told some sort of joke. "Little blighter probably has a whole family and I aim to get a shot," he said, patting his camera.

"That might not be such a good idea. If you get more than twenty feet off the road, you're on private property."

He looked around, craning his neck. "What's this then? A farm of some sort? I can't think anyone would care if I slipped around the shrub and muck in search of a tiny bird. I don't mean to damage any property or let the livestock loose."

Tom took out a pen and tablet. With his pen he pointed to a No Trespassing sign on a post just a few yards up the road. "In fact, it's a family home on a piece of acreage and there isn't any issue of you doing damage. It's an issue of them deserving the privacy they invested in."

"I don't even see a house!" he protested.

"If you slip around the brush and muck for long, you'll eventually run into a house. Can I see some identification?"

The gentleman opened his satchel, pulled out a wallet and handed it to Tom. "I must inquire once again, Officer, have I committed a crime?"

Tom flipped open the man's ID. Paul Faraday. San Jose address. He copied the information onto his small tablet and handed the billfold back. "Not that

I'm aware of, Mr. Faraday. I just like to know who's come to town. Where are you camping?''

"I'm actually thinking of visiting your bed-and-breakfast tonight. I could do with a cup of hot tea and a soak."

"Have you been camping around here?"

"I spent one night in Redwood Valley. In search of a crafty little bobolink."

"What campgrounds?"

He shrugged and smiled, his teeth large. "I can't remember, frankly."

"Maybe you have a receipt?" Tom asked.

"I wouldn't have saved it, Officer. I get the impression you're quite annoyed with me for something, and I can't imagine what."

Neither can I, Tom almost said. But instead he put out his hand to shake with the gentleman. "I like to meet the visitors," he repeated. "You be careful not to wander too far back into the forest, now. We have bears and mountain lions, and it's not at all unusual to run into enclaves of squatters, from mountain folk to pot growers. I wouldn't vouch for the friendliness of either."

"I'll be wary."

"And mind fire laws to the letter. It's been a dry summer."

"You have my word," Mr. Faraday said, getting into his truck to make his escape while he could. "Thank you for your time, Officer."

"Watch those No Trespassing signs, Mr. Faraday.

There is a misdemeanor charge for ignoring them. It would be inconvenient for you.''

"I'm sure.'' He laughed. "I'm sure. Good day to you then,'' he said, starting his engine. He stuck his arm out the window to wave as he drove away.

Tom watched him go, then lingered in the area for a while to make sure the man wasn't skulking around. When Tom got home, he found that the long wooden table used to feed his wife, five children, mother and father was set with only two places. He smiled in satisfaction. Ursula brought in their lunch on a tray—sandwiches, salad, tea and chips for Tom.

"Your father has taken your mother to Rockport to buy fish for dinner and the children have all eaten and run off. Johnny has made new friends—the Forrest twins. He's proudly showing them his fort and the woods.''

"Are we really alone?'' he asked.

"As alone as one can be with five children on the loose. Tanya is baby-sitting on the other side of the valley, but the others and all their friends cannot be trusted to stay away.''

He bit into his sandwich and said, "I'll savor the moment anyway.''

"The nicest part of my summer is having lunch with you,'' she said. "I can't believe the season is about to end so soon.''

"You love to teach,'' he said.

"I love to spend time with you as well. Tell me

about the criminals you've apprehended so far to-day.''

"I gave a bird-watcher some trouble on the way home. He was creeping around Myrna Claypool's property. I didn't like the looks of him. I had half a mind to tell him he could find that pesky little ruby-crowned kinglet on the other side of town, but then he'd know I know as much as he does.''

"He's looking for a ruby-crowned kinglet?'' she asked, puzzled.

Tom nodded and said, "And a bobolink.''

Ursula sat back in her chair, her mouth open in disbelief. "They're everywhere,'' she said, and he nodded. "He's up to something,'' she added, and he nodded again. "He's not very smart, either.''

"You'd think he'd at least name a bird that isn't indigenous to the area.''

"What an idiot,'' Ursula said, picking up her sandwich.

Tom shrugged, but his thoughts had wandered back to the years his father spent making him memorize every bird, plant, star and animal. All of Tom's siblings had been so taught and then Tom's children and wife, for Ursula's education had not been linked to the land and sky.

"You're obviously Native,'' she went on, "and that foot-long ponytail might suggest some old tribal ways, including an education in nature. What a dope. I hope you got a license number.''

Tom chuckled. "Yes, Ursula.''

But that afternoon he called June. "I have a favor to ask," he started. At her groan he said, "Just a small one. I found an alleged bird-watcher skulking around near your aunt Myrna's house. He was as phony as a wooden nickel, complete with fake accent. At least I think it was fake. I ran him off and told him he was getting too close to private property, but I wonder if you'd drop in on Myrna, tell her to keep an eye out for him and to call me or one of the boys if he seems particularly drawn to her property."

"How do you know he's a phony?"

"He was looking for a kinglet and a bobolink. He might as well have been hunting sparrows."

"He named common birds to a Native?" she asked, astonished. "Isn't that sort of like naming organs to a doctor?" She didn't give him time to answer. "Why didn't you stop in and see Myrna yourself?"

"I could have done that, but to tell you the truth, I was a little afraid she might go looking for him, have him in for tea...or martinis."

"Yeah, I see the dilemma. I'll drop in on her, make sure she understands she should be careful. Do you think he could be a bothersome fan?"

"I wouldn't rule out anything," he said. Except that he's a bird-watcher, he thought.

Myrna Hudson Claypool was Elmer's older sister and had raised him since he was an orphaned two-year-old. She had been only fourteen at the time, but seventy years ago it wasn't so odd for a fourteen-year-old girl to be a mother. Their parents had left not only the big house on the hill overlooking all of Grace Valley, but plenty of money.

Myrna didn't herself marry until Elmer was through medical school and settled with his own wife, and then it was a traveling salesman named Morton Claypool whom she chose. She never had a problem with Morton's travels, which took up four to five days of every week. It was almost as though she didn't want anyone who was going to be around too much so that it might distract her. Myrna had, late in life, turned from an avid reader to a writer of Gothics and mysteries and, finally, suspense novels. It was sometime during June's senior year of high school, some twenty years past, that Myrna was either widowed or abandoned or quietly divorced. No one knew which. All they knew for certain was that Morton was gone and Myrna had assured her family that he wouldn't be coming back. No one pried because it seemed fairly obvious that Morton had run off…or wouldn't she have at least held a memorial? She was rather proud of the large monument-type headstones she'd supplied her parents, so surely she'd have wanted a similar thing for her spouse. But pressing her on the subject seemed destined to humiliate her, so when she expressed her desire to not discuss it further, they— the family and close friends—allowed the subject to drop.

The town talked, plenty. But not to Myrna. Everyone loved Myrna. And even though she didn't talk about Morton's disappearance, there was a recurring theme in her novels of a philandering husband being killed by his scorned wife, the wife most often getting away with the crime. Each time Myrna revisited a variation of that plot, the poor husband suffered a death worse than the one before. Elmer had even confessed to June, in complete confidence, that he'd walked around the grounds at Hudson House in search of any freshly turned soil.

Myrna was a sweet old thing, still getting out a suspense novel every year despite the fact that she was eighty-four. She still drove a 1979 Cadillac, drank a martini or two a day, played poker with a bunch of old-timers and won more than anyone else, and employed the elderly twins Amelia and Endeara Barstow simply because no one else would.

She was also as eccentric as a peacock and Tom was right to fear she'd go looking for the fake bird-watcher. Myrna was not dense or forgetful or naive. In fact, she was as sharp as a tack with what Elmer referred to as a "dangerous memory." However, she did happen to lack cynicism—a strange thing for the author of so many grisly murder stories.

A few years back a couple portraying themselves as her most ardent fans and a brilliant writing team themselves had shown up at Hudson House with a back seat full of every book she'd ever written—over sixty. They'd insinuated themselves into her home where they were going to presume upon her hospitality for as long as she'd allow it. They were clearly taking complete advantage, going through her things, asking her questions about her wealth and ringing up lots of long-distance charges. While they didn't exactly fool Myrna, she allowed herself to be manipulated by a couple of pros.

It was Amelia and Endeara who blew the whistle on them. They refused to wait on them and went to June, who went to Elmer, who went to Tom. Otherwise, who knows what might have happened. The enterprising writing couple was ousted, and fortunately for them, they were gone before Tom found out they had a long record for conning rich elderly people.

"Aunt Myrna, you *must* be more careful," June had scolded.

"I was being *completely* careful," she replied. "They were fascinating! You can't believe how stupid they thought me, or the wild tales they told me to keep me off their scent. I'm not exactly sure what their long-range plan was, but in the short term, they were trying to figure out just what I was worth. I crept around the house planting old bank statements, canceled checks and investment records for accounts closed years ago." She cackled happily. "Must've made them drool. I wonder if they were going to try to get into my will, or if they were just going to kill me and rob me."

June had gasped. "How can you talk about that possibility so calmly?"

Myrna had patted her arm gently. "I guess I just see it all as research."

And, sure enough, a couple of books later a husband-and-wife con-artist team were rubbing out little old ladies for their fortunes, but eventually found themselves captured by one of their victims, herself a skilled murderess. Myrna was getting more shocking by the year.

On her way home from the clinic June dropped by her aunt's house. Amelia's car was still in front of the house and it was she who opened the door. "Is my aunt Myrna receiving?" June asked.

Amelia simply turned and walked into the great house, leaving the door open so that June would know to follow. The Barstow twins were not only the biggest grumps in town, they bickered so fiercely with each other that Myrna only allowed one of them to work for her at a time. Essentially, they job-shared.

The door to the den that Myrna used as an office was ajar and she peeked in. Myrna was hunched over her laptop computer. June tapped lightly and Myrna glanced at her watch as she looked up to see June. "Gracious! Where has the day gone?" She pulled off the reading glasses perched on the end of her nose, pulled the pencil from behind her ear and stood slowly. Stiffly. She took a moment to stretch out the kinks.

"You must be on a roll," June observed.

"Darling, sometimes they just write themselves. This one isn't going to let me sleep till it's over."

"If you're too busy..."

"Nonsense. I have to stop. I don't want to burn out, you know. Besides, I think it might be time for my martini. Join me?"

"Maybe for half a glass of wine. If you're sure you're not too busy."

Myrna laughed, her loud, joyful cackle. "There are two things I'm never to busy for. My five o'clock martini and you, my dearest."

"It's almost six," June pointed out.

"So it is. I might have to have two martinis." Myrna looped her arm through June's. Her steps were slow and creaky as they walked toward the kitchen.

"You shouldn't sit so long at the computer," June said. "Get up and walk around, at least once an hour."

"Lord, June, don't you think I do? I'm eighty-four! I can stiffen up in ten minutes. Amelia!" she called toward the kitchen. The woman stuck her head out. "Bring us drinks in the sunroom. June will have a glass of merlot."

"Chablis," June corrected.

"She'll have merlot. It's better for her heart."

"Merlot," she accepted, knowing she'd only have a few sips anyway. "I did stop by to talk to you about something specific." They came into the sunroom, an addition to Hudson House that was only fifteen years old. It stuck out of the north end of the house, seventy-five percent glassed-in porch, so that it caught the morning and afternoon sunshine. At six, the sun was slanting over the tall trees to the west and casting a soft light into the room. Dust motes floated in the soft rays of dusk light. Amelia and Endeara, for all the hours they spent at Hudson House, weren't much for housekeeping.

Myrna took another leisurely stretch before sitting in a large wicker chair. "Specifically, what?" she asked.

Amelia arrived with drinks on a tray and a little bowl of Goldfish snack crackers.

"Tom called me earlier today. He said he'd run some bird-watcher off your property. He'd parked on the road and—"

"Yes, I met him." Myrna closed her eyes and took a tiny sip of her martini. She smacked her lips, then opened her eyes. "Faraday. Nice fellow. I told him he could bird-watch, but not around the house. The Barstows get all excited if they see anyone lurking about. And I told him to take special care by the hydrangeas. They're delicate."

"You *talked* to him?" June asked.

"Yes, June. He knocked at the door."

"You shouldn't be answering the door!"

Myrna looked both bored and annoyed. "June, I don't even *lock* the door."

"Well, you should definitely lock the door!"

"You don't lock *your* door!"

June made a face. She was locking it now, now that she had a secret lover who sometimes appeared as though out of the mist. Her secret lover might be an expert lock picker, but her father wasn't. "Well, you're a famous author. You remember that couple, what was their name?"

"I'm not famous. Everyone but the neighbors thinks I'm dead. They think other writers are writing my books. Why, at my last signing in Garberville, there were only two people I haven't known for over twenty years!"

"But you let him in? You talked to him? I don't think he's really a—"

"Actually, no, I didn't invite him in. I felt badly about that. I told him I was quite too busy to have him in, but he should feel free to bird-watch on Hudson land, as long as he didn't hurt anything and stayed off the hydrangeas. He said the police had run him off, so he wanted to be sure to ask permission. He seems a perfectly nice young man."

"But Tom doesn't think he's really a bird-watcher, so now will you lock your doors?"

Myrna sipped her martini and said, "If it'll make you feel better, June." By her expression, she had absolutely no intention of doing so.

Tom was almost home for dinner when he was radioed by Deputy Ricky Rios that Ray Gilmore had called the police department, irate. Ray had a modest garden and henhouse that someone had raided, robbing him of eggs and ripe tomatoes.

Tom was nonplussed. "What does he want me to do? Read a fox his rights?"

"He says some kids have been throwing eggs and tomatoes at vehicles on 482, just about two miles north of Rainbow."

That perked his interest. "That so?" he asked as his foot came down harder on the gas pedal. "I'm not far from there now."

A road heavily traveled in the country, 482 cut through a hill that rose up sharply on each side of the road. Tom slowed to look around just as he entered the pass. Before ten seconds had gone by there was a large splat on his windshield. Runny yolk ran down into the wiper tray.

"I'll be goddamned," he swore in disbelief. He slammed on the brakes, spun the Range Rover around and jumped out of the car in time to see the foliage ripple all the way to the top of the hill as the culprits made away. "That's balls," he said aloud.

But no one knew the hills and roads better than Tom. He drove his SUV down the road a bit before he pulled it over to the side, got out and locked the door. He picked up a path that would cut around to the opposite side of the hill. He crouched a little, keeping low, as he crept along the path. He saw a flash of light-colored clothing—a shirt or a jacket— as a kid darted across the stones of the creek bed, coming right for him. Tom put himself behind a tree and just waited. When the moment was right he stepped out and scared ten years off the life of the vandal, who dropped the eggs he carried in his pulled-up shirttail. They splattered on his shoes and washed down the stream between the rocks.

"Dad!" cried Johnny Toopeek.

It was an instinctive move on Tom's part, a combination of shock and anger. He reached right out and grabbed his son's shirtfront and gave him a shake. "You?" He couldn't believe this!

"Dad, hey!" Johnny yelled.

"You'd throw things at moving vehicles? Like you don't know how dangerous that is?"

"No way, Dad! Gimme a break here!"

Tom let go. Johnny was getting pretty big. At fourteen he was tall, and his feet were already size elevens. Tom looked at those feet. "The evidence may be circumstantial, but it's all over your shoes."

"Yeah, well, I was taking the eggs *back*. But thanks to you..."

"Back where?" Tom wanted to know.

"To Mr. Gilmore's house, although I don't know how old they are or when they got taken. Let's just say I put a stop to it, okay?"

"Who'd you stop, exactly."

"It ain't important, okay?"

"It's my main concern at the moment."

"Well, I don't snitch, so I guess I'm grounded or something."

Tom tapped his foot and seethed. "Whoever you're protecting just hammered the police car."

"No *way!* Are you *serious?*"

"He said that with school being the struggle it was, with me making a decision like medicine without even telling him…well, I guess he felt he couldn't measure up. And he felt I had abandoned him."

Elmer made a face and shook his head in apparent disgust.

"Well, you can appreciate how that could happen," June continued. "We were young, but we *were* talking about getting married. And then I took a fork in the road without even calling or writing to him about it. I changed all my plans, so he changed all of his. And, I wasn't going to tell you this, but he claims to have felt terrible about it ever since."

Elmer laid his fork down next to his plate and stared hard at his daughter for a long-drawn-out moment. "There seems to be at least one thing about Chris Forrest you've forgotten," he finally said. "Most of the time he's full of shit."

Eight

The last patient of the morning had left the clinic and June fancied something sweet; maybe a little trip to the bakery would satisfy. As she was leaving the clinic she almost tripped over Julianna and Susan in deep conversation right outside the door. They hushed and bolted apart guiltily.

"Uh-oh," June said. "What are you two up to?"

"Come with us and find out. Unless you're chicken," Susan invited.

Every instinct told June to be chicken this once, but these two intrigued her. And if she was honest, she was a little bit jealous of their fast-and-firm camaraderie. She had good friends, sure, but there was something very special about the bond between the two women. It made you want to play.

"Chicken?" June asked. "Who you calling chicken?"

"We're going to see the new preacher," Julianna said. "To tell him what we did to the old preacher."

June gulped. "Why? Why not leave well enough alone?"

"I can think of about fifteen hundred reasons," Susan said, citing the approximate population of Grace Valley.

"I brought a cake," Julianna said. "That should make it go down easier."

They found the pastor in his office, sitting on the floor, sorting through a mound of papers. The place was in terrible disarray, the new pastor's things tossed into a room left a mess by the previous pastor. He looked up to see three women standing there, looking down at him, and at first it made him frown. Then he smiled cautiously. "Has the women's circle come to help?"

"Um, well...if a cake helps, then we have," Julianna said.

"Actually, Pastor, we were hoping you'd have a minute to talk," Susan said. Harry Shipton got clumsily to his feet, accidentally knocked a few folders from a nearby chair and watched helplessly as even more papers fanned out over the floor. He bent his long legs to stretch, clearly stiff from having been cross-legged on the floor for a while. He was lanky, but had a handsome face, younger than his forty-something age.

"We met a week or so ago," she said, sticking out her hand to renew the introduction. "Susan Stone. And my boss and friend, June Hudson." He nodded to June. "And the baker is Julianna Dickson."

"How do you do," he said. He peeked at the cake and his warm smile became a grin. "I don't keep a very nutritious diet. Cake is perfect."

"We should get this over with, Pastor," Susan said. "We have something to tell you."

The minister half sat, half leaned upon his cluttered desk, crossed his arms over his chest and said, "Shoot."

"I don't know how much you know about our last minister…"

"That would be Jonathan Wickham?" he offered.

"The same," Susan said. "Well, we want you to hear it from us. We ran him off. Julianna and I. June wasn't really in on it till the end."

"But I didn't disapprove," June said. "And when it came down to it, I participated. Besides, he wasn't really run off. He was boycotted."

Harry tilted his head, listening, but said nothing.

"Jonathan was a notorious flirt. An awful womanizer. He was always making passes. And at married women, too," Julianna said.

"Driving his wife crazy," Susan added. "Offending the entire congregation, except for the old men in town. They just laughed at him, which made it worse."

"We had a lot going on in town at the time that wasn't real woman-friendly," June said. "One young pregnant woman was battered into an early and critical childbirth by her husband. Another woman, the mother of five, barely escaped a life of terrible abuse when she… Well…" she said in frustration, "when she whacked her abusive husband over the head with a shovel and killed him."

Harry winced. "What happened to her?"

"Oh, she was acquitted," Susan said quickly.

"She works part-time as a waitress at the café. You'll run into her soon if you haven't already. Her name is Leah."

"Acquitted?" he asked.

"Acquitted," the three women said in unison.

"The climate wasn't real patient toward men who didn't respect women. So…"

"So…we tried talking to him," Susan said. "Julianna and I and another young mother he'd made passes at, but he blew us off. Clearly he wasn't interested in better manners."

"He had an affair with a very vulnerable young woman," Julianna said. Then, remembering that Harry Shipton was single, hurriedly added, "No one here stands in judgment of romance, Pastor," which caused Harry to smile, though weakly. "But Pastor Wickham was clearly on the prowl."

"He took such advantage, whenever he could!" Susan added.

"We weren't real sure what to do," Julianna said. "We could have written letters to the *Signet*, in hopes of having him removed…"

"But we were in search of a bigger solution than having his hands slapped. We wanted Pastor Wickham to understand that he was in our church, not that we were in his." Susan clamped her mouth shut suddenly, put a hand over her lips and began to flush. "I mean…"

"That's what she meant," June said, before Susan could try to wiggle out of that statement. "And it turned out that most of the congregation agreed, because at the first suggestion of a boycott, no one went to church, and Jonathan and his family left us."

"He had become such a problem for the women of this church," Susan said. "He was always asking young married women if they'd like a little private counseling, that sort of thing."

Harry's eyes widened in surprise. "That's bold for a single minister, much less—"

"We wanted to tell you ourselves, before you heard it from someone else," Julianna said. "We're not really a bunch of hardheaded, bossy women."

"Even if we are, we're not mean-spirited," Susan said, shaking her head.

"It's been said that we're dangerous to cross, but that's such an overstatement," Julianna put in. "I mean, we're the most reasonable women in town! Don't you think, June?"

June nodded. "Absolutely. Extraordinarily reasonable."

"So if you hear rumors, gossip about us… Well, if you could just not believe the worst, or maybe even—" Susan said.

"Ask us! Yes, ask us to clarify before you start thinking we're the scariest women in the whole world," Julianna continued.

"Honestly, we want you to enjoy your stay here. I mean, you're a single man, right? No reason for you to be afraid to ask a woman for a date, based on what you've heard about the women—" Susan stopped talking as she noticed Harry's frown. "You know what I mean."

Harry straightened, standing from his perch on the desk. A pile of books seemed to topple from the surface for no apparent reason. It was almost as though things fell or scattered just because he was near. "You must have had your hands full," he said to them.

Julianna sighed deeply. Susan shook her head and said, "You don't know the half."

"Well, not to worry. I'm not very good with the ladies," he said. "I have an ex-wife who will be happy to attest to that."

"But Pastor Shipton, we don't mean *you* shouldn't flirt or date or—"

He held up a hand. "Please. Harry."

"Fine, Harry. By all means, you're a single man. But we'd appreciate it if you'd—"

"I'll try not to force you into a repeat performance of the boycott," he said in good humor.

"We could even tell you who some of the single women in your congregation are," Julianna offered hopefully.

"I imagine I'll run into the single women in church one way or another, but I hear there's a fantastic poker game in town. Any possibility I could get in on that?" He rubbed his chin. "Might be a safer bet."

As the last days of summer gave way to fall, June saw Harry Shipton at the café from time to time, visiting with the locals and getting on just fine. He'd found the poker table for himself—Elmer, Myrna, Sam Cussler, Burt Crandall and Judge Forrest. They'd continued to meet at the café because of the commotion at Judge's house, but then Harry stepped in and offered the parsonage for their weekly game.

"The parsonage, huh?" Elmer said. "You think that'd be all right? Gambling and all, right under God's roof?"

"As long as you tithe, I don't think anyone will make a fuss."

"Pastor, I think you're going to fit in right well around here," Myrna informed him.

As the days passed, it became even more difficult for June to guess what was going on with the Stones. One day she'd swear they were all made up, the next day she'd feel the chill in the air. She'd learned, through the local grapevine, that the whole thing had started at a card game when John and Mike lost their heads, started joking around and ended up insulting their wives. Oh, they probably hadn't meant to be insulting, but they hadn't meant to be stupid either, and now the two of them were in serious hot water. Jessie had whispered to June, "Every time John opens his mouth to apologize, he manages to say something to make things worse."

At the Dickson house, rumor had it that Mike had tried to explain to his mother why Julianna was so upset with him. June heard it from her dad, about fifth or sixth hand, but Mike had said something like, "You know what I was saying, Mom, that Julianna doesn't want to work, she wants to take care of me and the kids and the house.'' Grandma Dickson, who had worked hard all her life in the aforementioned— or would that be the *not* mentioned?—career field, went pale and wondered how she had failed to train up her son better than she had. She was now also miffed. And the one thing you want to be careful about is not to piss off the help. Now those two men were paying dearly. But the women seemed to be holding up just fine.

School had started, the temperature dropped and the valley settled into a favorite time of year. The Grace Valley High School football team, loaded with the sons of loggers, fishermen, farmers and vintners, hardworking and very physical men, always made a good showing. The town supported the team well, and not just the parents of high-school students. The bleachers were full for every game.

Another hallmark of fall would be the harvest festival, the celebration of the coloring of the leaves. Local merchants and organizations swung into gear for a town party that would last a weekend and draw vendors and visitors from near and far. Even June's quilting circle, the Graceful Quilters, would auction a specialty quilt, one in which landmark buildings— houses, barns, churches, et cetera—were sewn into the squares. It was a quilt of Grace Valley.

On one particularly beautiful, crisp fall day, June received a call at the clinic from Ursula Toopeek. ''Are you going to quilting Thursday night?'' she asked.

''Oh gee,'' June hedged. ''I'm on call, so it's iffy.''

"Listen, June, get out of being on call and go to quilting. Birdie thinks you're avoiding her because Chris and the boys are staying there, and you can't allow that. She's not very young and she's one of your very best friends."

"I haven't been avoiding her!"

"Are you sure?"

No, she wasn't, but she said, "Of course not! There's been a lot going on."

"There's always a lot going on. He's been back, what…four weeks or more? You can't avoid him forever."

"Really, I've been busy. And besides, I'm not avoiding Chris. I've actually seen him and talked to him a couple of times." This was quite a stretch. Chris had seen her slop ketchup and mustard on her shirt and visited her at the clinic once. Those were the only two times they'd spoken. She'd seen him, that was the truth. His eyes had twinkled and he'd winked as though they had a secret, and she hated that.

In the weeks that Chris had been back, June had found excuses not only to miss the quilting circle, but also church, which the Forrests attended, and football games. It wasn't done consciously; it was just a kind of withdrawal. If Chris had been back four weeks, then Jim had been gone longer. Chris was lurking, ever present, suggesting with his sparkling eyes that they could "start over," while Jim, far away and working undercover, had not even found the opportunity to phone.

"Come Thursday night," Ursula insisted now. "Trade on-call with John. He doesn't have anyone at home who'll talk to him anyway."

This made June laugh. "I guess that little spat is all over town."

"Well," Ursula said, "John's been buying lots of flowers lately."

June knew she had to do it—resume her quilting with the circle. It had always been one of the most relaxing and pleasurable parts of her week. And June, a master of sutures, was an excellent stitcher. But quilting was less about stitching and more about coming together. There, with their hands joined by the fabric, these six women gave each other spiritual grounding. They were dear friends, each one. There was Ursula Toopeek and Tom's mother, Philana, Birdie Forrest, Corsica Rios, Deputy Ricky Rios's mother, and Jessie from the clinic. When she added together the number of years she'd been friends with each one, it was over a hundred years of friendship.

She could not stay away on account of some man.

Ursula had brought to mind the Flower Shoppe, and a call June had been meaning to make. Justine Cussler, the shop's owner was both a patient and a friend. Despite the age difference, Sam and Justine made a good-looking couple. Sam was a handsome and fit gentleman with white hair, a tanned face, blue eyes so young and bright they looked as though they might crack, and a keen sense of humor. Six months ago Justine had been a morose young spinster with a sour attitude, but Sam had brought her to life and she glowed with happiness.

There was but one pall on their union—John had been forced to remove a malignant ovarian tumor. Fortunately he caught the cancer early and Justine's chance for survival from this volatile disease was good. John had even managed to salvage the other ovary, at Justine's insistence. Justine was determined to have a baby. John and June had tabled the discussion as to whether that was such a good idea or not because Justine faced a year of chemotherapy before she could even consider a future pregnancy.

The bell on the flower shop's door jingled when June walked in, and Justine came from the back. "Well, stranger. I haven't seen you in a while," the younger woman said.

June's immediate reaction was Uh-oh. Justine's skin was pale and she had dark circles under her eyes. She looked to have lost a few pounds. It was hard to tell if her hair was thinning because she had it pulled severely back. "I've been meaning to drop in on you for weeks. Are you getting ready for the fall festival?"

"I'm behind, but I plan to sell dry-flower wreaths at a booth. Like last year."

"Is your dad going to sell fresh flowers?" June asked. Justine's father, Standard Roberts, was the biggest flower grower in the valley. He shipped fresh flowers to flower shops all over the West.

"Same as always." Sam stepped into the door frame, wiping his hands on a towel. His usually chipper demeanor seemed to be sagging. He simply nodded hello, and June, who had known Sam all her life, knew there was a problem.

"How's the chemo going, Justine? Have you been feeling okay?"

"Oh, I have my ups and downs, but everything's okay."

"What's the doctor saying?"

"Same old stuff. You know. I'll just be glad when it's all behind me."

"I know you will. Well, how about a nice bouquet for my office. Something with fall colors to get me in the mood."

"I've got something made up in the back. I'll get it."

When Justine edged past Sam in the doorway, he barely moved, keeping his eyes connected to June's, his mouth turned down. It was painful to even look at him, for Sam unsmiling was such a rarity. It meant something devastating. June feared the worst, that treatment wasn't going well and the cancer was advancing.

Justine brought out a bouquet of yellow and red and brown accented with large maple leaves in fall hues. "Perfect," June said, her voice well trained in not giving away her concerns. "How much?"

"Twelve?" Justine asked.

"How about fifteen?" June countered.

Justine laughed. "You're supposed to negotiate me down, June. You're not doing it right."

"I'm surprised you're not out of business, the way you give your beautiful flowers away."

"I don't give just anyone the bargains. If it makes you feel any better, Steph Reynolds was in earlier for a centerpiece for that ten-foot dining table of hers and I gouged her good."

"Well, thank heavens," June replied, taking the flowers and handing over a five and a ten. "Take care of yourself. If you need anything, Justine…"

"Thanks, June. I'll be fine."

June left the flower shop, flirting with ideas about how she'd get Sam alone and ask a few questions. Maybe Elmer could wiggle some information out of him at weekly poker, out of earshot of the others. If the chemo was making Justine extremely ill, there were counteracting drugs, to help her with fatigue and nausea. There was even pharmaceutical marijuana, but she'd have to communicate with Justine's oncologist. Stoicism, saying everything's going to be all right and I'll just be glad when it's over, is no way to go through cancer treatment.

"June?"

She was almost to the clinic when Sam came up behind her. "Sam! I was just wondering how I was going to get you alone and ask you a few questions about Justine. She's looking a little peaked. She should tell her oncologist if she's—"

"She hasn't been to the oncologist. She's stopped the chemo."

June was speechless. This couldn't be! It was so dangerous. Especially in the case of ovarian cancer, perhaps the most dangerous for a woman. "But Sam, you can't have let her do that!"

"I didn't know. She lied about going to the doctor."

"Oh God. But she doesn't look so good. She needs to get in right away, let us see what's wrong."

"We know what's wrong, June. Can't you guess?"

She frowned in confusion. Guess? The woman looked ill!

"Justine is pregnant. She stopped chemo, had her IUD removed and got pregnant almost immediately. I don't know that she had even two chemo treatments."

"But Sam, maybe she's not pregnant. It was a pregnancy scare that caused John to find the tumor, haven't you reminded her of that?"

"Believe me," Sam said tiredly, "it's hard to know what to do."

"Let me think about this," June said. "Let me talk to John. Maybe he'll have some ideas. But you can't force treatment on a person, so the options are pretty limited."

His eyes glistened slightly. "I just hate the thought of being widowed again. So soon after we…" He looked away uncomfortably. "She's going to kill me when she finds out I told."

"If she is pregnant, she can't expect to keep it secret for long," June said, matter-of-fact. "I don't think she thought this one through."

"She didn't think at all," Sam said. "It's like an

obsession. She's driven. Like she needs this more than she needs her own life.''

June touched Sam's arm in sympathy and commiseration. "I hope she isn't obliged.''

June put her flowers on the reception counter and Jessie said, "Tom Toopeek called. He said he needs you at the police department at your earliest convenience.''

"Is someone hurt or sick?''

"He wants you to look at some bones, I think he said.''

"Bones? From…?''

"He didn't say. Can I come?'' Jessie asked excitedly.

"You'll have to ask if Susan will answer the phone. Or even John.''

"John's not here. He's gone to the hospital and will be back in an hour, and Susan has gone over to the café. Can't I put it on the machine? Please?''

June caved. "Sure,'' she said, enjoying Jessie's excitement. "Come along then. We'll call it on-the-job training.''

"Thanks!''

Jessie was a work in progress. A high-school dropout, she'd taken the job at the clinic to appease her father who insisted that if she wasn't going to go to school, she had to work full-time. It didn't take any time at all to see that Jessie was extremely smart; she did the job of five secretaries.

Jessie had a gift for sewing and quirky fashions, so

she'd always believed that she'd break into the clothing industry as an avant-garde designer. Her father was an artist, a painter, and Jessie had inherited a beautiful drawing hand and flair for color. But then she'd witnessed some medical treatments and procedures and fallen in love with medicine. Now she was finishing her GED and applying to colleges. She had miles to go, but Jessie wanted to be a doctor.

This discovery had changed her remarkably. Last spring found the girl dressed as a Goth, her head shaved, her lips and nails colored black, pierces all over the place. This fall she was a foxy young lady whose normal hair color was a peachy blond and many of her pierces were no longer in use.

"Do you do this often?" she asked June. "Look at bones?"

"More often than you'd think. People run into old bones in their gardens or cellars and they worry that they've stumbled upon some hidden human grave, but the remains are almost always those of an animal. A big dog, a deer. Even a horse or cow."

"Can't they tell by the skull?"

"If it's been a long time and the bones get separated, they can't."

The police department was located at the end of the block in a small, brick, three-bedroom house. The living room was a reception-waiting area and the dining room was divided with a counter behind which sat the desk, computer, radios, fax and phones. One of the bedrooms made a good-size office for Tom, and the others were holding cells.

June found Tom standing in the driveway behind his Range Rover. Parked next to him was a tan truck and supposedly its owner, a tall redheaded gentleman with a camera hanging around his neck.

June walked up to them. ''Hi, Tom, what have you got?''

Tom didn't speak. He didn't introduce his companion, either, but silently went to the back of the man's pickup. He pulled down the back hatch and drew toward him an old army blanket. He gently opened it to reveal four bones. June picked up the largest. It was old, but she had no idea how old. It was clearly sawed off on one end, but the other three smaller bones were whole. Unmistakably, they were human.

''Humerus,'' she said. ''Rib, clavicle, and probably metacarpal.'' She tapped the back of her hand. ''Palm bone. The humerus has been sawed or hacked through.''

''You're certain?'' Tom asked.

Jessie reached around June and lifted one of the bones, examining it, turning it to and fro, feeling the texture of it.

''I'm certain they're human bones,'' June said. ''But old.''

''You have any idea how old?''

''I really don't, but that isn't difficult for a pathologist or forensic anthropologist to figure out. Where'd they come from?''

Tom glanced at Jessie. "I'd like this to be confidential." He then glanced at the tall man. "For now."

Jessie made a face. "I work in a doctor's office, Tom. I keep secrets all day long."

He looked back at June. "They came from your aunt Myrna's backyard."

After the shock of the news settled a bit, June was introduced to Paul Faraday, the bird-watcher who'd been poking around Hudson House.

"I didn't realize how close to the house I was getting, but I did have Mrs. Claypool's permission," he said.

"Bird-watching," June said. "Shouldn't you have been looking up?"

"Actually, I tripped over the bones. One of them, at any rate. So I dug around with my hands a bit and unearthed a few more. But I stopped. Didn't want to let on, you know."

"My grandfather built that house over eighty years ago, Mr. Faraday. Those bones might have been there many years before that. This area was all part of the gold rush. There were settlers and boomtowns all over the place. Natives, Spaniards, squatters. In any case, years back, people sometimes felt inclined to bury their own dead on their own property. These could be the bones of an Early American from the nineteenth century or even a hired hand or domestic from the early 1900s."

"Not to mention a Native American," Tom added.

"Where exactly were the bones?" June asked.

"I believe they were under the rhododendron. We'll have them examined, won't we?" he asked.

"I'll take care of that," Tom said, taking the blanket from him. "I'll have it done by the county."

"But I'd like to know, of course," Faraday said. "Since I found them."

Both June and Tom stared at the man in some confusion. What was his interest in old bones, even if he'd found them? "I can arrange to let you know, when the investigation is complete."

"Very good. How long do you suppose it'll take? I plan to be around the general area for the next few weeks. Until the weather turns."

"I have no idea. Leave a number inside with my deputy, Ricky Rios, and we'll give you a call," Tom offered. "Now that it's necessary to investigate the bones and the area, you are ordered to stay away. Even with permission of the owner, the area will be sealed off. Do you understand?"

"Oh certainly. It's a potential crime scene," Faraday said, puffing up a bit.

"That isn't what I meant. In fact, I find it highly unlikely. I just don't want the area disturbed."

"I do understand," Faraday said. "Shall I go tell Mrs. Claypool that I've found bones on her property?"

"Why don't you let me handle that," June said. "She's my aunt, after all."

"Charming woman, Mrs. Claypool. We had tea just days ago."

"Did you, now?" June asked. "How was it you had tea?"

"I thought the least I could do was stop by and say hello, since I was haunting the grounds, so to speak. Most understanding. A delightful lady. Quite a sense of humor for an old girl."

"Hmm," June said.

"I'll be off then," he said. "I'll check back with you before I leave the area to head for home, Chief Toopeek. If you haven't discovered anything about the bones by then, I'll give you my home number."

Tom nodded.

"Doctor. Miss," he said, bobbing in each direction. He then got into his truck. Tom and the women stepped out of the way so he could back out of the driveway and leave.

"I've already got his number," Tom said.

"He's up to no good," June said.

"Are you going to speak to Myrna right away?" Tom asked.

"Sure. Not only should she know about this discovery, I want to ask her to stay away from this Faraday man. I don't think I like him."

"Will you also ask her if, in any of her books, she had a body buried under the rhododendron?"

June chewed her lip. "I think it was in *Dead by Dawn*."

Nine

Sometimes small towns can nurture their mysteries as affectionately as their secrets or their scandals, and that is exactly what Grace Valley had done with the disappearance of Morton Claypool.

June wasn't being glib or dishonest when she explained away the bones to Paul Faraday as probably belonging to a settler or Native. She thought it entirely possible. The one tiny glitch was that her uncle Morton had disappeared twenty years ago, had apparently never been heard from, and not long afterward, Myrna's murder mysteries had grown ever more grisly. This was a *tiny* glitch, because, first of all, no one could imagine Myrna hurting a fly, and second, the entire town thoroughly enjoyed the speculation, and Myrna knew it.

The facts were thus: Morton had been a traveling salesman who spent precious little time in Grace Valley, which seemed to be the preference of Morton and Myrna alike. They were not exactly young when they married—Myrna herself was already in her forties and had been writing Gothic novels for almost twenty years. She had not been well known in those days, as her books were published in library editions in small numbers. Fame would come much later. But raising Elmer and getting him through medical school had been her first life, writing her second and Morton her third. Though no one ever asked, it was probably convenience more than passion that brought them together in the first place.

Morton was an amiable fellow, well liked by almost everyone even if he was understood by few. He sold office supplies, for which there was very modest need in the valley, far greater need in larger cities. Myrna actually met him in a bookstore in Redding. They corresponded for a time and then married on a weekend trip to Reno. She brought him back to Grace Valley and said, "Meet my new husband, Morton Claypool," without anyone, even her beloved brother, ever knowing she was courting.

Over time, Morton was in Grace Valley less and less, but who was to notice? June was barely conscious of this, being a young teen with concerns of her own. Elmer and his wife noticed and, of course, asked Myrna, "Is there any trouble between you and Morton?"

"Why in the world would you ask that?" Myrna countered.

"We see him less and less," Elmer had said.

"And to you, that would translate into trouble?" she wondered aloud.

"Well, he's your husband. What would it mean to you that he's here less and less?"

Myrna had shrugged. "More time to myself, I suppose. I have a book due in six weeks anyway. I have little time for domestic fuss.''

Many a family might have pressed the issue, but Myrna was independent, eccentric and, above all, proud. Elmer and Marilyn took that to mean that Myrna and her husband were not as invested in each other as they had been, that Morton had permission to move along if he so chose. When June was a senior in high school, Myrna said to Elmer and Marilyn, ''I've lost track of Morton altogether. He's been gone for several months now.''

''Are you worried?'' they'd both asked.

''Not in the slightest. If there were bad news, I'd have been notified. And it's just as well I haven't been. I must admit, I haven't been entirely pleased with Morton lately and I don't feel inclined to waste a lot of money on a fancy funeral.''

''You've separated then?'' Elmer had asked.

''Well, if he's not here, I guess we have.''

''What about divorce?''

''Why bother? I certainly wouldn't want another husband. Besides, wouldn't I have to dig him up to manage that?''

Elmer really didn't find anything ominous in her query about digging him up. His gentle sister was a tad dotty, but no murderess. Much later Myrna appeared to kill him off in her books, over and over again.

Everyone in Grace Valley assumed that Morton had wandered off, perhaps found a woman who would make him eggs in the morning, or possibly he'd found a job that was a tish more exciting than

selling pencils and typing paper. As for the speculation that she might have had enough of his long absences and done him in? Myrna was not only unanimously loved, she was thought of as gentle, despite
the bloody novels. And it was *she* who belonged to
Grace Valley. She was an icon. Her father had
founded the town. Morton was the newcomer. People
who know small towns know that you can be a newcomer for twenty years without ever quite being one
of them. People would worry a lot if something happened to Myrna, but they didn't worry overmuch
about Morton.

When the bones were found under her rhododendron at the far south end of her huge yard on top of
the hill, June went immediately to her dad and said,
"Some bird-watcher found four human bones on
Aunt Myrna's property."

Elmer got a look near panic and said, "Shoot!"
Then, in a soft yet urgent tone he said, "June, I
checked under the rhododendron."

An emotional picture of little, skinny Aunt Myrna
in handcuffs and leg irons came to June's mind and,
unbelievably, she got all teary. Her nose pinkened and
dripped. "Oh, Dad," she sniveled. "What if she's in
trouble? Real trouble?"

"June?" Elmer queried, confused. "Are you crying?"

"Jeez," she said, turning away in embarrassment.
She was so much tougher than this. She didn't dis-
solve into tears like some schoolgirl. "It's just that
the picture that came to mind..."

Elmer grabbed both of June's upper arms and gave a squeeze. "She can't ever be in so much trouble that we can't help her, June. Not after all she's done for us."

"Sorry," June said, sniffing. "This is no time to fall apart."

"That's for sure. Not with *bones* in her yard, for God's sake."

June and Elmer went to Myrna's house together, mostly as a show of force. It would be nice if eccentric old Myrna would take things seriously for once. Elmer rang the bell.

"I know it's blasphemous to think this way, but every time I come to this big old house, I can't help but hope I die ahead of her."

"Dad!"

"Well, think what an ordeal it's going to be to clean it out one day," Elmer said. "I don't believe Myrna has ever thrown anything away."

They both gulped and looked at each other. Perhaps not even Morton?

"I used to love to come here as a child," June said, changing the subject. "It was like playing in a museum. I could stay busy for days and never find the end of the treasures. But I sure don't want to have to do that now."

It was Myrna herself who opened the door. Her reading glasses dangled on a rope around her neck, a pencil was stuck behind her ear and she had a well-worn paperback thesaurus in her hand. Her white hair was electrified, escaping her bun in little springs, and she had two dark spots of rouge on her cheeks that matched the red of her lips. "Well, look at this!" she said, clearly surprised. "If it's the both of you together, this must be serious."

"As a matter of fact, it is," Elmer said. "Who's on duty today? Endeara or Amelia?" he asked as he entered.

"It's Amelia, but she's upstairs watching her soap opera. The hospital one. I hope you don't want anything too complicated, because if I call her down to the kitchen to work, she'll be in a foul mood all the rest of the week."

"Good, let her be. We'll go in the kitchen and brew some tea or something. We have to talk about this Faraday fellow."

"I might have known," Myrna said. She leaned toward June to give her a peck on the cheek. "Hello, dear. Are you upset as well?"

"We're neither of us upset, Myrna," Elmer said, but he said it tersely. "Concerned is all. June tells me you've had that Faraday fellow in to tea."

"My goodness, the speed of gossip isn't getting any slower in this town, is it?" Myrna looped her arms through June's and Elmer's and let them guide her to the kitchen.

"You don't even know him," June pointed out. "He could be a thief. Or worse."

"Oh, he's not a thief. He's just what we used to call a nosey parker. Now, what's this all about?"

"In the kitchen," Elmer said.

The kitchen at Hudson House was huge, originally designed to cater dinner parties for large numbers of guests. Charles Hudson had been a rich banker from San Francisco who fell in love with the area later known as Grace Valley. He built the house for his young wife and expected to entertain many friends who would stay for long periods of time. He had not scrimped on space. Myrna, following suit, had always opened her home to guests for dinner parties, committee meetings, any event that justified the space.

Elmer closed the kitchen door. "This is going to be a shock. Sit down."

Myrna sat at the kitchen table. June moved to put on the kettle. Elmer sat across from her and said, "Faraday found human bones in your backyard."

"Oh! Is *that* all," she said, relieved. "They're probably the remains of some old prospector."

"Very likely," Elmer said. "But Myrna, it's going to demand an answer to the Morton Claypool question."

"I don't see why. They wouldn't be Morton's remains."

"You're quite sure?"

She leaned forward, a bit impatient. "Don't you think I'd have *noticed?*"

"They were under the rhododendron," June said from the stove. "Definitely human remains."

"A skeleton?" Myrna wanted to know.

"No. Actually, just a few bones. Which leads to the question, did some old prospector die, dismember himself and scatter his remains around the yard?"

Myrna shrugged. "Daddy did not intentionally disturb any graveyard or burial ground when building Hudson House, but that was a long time ago, you know. It's possible the builders were less than cautious when they were excavating for the foundation. We have an ample cellar." She rolled her eyes. "I haven't been down there in years. The steps creak as bad as my knees and I'm not sure which will go first."

"Did you hear me, Myrna? It's time to take the question of what became of Morton Claypool seriously. You're going to have to stop hedging for the fun of it," Elmer demanded.

"Elmer Hudson, how dare you!" she replied. "You don't really think I do that on purpose!"

"I'm absolutely sure of it! You enjoy alluding to having done him in. You write about women who kill their husbands all the damn time."

"Now, that's simply not true! My last two books had male killers." She smiled snidely. "You don't read my books, do you, Elmer?"

"I buy them," he said.

"I read them," June said. "And Dad is right, Aunt Myrna. You're going to be asked a serious question and you'll have to give a serious answer or there could be problems. You have a missing husband! Human remains have been found in your yard! You may not always write about women bent on revenge who get away with murdering their husbands, but you have enough times to get the tongues wagging." June stopped and looked at Myrna, who positively beamed. "Look at yourself! You think it's fun."

"Now, don't be ridiculous. I'm just proud as can be that you read my books." She sneered at Elmer. "Not everyone does."

"All right, all right... Talk to me about Morton, Auntie. Please," June implored.

"May I have tea first?"

"Of course," June said. Then she realized that Myrna wasn't being shy or decorous; she wanted time to drum up a story. "No, wait. The water has to boil. I'm fixing the tea and you will have it the second it's ready. For now, just tell us about Morton before Amelia is finished with her soap opera."

"My, but you're impatient."

Elmer leaned into Myrna's space. "Hardly," he said sternly, a tone rarely taken with his sister. "We've waited over twenty years."

Myrna sighed deeply, as if bored. Then she shook a bony finger in Elmer's face. "You're the only person I'll allow to take that tone with me, you know."

"I might not be, by the end of this. That Faraday fellow turned the bones over to the police, you know."

"Ach, Tom Toopeek! Well, I daresay he knows the score. He's not likely to overreact to the extent the two of you are."

"Myrna!"

"All right, all right. But you're going to be so disappointed. It's a terribly dull story." She took a breath. "Morton saw himself as suave, but, of course, if you remember him at all, you know he was terribly boring. Very sweet, but boring. If he hadn't had his job selling paper supplies to businesses, he'd have had absolutely nothing to drive him. Morton was a sincere man, and smart in his own way. Our favorite thing to talk about were the books we read. He was an incredible reader. He particularly liked my books, which drew me to him, I suppose. I could nearly use him for research—he read so fast and remembered everything. But strangely, he never could apply anything he learned. No matter how hard he worked at his small business, he was never successful. He lost things, mismanaged customers, handled his records badly. He was something of a brilliant dunderhead. You know what he was? He was steady, that's what!

"We had but one area of disagreement that was serious. I wouldn't even consider letting him help me manage my inheritance and earnings. He had investment and business ideas, but I *couldn't!* He was perfectly useless. He'd have bungled it all, so I kept making excuses and kept control. It bothered him. But he seemed to get used to that idea, over time.

"Morton was easily distracted," she went on, "and no one around Grace Valley seemed to notice that there were periods of time he wouldn't appear for months. I suppose I contributed to that illusion by saying things like, 'Oh my, you've just missed Morton,' when in fact he hadn't been around in quite a while. Then for a period of months he'd be around every week." Myrna leaned into Elmer's space and whispered, "I suspected other women."

"You should have told me," he said.

"Why? This didn't seem to be a problem for Morton and I."

"Myrna, you're an intelligent woman. What about things like *disease?*"

Myrna looked stricken. "You don't imagine I'd sleep with a man who spends weeks, if not months, gone off to unexplained places? Morton was the dunderhead, not I!" She straightened indignantly, brushing invisible lint off one shoulder. "Besides, he wasn't nearly as accomplished as he thought he was."

"So...he was not such a good husband?" June asked. "Were you unhappy?"

"June," she said earnestly, "it depends entirely on what kind of husband you need. Since I hadn't imagined having any kind of husband at all, Morton wasn't really much trouble. And I've always enjoyed talking books." She looked skyward. "I really don't know what happened to Morton. Suddenly he was gone. There was no getting him back." She looked at her brother. "I confess, I didn't try. I knew we'd both be better off if we just let things lie. But I assure you, I didn't chop him up and plant him in the garden!"

The teakettle whistled and June prepared tea. As she passed a cup to Myrna, she said, "But Aunt Myrna, why have you seemed to kill him off in book after grisly book?"

Myrna looked at her as if she were a total dunce. "My dear child, do you think story ideas grow on trees?"

* * *

The quilting circle always met at Birdie's house because it was centrally located and because she was the most senior member. She was just shy of being the eldest as well, but Tom Toopeek's mother, Philana, was older by a couple of years. They would not have wanted to meet at the Toopeeks' house, however, because there were so many distractions there. Quilting, Birdie always said, is a quiet sport.

There was an unenforced rule that everyone would bring some sort of dish or snack and Birdie would be obligated only for coffee. It was not an enforced rule because there were times a person was too busy and rushed to even stop by the bakery for a little something. Thus, about half of them would remember to bring something, and June least of all.

But June, who had been absent for a month, felt the need to make amends, so she was up at 5:00 a.m. putting a chocolate cake in the oven. For her to bring something, given her chaotic schedule, was something in itself, and for it to be homemade reinforced the message that she was sorry to have been away. And while she preheated the oven and mixed the cake, she realized how she had missed them, how she longed for the company of her friends. She had been lonely, after all.

As if that thought carried a message across the country, the phone rang. Somehow she knew. In some psychic way, she never for a second thought her cake would be ruined by a medical emergency. She picked up the receiver and heard the rich, deep voice of Jim.

He said, "God, how I've missed you. Are you still my girl?"

She felt a warm flush pass through her. The sound of his voice, so familiar yet far from memory, filled her with new longing. And then a bizarre thing happened. When she wished to murmur back to him in loving tones, instead she sniped, "Barely."

"Uh-oh. Did someone wake up on the wrong side of the bed this morning?"

She took a breath and begged herself to be rational. It was not like her to be waspish. "Do you have any idea how many weeks I've waited for a call?"

"I'm sorry," he said patiently. "I've wanted to."

June sighed. "No, I'm sorry. I don't know why—"

"It's tough, this situation we've gotten ourselves into. I understand, June."

"You can't understand because even I don't understand. It's just that—" She couldn't finish. Just that *what?*

"I didn't want it to be so long," he said. "I know I miss you as much as you miss me. More, probably."

"Are you in danger?" she asked.

"No. Really, no. I mean, that may come before we're finished here, but at the moment everything's cool."

"If it's *cool,* then why couldn't you at least have gotten a message to me that you're all right?"

She was stunned. Where had that come from? She had been missing him, but she hadn't been in any way angry. Or had she? Had she stuffed down some penetrating anger that had bounced up at her without any warning?

"June..."

"Oh God, Jim, I'm sorry! I'm so sorry! I guess I've been more upset than I realized. It's probably because of my aunt. She's in trouble and just yesterday I was in tears about it. You don't know this, but I'm hardly ever in tears about anything. Jesus, forgive me. Yes, yes, I miss you, too."

He was quiet a long moment, then she heard him sigh. "What kind of trouble?" he wanted to know.

"Somebody found bones in her backyard. Human bones. And, well, her husband disappeared about twenty years ago and she's a writer and in several of her books over the years she's killed off a husband or ten and buried them in the... This sounds really, really bad, doesn't it?"

"Oh man," he said.

"Maybe I've run into something I really can't handle," June said softly. "Little frail old Auntie Myrna in chains..." She sniffed quietly.

"June, are you crying again?"

It was not necessary to admit it, even though she muffled some of her tears in a handy tissue.

"I was so happy with you," she said. "For such a short period of time." And then it came again, the tears.

"Oh brother," he said. "Look, try to get a grip. This isn't going to last forever. And this is it, you know. The last time."

"And you're coming here?" she asked ridiculously.

"Where else would I go?"

"How do I know? You haven't even called in a month!"

"I'm *undercover!*"

"Where we need to be is under the *covers!*" she nearly shouted.

Fortunately, what she heard in response was his deep laugh, rolling through the phone line to meet her. So she joined him, laughing at how stupid and out of control she was.

"I have to go," he said when they finally stopped.

"Already?" she whined. "But you only just—"

"Listen to me, this is important. I'm not going to take any unnecessary chances, because I want to come back to you. You understand? So if I can't call you, that's just how it is. It doesn't mean I've stopped wanting you."

She wanted to tell him, "Say you love me again." But instead she said, "I understand." And she wanted to say, "I love you, Jim." But instead she said, "Please be careful."

"I will. Aunt Myrna will be okay, June. And I'll be back with you soon."

They disconnected and June drew a ragged breath. I'm losing it, she said to herself. Finally, there was just too much pressure. She blew her nose. She needed a long, hot shower to wash away the mood. She took her time, trying to get her thoughts on track.

And when she got out of the shower she was greeted by the sweet-smelling smoke of burning chocolate cake.

The women of the Graceful Quilters made something of a fuss over June and Sadie. They would never know how much June needed the extra attention, after the way she'd started the day, and Sadie never turned down a pet. It wasn't as if she hadn't seen them, for she saw them all the time, in various settings around town. But it was different seeing them here, in a quiet room, alone, sharing secrets and trusting the confidentiality of the group. She presented them with a chocolate cake made by Burt Crandall at the bakery and confessed it was her second cake of the day. And then she noticed that her darling Birdie was looking positively haggard.

June's bond with Birdie went back to her infancy. Birdie was June's godmother, her deceased mother's best friend. There wasn't a thing June couldn't tell Birdie, or ask Birdie, except on the subject of her son, Chris. Both Birdie and June had some ragged edges where he was concerned.

Sadie was relegated to the kitchen, where she cozied up to the radiator. When they all sat down to quilt, Corsica asked, "Where are your houseguests tonight, Birdie?"

"Chris put some money on a house out by Roberts's flower fields, not too far from the Toopeeks', but it's not habitable yet. It's been vacant for years and needs lots of work. Judge, Chris and the boys are doing repairs out there tonight while we quilt."

"They need to get their own place," Philana said, not looking up from her stitching. "It would strain anyone to have so much clutter and confusion."

"You live with five grandchildren!" Birdie argued.

"But I always have done," Philana said.

That was it, June realized. Birdie was exhausted by the unaccustomed complications of long-term house-guests.

"Chris was always a lot of trouble," Birdie said quietly. "Oh, I couldn't ask for a better son. But he's busy. Always busy. And now there are three of them."

"When do they expect to be in their own place?"

"Not quite soon enough," Birdie said, and the tension was broken by laughter.

They shared the news of the town, talking first about Charlotte's shaky recovery at home with Bud waiting on her, then about Jessie taking her GED test in two weeks to complete her high-school diploma. Harry Shipton came up, along with his gangling good looks and love of poker. Finally the bones in Myrna's yard surfaced as a topic, and it was unanimous that they could not be any relation to Morton Claypool. Justine's pallor was mentioned with worry, but June held silent about the possibility of pregnancy, and before she knew it, they were putting away their quilt and having a cup of coffee. It felt so good to be back among them, nurtured and nurturing.

The spell was broken with the crashing disruption of four males bursting into the house, the gamy odor of hard work at carpentry accompanying them. June gave Judge a kiss on his weathered old cheek, said hello to Chris and the boys and quickly made her excuses. But it was not awkward because all the women dispersed. No one wanted to linger over coffee and cake with the men present. The twins headed for the kitchen where they made fast work of what was left of the cake, calling to their grandmother for milk. Sadie was up and wagging hopefully, but the boys ignored her. What manner of boy didn't stoop to pet a wagging dog? June wondered with a frown. "Come, Sadie," she called. "Time for us to go."

They all said their goodbyes on the porch, June being the only one on foot. Corsica and Jessie had ridden together, as had Ursula and her mother-in-law. Birdie went back into the house to attempt to regain control of her kitchen, while June headed down the street to the clinic where she'd left her little truck. The nights were cooling down faster as mid-September approached and she shivered in the chill air. As she passed under one of the two street lamps, she heard her name.

"Hey, June. Hold up."

When she turned, Chris came out of the darkness toward her.

Ten

It's not fair, June thought. She was moody, teetering on some weird emotional precipice. And lonely. So lonely with Jim so far away and who knew when, or God forbid, *if* he'd be back. And in that condition she had to view Chris walking toward her, approaching her with that damn confidence of his, that sexy grin that had sucked her in as a girl and would threaten the chastity of a weaker woman now. I'm vulnerable! she wanted to shout. Don't mess with me!

"I just wanted to tell you that I was glad to see you at Mom's tonight," Chris said. "She was complaining about hardly seeing you lately. She wouldn't admit it, but I think she was secretly blaming me."

"I've been really busy," June said. "And so has Birdie."

"Yeah. She's doing too much."

"She's looking a little tired, Chris…"

"She's not used to having a houseful of people."

"People? Guys, Chris. A cranky old husband, a grown son who's just left his wife, and teenage twin boys. There's enough testosterone in her house to grow a beard on a melon."

That made him laugh. "You're right. But we'll be

out of her hair soon enough. As soon as the house I just bought is livable.''

"You're absolutely staying then?" she asked.

They stood under the street lamp on the dark, deserted street. It felt like a spotlight.

Sadie, enjoying her freedom, pranced back and forth across the street, paused beside June briefly, then pranced off again. The world was a place of plentiful smells for a collie, but she always circled back to make sure June wouldn't leave without her. "I'm absolutely staying. Which is why I wanted to talk to you. For just a minute." He glanced over his shoulder at the café as if looking for a haven and a cup of coffee, but it appeared to be closed. George didn't keep regular hours, but if anything was going on—like a town meeting, high-school ball game or special event—you could count on him to be open. He was just about the only game in town. But on this ordinary Thursday night, it was lights out at 9:00 p.m.

"I was just heading back to the clinic for my truck, then home. I have an early morning and…"

"I'll walk you," he said. But he didn't just walk alongside. He took her elbow and steered her in that direction. Out of the spotlight, at least. "I'm really bothered by something. When are things going to be easy again between us?"

"Aren't they?" she countered, knowing that once again she was faking. There was an unmistakable edge to her voice.

"Seems like we'd run into each other a lot more

than we have lately. And when we do, it's a little tight. Tense. Am I imagining that?'' he asked.

Chris. He always had been smooth. Even when he was just a kid.

"One of the things I'm most grateful for,'' he went on, "is that everything here is the same. Undisturbed. Even the new businesses haven't seemed to upset the balance of things. The town looks the same. The people are the same, except maybe a few years older. Even the trails, back roads and farms are just like they were when I left. The only thing that's different is me and you. I mean, the way you are with me.'' He stopped in the street, forcing her to stop too, and looked into her eyes. "Is there anything I can do to make things flow a little better between us?''

A memory was awakened in her. Before they were boyfriend and girlfriend, before they were young lovers talking about marriage, they had been best friends. June, Chris and Tom—and sometimes Greg Silva, when he didn't have to help on his dad's farm. They had played hard, camped out, trusted each other and talked about crucial things—their fantasies for the future, their fears and problems and deepest desires. Once they had all cut their hands and became blood brothers, forgetting June was the girl.

Was he still someone she could talk to?

She sighed in defeat. "Okay, I admit it,'' she said. "You disrupted me by coming back. Especially the way you came blundering into my life asking if we could try again. Jesus.''

"Disrupted, huh?" he asked, grinning from ear to ear. "I bet you wanted to kill me."

"Kill?" She laughed slyly. "Don't be silly, Chris. Death was too good for you."

"Aha!" he shouted as though victorious. He spread his hands wide. "The lady admits to violent thoughts! I knew it!"

"Well, I'm pretty much over those fantasies red with your blood, but I might still be a little tense. I don't think that's too unreasonable. I think it's going to take some time."

The look that came over his face was like sheer bliss. Incredible relief blushed with deep happiness. "God, that takes a load off my mind. I know I don't deserve much consideration, but it hurt to think you might never forgive me. What would I do if I lost you forever, June-bug?"

I would know how that feels better than you, came to her mind. But she didn't say it. Instead she walked on toward the clinic. She always preferred to hold her tongue for the sake of peace rather than speak up and risk discord. She was never sure whether this was a virtue or a character flaw. *Am I of generous spirit or a big fat chicken,* she asked herself. Again, his hand was on her arm, steering her through the darkness.

"There were plenty of times over the years that I fantasized about what it would be like when I came back, but I honestly didn't know if I'd ever have the guts to do it. I left a lot behind, you know."

Not the least of which was a wife, she thought. But again, silence.

"I had my own little neighborhood insurance office. Fortunately, Bob Hanson over in Rockport is going to let me into his shop."

His hand on her elbow actually felt *good*. What was *that* about? Just more of that loneliness creeping into the picture? She said, "Job, house, school for the kids. You're just about all set, aren't you?"

"I thought I'd put up a little booth during the harvest festival. Bob hasn't done that in the past, but he thinks it's a good idea."

"I agree. How are the boys liking it here?"

"So far they love it. They haven't had this kind of freedom in their young lives. Where we lived in San Diego they were limited to the neighborhood, park and school. Here, it's like all of Grace Valley is open to them."

"Like it was for us" she heard herself say.

"It was a great way to grow up, wasn't it, Junebug? We sure can't complain of the childhood we had in this town."

"It's not a bad adulthood, either."

"I hope you don't mind me asking, but how is it you didn't get married?"

She laughed hollowly. "Who was I going to marry, you nitwit?"

"Well, hell, you were away at school for about ten years. Didn't they have men where you were?"

"Yeah, they had men there, but do you have any idea what medical school is like? Or internship and residency?" They reached her truck and she stopped. Be fair, she told herself. Getting along is better than being bitter. "Actually, I had a couple of close calls. But in the end, neither of them would have wanted to come here with me, and this was exactly where I've always wanted to be."

"That's true, huh?" he said as if he'd just remembered. "There were lots of kids we went to school with, farmers' kids and loggers' kids especially, who couldn't wait to shake the dust of this dumpy little town off the soles of their shoes, but you always said this was the only place you ever wanted to live. So, you couldn't find a small-town type to fall in love with?"

She shrugged. "There weren't a whole lot of med students who just couldn't wait to move to a tiny little burgh where they'd be paid in vegetables or eggs. But for me, it's the perfect life. Most of the time." She opened her truck door. "I'd better get home, Chris. I've had a long day. I was up at 5:00 a.m. burning up a cake."

"What?"

She shook her head in exasperation. "Long story. The phone rang, I got distracted, I was baking a cake for quilting, and—"

"Little accident?"

"Big smell. I left all the windows open to air the place out. I hope I don't find Mama and Papa Bear eating porridge in my house. Where is that dog? Sadie!" she called. She gave a whistle and was immediately rewarded by the sound of Sadie's tags jingling. "Good girl," she said as the collie jumped in.

Chris put a hand on June's shoulder. "Well, look,"

he said, kind of stumbling. "Thanks for giving me, you know, a few minutes. I just couldn't stand the thought that we wouldn't be, well, good friends at least. You know?"

"I know," she said.

"For now, anyway." He leaned toward her to give her a friendly hug and peck on the cheek, but once he got close, he slowed way down. Hovered. His lips against her cheek, his hand on her shoulder. Cautiously and slowly, he slid his lips around to hers, his hand moving from her shoulder to her chin to lift her face to meet his.

She would ask herself later why she allowed this, for to lead Chris on would be a huge mistake, with him in this condition of wanting a second chance with her. But she was curious, and okay, lonely. What could it hurt to kiss him to be sure she didn't feel anything for him anymore? Absolutely sure?

But she felt something. She wasn't sure what it was. Perhaps memory, perhaps longing, perhaps vulnerability to the old boyfriend, or maybe she was just a cheap hussy who couldn't resist the most attractive, single bachelor the town had to offer at the moment.

Damn, she thought, kissing him back. Some things never change, and Chris's lips had not. He had always had great, soft lips that moved familiarly over hers. If her life weren't so complicated right now, it would be very easy to fall back into a routine with him. This was just what she remembered, and it felt good. But with the good-feeling kiss came the memory of what kind of boyfriend he'd been. When he tried to part her lips with his, she pulled back.

"I'm sorry," she said, and immediately thought why am I sorry? "I shouldn't have let you do that because…well, you know. I don't want to have a romantic, you know—" She stammered and stuttered and couldn't spit it out. "I was just curious. Curious, not interested. Think of it as…old time's sake."

He grinned down at her, but she could see in his smile that he thought he'd scored one. "It's okay, June-bug. Don't be sorry. I'm sure not sorry."

"Chris, listen, you mustn't think—"

"Hey, don't worry! I'm a patient guy!"

"But—"

She was cut off by the lights from a vehicle that was heading straight at them. There was a loud whoop and the police SUV pulled up. Ricky Rios rolled down the window. "Mr. Forrest? Chris? You have any idea where your boys might be?"

"At home, brushing their teeth and getting ready for bed, I hope. At my folks'."

"Well, sir, your mom thinks they might've come in the front door and gone right out the back."

"Damn the little shits. Is she worried about them? They probably just—"

"No sir, she didn't call me, I went by the house. Someone was egging some houses over on Fourth Street. The back door to Burt's bakery is jimmied open and it's just a half block from Judge and Birdie's, and—"

"Okay, Ricky, let's see if we can rein 'em in,"

Chris said, walking around the SUV to the passenger side. "Little devils sure can find plenty of trouble in just thirty minutes, can't they? Bye, June. I'll catch you later."

There will be no catching, she thought. "Good luck," was what she said.

June woke up earlier than usual the next morning, and the very first thing on her mind was that she had kissed Chris while she was seriously involved with Jim. Why had she let that happen? Was it because no one knew about Jim? Was it because he was invisible to everyone but her? and second, mystical—almost nonexistent?

But if she examined her feelings for Jim, they were bold. She was pretty sure she was in love with him.

The hell of it was, with Chris she had history, and with Jim, uncertainty. With Chris there was unfinished business, and it was high time there be closure. With Jim there was hope, but it was clouded by distance and time.

She sat up and shook her head. Maybe it was a good thing that she had to deal with the Chris issue, before she made a permanent commitment to Jim. It gave her a little time. Though she hadn't pined over Chris all these years—her first love, her first broken heart—he had never been very far from her thoughts. But now she had time to reckon with this issue once and for all, close it out, be sure she was done with that whole thing. She would be smart; this would finally be over.

She showered and dressed, though it was not yet dawn. The prospect of beating everyone else to the clinic appealed to her. She wanted to think, undisturbed and undistracted, about the kind of life she wanted. She couldn't help but feel, deep down, that she was on the threshold of a new beginning. And she did her best thinking while alone at the clinic.

To say she had a special feeling about the place was an understatement. When she had come back to Grace Valley, her dad was still practicing out of his house, and that's where she began her work in the valley. But the little country doctor's office in his home was not even close to accommodating the growing population. Elmer had been thinking of moving his practice over to Rockport, near the hospital; June's idea was build the clinic. She'd been dreaming of just such a clinic for the town for as long as she'd been studying medicine. And the town rallied to support the construction, each person in whatever way possible, no matter how slim their means. Free tile for the floor, a little gratis construction work, donated supplies, a few dollars tossed into the hat. In the end it was Aunt Myrna who secured the building loan and guaranteed it. She also bought the ambulance after June wrecked her Jeep on a dangerous curve while out on an emergency call. Myrna was loaded. And how loaded only she knew for sure.

When June pulled into town, she noticed that the café was already open—a good hour early. And next, with a bit of disappointment, she saw that she wasn't the first to arrive at the clinic. The ambulance was already parked outside at this predawn hour. The building was dark, however, and when June and Sadie got to the back door, she found it locked.

She opened the door and flipped on the hall light. "John?" she called, but there was no answer. The first room to her right contained two beds and functioned as a recovery room for patients who had outpatient procedures that required sedatives or local anesthesia. The other rooms held examining tables and gurneys. In one of the beds, sleeping in his clothes, was John Stone. He must have had a patient in the middle of the night and decided not to go all the way back home, June reasoned.

She glanced at her watch; it was almost five-thirty. Since George had the café open and her stomach was growling, she decided John could probably also use a cup of coffee and a treat. June and Sadie beat a quiet retreat.

The clinic had a coffeepot, of course, but it wasn't used very often because June's ritual was to walk across the street where her coffee and morning pastry were always free, a custom that brought George much pleasure. He would let her pay for lunch and dinner, but he took care of the doctors, the law and the clergy. And they took care of him.

"George?" she called. She heard some clamor in the back, behind the grill.

"Morning, June, morning, Sadie," he called. "It'll be a minute 'fore she's brewed."

"What are you doing here so early?"

He grunted angrily. "Some little heathens threw

eggs at the front window. Ricky Rios was doing his drive through town, spotted the mess and called me. He figured I'd want to get it washed off before the start of business, which I did. That's the second time.''

''No way!'' June exclaimed, then remembered the night before. ''George, do you have any idea who—''

''I've got a pretty good idea, considering we ain't never had that kind of trouble around town before those two little hellions and their daddy moved up here from San Diego.''

''I wonder, does Chris *know?*''

''Don't think there's much mystery about that. He knows. He just don't take it too seriously. But he will. Because if I catch 'em, I'll see 'em arrested.''

All June could think was poor Birdie. No wonder she was looking so tired. They weren't just a handful, they were *bad!*

''Little bit early for you, isn't it?'' George asked.

''It is. I was awake before five. And John's already in, so I'll take him a cup and whatever pastry he likes.''

''He usually favors the bismark. Let me get your bear claws. You all running a special today or something?'' George asked, going back behind the grill while the coffee perked.

''No, I just couldn't sleep and John was on call last night. He must have had a patient at the clinic—he's conked out on one of the beds.'' June sniffed the air. ''George, what is that awful smell?''

George peeked around the counter, his face wrinkled in question. "Smell?"

June put a hand on her stomach. "*Blllkkkk!* What is that? It's putrid."

"I'm just frying up a little bacon, is all. I thought I'd beat the rush, have some breakfast."

"You'd better check that bacon or I'm going to be treating you for food poisoning later today. I think it's gone bad."

George sniffed. "Smells okay to me, June. You sure?"

"I have a good nose," she said. "Is that coffee ready yet? Can you cheat the pot so I can get out of here?"

"Sure thing, June," he said, hurrying back around the grill. "Gee, it sure don't smell that bad to me. But if you think so, I'll pitch it and start again."

"Do yourself a favor," she said. She took her coffees and sweets and got out of the café before she turned green. George made a mean pie, but he'd never been much of a cook. Passable was all.

She went into the room where John slept. She sat on the stool between the two beds, her tray of coffees and pastries on her lap. She hadn't turned on the light; she didn't want to startle him awake. The only light in the room came from the hall.

He opened one eye and peered at her.

"Late night?"

He groaned and pulled the blanket over his head.

"I brought you coffee and a bismark. George said that's your usual. He's frying up roadkill over there and it stinks to high heaven, so be glad you got room service.''

John groaned again and slowly came to a sitting position. Known for his *GQ* good looks, John was rumpled, bristly and his hair was spiky.

"Gee, you don't look that great first thing in the morning, do you?" she observed.

He reached for a cup of coffee, took a sip and scratched his head.

"So," she said, "who was in?"

"In where?" he asked.

"Here. What brought you to the clinic?"

He looked at her with a hard, level stare. "I was tired of the lumps on my couch."

Her mouth fell open. "No way!" she said when she'd recovered. There were tiffs and then there were tiffs. "Haven't you two made up yet?"

"We have brief cease-fires. Then I try opening my mouth again."

"Jesus, John! You must have really stepped in it good!"

"You can't imagine..." He sipped his coffee again.

"What the hell did you say?"

"I'm not sure," he said. "It's just that, when I try to address the subject of women and work, work and women, I screw it up so bad, it's to the point now that I'm lucky to be *alive*." He reached for the bismark, held it with the napkin it came in and took a bite. Red jellied filling bubbled to the top. "I tried a new approach. Guess how this one worked. 'Susan,'" he quoted, "'I don't want you to have to endure the stress of working outside the home. I want to take care of you. I want you to have everything I can give you and I don't want you to worry about all the pressures of a medical career.'"

June leaned forward on her stool, astonished. She frowned. "John, you didn't say 'worry your pretty little head,' did you? Because I'd be picking shot out of *your* butt, if you had."

He sighed in helplessness. "I might as well have."

She couldn't help but laugh. "God, are you stupid. 'I don't want you to have to worry about being an adult, dear,'" she mocked. "'Just let Daddy do all the worrying and you just rest your teeny, tiny little brain.'" John frowned. The deeper his frown, the harder she laughed. "'And while you rest your teeny little brain, do you mind doing the housework, laundry, shopping, ironing, cooking, landscaping, child care. And could you manage the budget, write to my parents and get the car repaired? Thanks, and don't fret, honey. I'll worry about the *important* things.'" She howled. She thought she was extremely funny.

"I didn't mean that," he said darkly.

"Tell me something," she asked. "What did Mike Dickson do to get himself in trouble?"

"I probably shouldn't tell you."

"I don't think Julianna wants to get a job other than the one she has, so—" John began to color, his cheeks slowly growing crimson. "Oh, no!" she said. John nodded. "Mike commented that his wife didn't want to work, she wanted to take care of him, his house and his children. Like his mother had."

June erupted into hysterical laughter. "Five kids! An orchard, farmhouse and an extended family living on the property! God! Sounds like a paid vacation to me!"

"See, that's the thing," John said pleadingly. "It's all semantics. That's not what we *meant.*"

"John," June said, tears beginning to show on her cheeks. "You guys need to go to remedial husband classes. The two of you are as dumb as a box of hammers."

June was in the middle of a quiet Friday morning at the clinic when Mrs. Lundgren, a surgical nurse from Valley Hospital, called. She overheard Jessie trying to explain that she didn't know where a patient who hadn't kept an appointment for a surgical consultation might be. There were no patients in the waiting room, Susan was at her desk filling out a schedule and June was scribbling in a chart. Jessie put the caller on hold and looked at June pleadingly. "June, this is about Mrs. Mull, and I don't know what to—"

"Here, let me," June said, taking the receiver. "This is Dr. Hudson," she said.

"Hello, Doctor, sorry to bother. Your patient, Mrs. Mull, hasn't kept up her appointments for presurgical blood work or her appointment with the plastic surgeon who's doing the next surgery. And, as far as I can see, there's no phone number."

"The Mulls have no phone," June said. "But they

live in town. Someone from our clinic could stop by and make sure she knows she has an appointment. Would that help?''

The secretary sighed impatiently. "I would think, since this is a *charity* case, that Mrs. Mull would be a little more courteous and conscientious."

Prickles went up June's spine and the hair at the base of her neck was electrified. "Mrs. Lundgren, do you have Jurea Mull's chart?"

"Yes, it's right here. With the appointment roster," she replied, her voice brittle.

"Did you read it, or do you only know that she didn't keep her appointment, that her surgery is free and that she was referred by me?"

"Dr. Hudson, I—"

"Let me save you a little time," June said, her voice getting louder. "There are one or two additional facts you should know. Mrs. Mull is having plastic surgery because at the age of five she took the bad end of a claw hammer in the face when her father was in the back swing of driving a nail. She never saw a doctor or had treatment. She's lived in the backwoods all her life, and for her to go to the hospital for major surgery probably took more courage than you or I will possess in a lifetime."

Susan stood up from her desk in awe, and John came into the reception area to see what the upset was about. They all stared at June in amazement.

There was a moment of silence. June could hear herself breathe.

"I certainly didn't mean to offend you, Dr. Hudson," Mrs. Lundgren said.

"Don't worry about me, but when and if you ever chance to meet or converse with Jurea Mull, treat her with the respect owed a person who has endured monumental challenges."

"Of course," she said meekly.

"And I will go to her house to find out why she hasn't kept her appointment."

"Thank you, Doctor," Mrs. Lundgren said.

June hung up the phone and thought, Well, I didn't have any trouble speaking up that time. She frowned at herself. She was doing a lot of things lately that came as surprises to herself. Oh, Mrs. Lundgren probably deserved to be taken down a peg, and Jurea most definitely was entitled to a champion or two along the way, but the entire conversation could have been handled with a little less venom and a lot more diplomacy.

So why was she smiling? Had it felt that good just to chew someone's ass?

She then noticed her entire staff staring at her.

"I'm becoming very strange," she said to them. "And I think I like it."

Eleven

The tiny two-bedroom house that the Mull family rented was not quite upscale enough to be called modest, but it was the finest thing they'd ever had. There was electricity and hot- and cold-running water—luxuries that had sent Jurea into an explosion of excitement. She had never dreamed she could live so well, which was an exhibition of perspective that many an American could use as a lesson.

Charlie MacNeil, the Veterans Administration counselor, had been able to fix Clarence up with a disability pension based on Clarence's PTSD, clearly a by-product of the war. It was the first time the Mulls had had a regular income. Charlie also managed to get the family furnishings, kitchenware and clothing from the Vietnam Vets charity. And finally, the kids had worked with volunteer tutors all summer so that they could enter school in the fall. It turned out that Jurea and Clarence hadn't done too badly with their ad hoc home schooling; Clinton was a mere two years behind and Wanda only one.

They had come so far, but as June pulled up to the little house she was reminded that, for Clarence at least, it had been too much, too fast. She hoped against hope that he had come back to the house in town, but his old truck wasn't parked anywhere in sight. Already disappointed, June went up on the creaky porch, followed by Sadie.

Clinton answered the door, and he beamed when he saw her. "Dr. Hudson, I'll be danged! What are you doing here?"

"I hope I'm not interrupting dinner or anything," she said. "I was looking for your mom."

"Ma ain't here, but come on in and sit. Say hello to Wanda."

"Can Sadie come in, Clinton? She's well behaved."

"Sure. We've been talking about getting us a dog. Come ahead."

He turned to lead the way into the house. Her powers of observation kicked in and she studied his gait. He had a prosthetic leg and foot made necessary by the below-the-knee amputation done in the spring. He did well on it; his stride was strong and even.

Clinton led her into the kitchen where Wanda sat at the table with her schoolbooks out. There was bread, cookies and chips open on the counter as though they'd had a cold supper while they did their homework. Wanda smiled at June, but her expression beamed with delight when she saw Sadie. She immediately kneeled on the floor so she could pet her. Here was a girl who could do with a pet, June thought.

"How's school going, Wanda?" she asked.

"It's going a little fast for me, but Clinton gets

most of it and helps me. I got to try harder than most, you know.''

"But do you like it?''

"Oh, yes, ma'am, it's the best thing. I even have a friend to listen to CDs with.''

"Wanda's in love with the Backstreet Boys,'' Clinton teased, grinning.

"Am not!'' she protested, coloring a little.

"Sit a spell, Dr. Hudson. Have a cookie with us,'' he invited, grabbing the package and unceremoniously plopping it on the table.

"Okay, but don't let me have more than one,'' she said, pulling out a chair. "I get going on these things and can eat the whole bag.''

"You can have as many as you want,'' he said. "Ma'll be sorry she wasn't here for your visit.''

"I need to see her, Clinton. When will she be back?''

He shrugged. "I got no way of knowing.''

"Do you know where she is?''

"She's back in Shell Mountain with Daddy,'' he said.

"For the day?'' June asked.

"No, ma'am. For the time being.''

June sighed and chewed on the cookie. They weren't getting anywhere fast. "Clinton, help me out here. She had an appointment with the plastic surgeon to schedule her next surgery and she didn't show up. The hospital couldn't call and remind her since you don't have a phone yet. Maybe I could give her a lift to the hospital tomorrow?''

Clinton shrugged again, as if he didn't get what June didn't get. "I don't know if she'll be back tomorrow. She said she had to see about Daddy because he's having a hard spell."

A cold dawning came over June. "Clinton, when did she go back to your old place in Shell Mountain?"

Clinton rolled his eyes upward, remembering. "Let's see. Right about two weeks ago now."

"But you didn't go. Why?"

"Oh, Ma didn't want us to go back there. She knew we were both intent on school and living in town. Besides, it's Daddy can't take change, not us."

"We like it in town," Wanda said.

A flash of squeaking fur streaked across the kitchen and under the cupboard. Sadie bolted after the little mouse but didn't stop fast enough; she skidded to a stop and banged her head into the cupboard door. When June found her breath again, she asked, "You don't have any rodents bigger than a field mouse, do you, Clinton? Because you know they carry disease."

"That's just Algernon, Doc. He lives mostly under the sink and we keep the food sealed up in that icebox. We had to keep our wits on the mountain so as not to get run out by the mice."

"Good, that's good. I hope Algernon doesn't invite his family in."

"I like the little fella, but I'm not above doing what I have to if he gets pushy."

"So, you and Wanda have been on your own for

two weeks? What are you doing for food? For money to buy food? Rent payments? That sort of thing?''

"Ma showed us where to sign Daddy's check and Mr. Fuller at the café gives us the money for it. He said he's glad to do it, but we should think about banking. Ma doesn't like the idea of banking, but I think Mr. Fuller is right. He said after I get settled in at school, if I get good enough grades, he'll let me have some part-time work.''

"Mr. Fuller is right, you have to get settled into school first, see how it goes. Now here's my next question. Do you have any idea how long your mother plans to stay on the mountain with your father?''

"No, ma'am, only that she said we're all right and he's not, so he needs looking after.''

"What about her face? Her surgeries? Did she mention that?''

"She did, Dr. Hudson. She said there'd be time enough for that when Daddy can abide it. She said he'd never have left her scared and sick, so she wasn't inclined to do that to him.''

"Hmm. I suppose I could go out to Shell Mountain and pay a visit.''

"You could,'' Clinton said uneasily. "But you'll want to have a care. I can't say what kind of temper Daddy's in. I don't know if he's het up or quiet. He's much like he was before we came to town.''

"He's not taking his medicine, is he?''

"I don't rightly know, Doc. Mr. MacNeil said that sometimes medicine like that can stop working, too, and has to be changed. But it's like starting over if it stopped working. You know what it took to get Daddy to try it in the first place. I'd've sooner wrestled a bull to the ground.''

"I know," June said. She was saddened to know Clarence was having his old troubles again, but knowing Jurea had gone to him was even worse. They might begin to feed off each other's disabilities again, as they had done in the past. That they had produced these children with few emotional problems, remarkable courage and relatively healthy self-esteem was miraculous.

"Clinton, you know Mrs. Rios, don't you? The social worker?"

He frowned. "Could be I met her in the hospital, but Mr. MacNeil's been doing most everything for us—like helping us into this house, getting us our clothes to go to school…"

"I know. He's a great guy, isn't he? Mrs. Rios is a wonderful woman, and she's a friend of mine. I'm going to have to tell them, Clinton."

"Tell them what?"

"That you and Wanda are staying here alone, signing your father's disability checks."

Clinton's face went immediately rigid, all trace of happiness or comfort gone. "Will they say I can't? Ma told me to, and I'm doing just as she said."

"I don't know what they'll say, Clinton. I imagine they'll want to talk to you about how you're getting on. And I want you to know, up front, that I'll be mentioning it, so you don't get upset and excited if they show up at the door, offering suggestions to help you out.''

There was definite pain in his eyes and June stole a glance at Wanda, who had been silent so long. She was back to stroking Sadie, but she had grown pale and looked afraid.

"Doc Hudson," he said gravely. "Don't go making trouble. All we want's to go to school."

John Stone was walking on eggshells around Susan. He had very little contact with Mike Dickson these days, but when they last talked, Mike confirmed he had not had a warm breakfast in weeks, and his bed was about the same temperature. Frosty.

June had left the clinic early to go see the Mulls and John putzed around until Jessie left. He then took a steadying breath and approached his wife. Coward that he was, he approached her from behind. She was busy filing charts. He took a long, agonizing look at her slim waist, her shapely legs. When she had to bend to put a chart in a low file drawer, he almost gasped. In days past, before he allowed himself to speak his mind, he might have taken this opportunity to grab her, spin her around and make lewd suggestions about new examination techniques. "Susan," he said to her back. "I need to come home. I'll do anything you want, but I have to sleep in my bed again."

She slowly rose and turned to face him, the sweetest smile on her face. For a second he thought he'd finally been forgiven. "Of course you can come home, John. It's your house. And in thinking about it, I suppose the bed is big enough, so we won't get in each other's way." She gave his hand a pat that a dumber guy would mistake for encouragement. "I don't think it's good for Sydney that we bicker."

"What do I have to do?" he pleaded. "I'm sorry. Didn't I say I was sorry?"

"John," she said patiently, as though speaking to someone mentally impaired, "I don't need you to be sorry. I need you to be changed. Cast off that old cloak of Victorian misogyny," she said dramatically, gesturing as though casting a cape off her shoulders, "and don the garment of the twenty-first century."

"I'm trying," he said pathetically. "But you spoiled me. And I'm forty now."

"I don't feel sorry for you, John. You're not going to somehow make this my fault."

"Why can't we just kiss and make up?" he wanted to know.

"Well, first of all, we tried that a couple of times. And you somehow dug your hole again. So, letting bygones be bygones isn't going to work, I guess. The better course of action is for us to go about our business, get along as well as possible for the sake of our daughter, and when you get your ass out of the seventeenth century, we'll get along all that much better."

"We need counseling. Should we call a marriage counselor?"

"Excellent idea, John. But give me a little time, please."

"Why?"

"Because I'm trying, but I'm still pissed."

How could she say that with a smile on her face? The past few weeks had been torture for him, and as each day ticked by she seemed to grow more beautiful, her scent more fragrant, her laugh more musical. Pretty soon he was going to die of wanting her.

"Okay," he said. "Should we go see Jerry? Or do you want to check out the new minister?"

"Well, Jerry thinks he was abducted by aliens, doesn't he?"

"He's not as insistent about it anymore, since people are kind of sketchy about getting counseling from him, but yeah. He admitted that to me."

"And the new pastor is divorced...so tell you what? Why don't you just work on you, I'll work on me, and when things cool off a little, we'll talk about marriage counseling."

"Shew," he said, losing his head and reaching for her.

She put up a hand to stop him and the sweet smile vanished instantly. "Don't get any ideas, John, or you'll be booking a room at the bed-and-breakfast."

He was getting smarter; he backed off immediately. "Want me to go pick Sydney up?" he asked with a tentative smile.

"Nope. I'll go. I want to check on Julianna. She has a very full day, not working with five kids."

Zing. Well, he deserved that, but Mike deserved it more. Mike was the one who said his wife didn't want to work. John's stupidity ran to the other extreme. He had learned to like having everything done for him so he could go about the pursuit of being the man of the family. His regret was enormous. Susan kicked the file drawer closed and picked up her purse to leave.

"I really am sorry," he said. "I am, and I do know what I did." She listened to him patiently. "I'm going to make this up to you," he finally said.

She gave his cheek a gentle pat. "Good, John. I'll look forward to it."

Tom Toopeek used the key that Burt Crandall had given him to get into the back of the bakery. He carried a flashlight and thermos of coffee and, without turning on any lights, found his way to Burt's untidy little office. It was good that the September nights were chilly because he'd need the coffee to stay awake and he hated drinking hot coffee on boring stakeouts on long summer nights. He had left a book and a battery-powered book light earlier in the day when he'd met with Burt.

There was egg throwing going on all over town, and the eggs were almost certainly coming from Burt's bakery. The door had been found pried open twice, and Valley Drive had been peppered with eggs. Tom suspected the Forrest twins, but although they'd been caught out after hours roaming the neighborhood, they had not been caught egging, and they denied any mischief or vandalism. They denied, Chris believed. Tom had not thought Chris naive until that moment.

Johnny Toopeek wouldn't divulge what his ex-friends were up to, but he was giving them a wide berth. It was as obvious as the nose on his face. He'd been excitedly drawn to Brad and Brent when they'd arrived on the scene, and less than a month later he was done with them. In the time in between, there'd been numerous reports of vandalism in Grace Valley, from eggs thrown at cars and houses and places of business, to dumped trash cans, tipped flowerpots, ravaged tomato patches and a couple of spray-painted fences. There was one other thing, and Tom hoped there was no connection; the Barstow sisters were missing their cat. Just remembering that made him frown blackly. He knew the boys were up to no good, but if he found out they had something to do with scaring or hurting someone's pet, he'd personally tan their hides.

It was a long while before he heard the sound of a creaking door and subdued whispers. He clicked off the book lamp and let his eyes adjust to the dark before sliding open the office door. Within seconds the back of the bakery was flooded with light as the door of the industrial refrigerator swung open. In the glow stood the boys, arms and legs too long and lanky for their skinny torsos, their jeans hanging off their flat butts, digging into the refrigerator for a big box of eggs. He watched them as they cautiously took the eggs, one at a time, from the box and placed them gently in a plastic bag.

He sidled around behind them to the back door of the bakery, blocking their escape. He flipped on the overhead light. The boys jumped in surprise, dropped their eggs and whirled, scanning the place for another exit.

"Forget about it," Tom said. "You're mine."

"Hey, man, we didn't mean nothing," one said.

"It was just a little fun, nobody got hurt!" said the other.

"Oh yeah, someone did," Tom said, pulling out his handcuffs as he approached them. "You did." He cuffed them, wrists to wrists, around a steel radiator in the kitchen. "Now don't try to move," he told them. "You might hurt yourselves or the radiator."

"You leaving us?"

"Just for a minute," he said, and went out the back door.

Birdie and Judge Forrest lived just down the block. As he expected, the house was dark. He could walk around the perimeter to find the opened window the boys had crawled out, but it was a moot point. He stomped up onto the porch and noisily rang the bell and banged on the screen. Pretty soon he had the whole party at the door. Birdie was in her chenille robe with some sort of pink plastic curlers in her silver hair, Judge in his pajama pants and brown leather slippers, his face all grizzly with late-night beard, and Chris in hastily drawn on jeans and bare feet.

"Tom?"

"Chris, I have your boys handcuffed to a radiator in the bakery. You'd better come with me."

Chris looked positively stunned. Then he said, "You *handcuffed* them? Are you crazy?"

"No, Chris, I'm not crazy. I caught them stealing."

Judge snorted and turned away, saying, "Ought to read the little beggars their rights." Birdie sighed in exasperation and followed her husband.

"What were they stealing?" Chris wanted to know.

"Eggs."

"*Eggs?* Well, for God's sake, eggs? You handcuffed them for *eggs?*"

Tom got a look of sheer impatience, which no one could affect better than a very large Cherokee. "They weren't planning to make an omelette. You want me to just lock 'em up?" Tom asked, more than a little put out that Chris had so little concern over them breaking the law. But then again, maybe that's how they'd gotten to this place in their young lives.

"Gimme a second," Chris said, retreating into the house. He returned in shoes and shirt. "So, you're trying to scare 'em, huh?" he asked Tom as they walked.

"No, but it wouldn't hurt if they got a little scared. Fact is, I was trying to hold them still until I could get you to the bakery. We don't question or cite juveniles without an advocate—usually a parent or guardian."

"So, now what? I'll take them home and they'll get—"

"We're going to the police station, Chris. There's been a lot of vandalism around town and I have a feeling these young men are responsible for all of it."

"What kind of vandalism? You mean, like egging?"

"And dumped trash cans, smashed flowerpots, some spray painting..."

"And you've decided it's got to be my kids? Why my kids?" he wanted to know.

Tom stopped walking. He was getting a little tired of this cat-and-mouse. "Do you have any doubts your kids are vandalizing property? Because I've been in this business for a while and one thing I know, they didn't just dream up this idea. They're experienced vandals who know what they're doing."

"You have some sort of proof of that?" Chris replied, defensive.

Tom lifted an eyebrow. "If I make a call to San Diego PD, will I find out these boys have been in trouble before?"

"Come on, they're boys! You know, boys will be boys?"

"These boys will be felons before long, Chris. They're bold, they're arrogant and they don't appear to have any remorse."

"Hey, that's pretty insulting talk. I thought we were friends."

Tom resumed walking. He said nothing, but what he thought was, the one who could stand a good scare is Chris.

"Lighten up, Tom! We were kids once! We pulled our share of pranks! We got in trouble! We weren't handcuffed or put in jail, for God's sake!"

Tom stopped again. "No," he said solemnly, "because what we'd have gotten from our own fathers would have made jail look like a day at the beach.

Maybe I should just turn these two over to Judge. He's no candy ass.''

"You calling me a candy ass?" Chris challenged, pressing his face close to Tom's.

Tom had not wanted it to come to this, but he wouldn't back away. The fact was, if Chris was spoiling for a fight on behalf of his kids, he was seriously misjudging the prospect of success. Tom was bigger, stronger, well trained and, by now, pissed.

Tom grabbed Chris by the front of his shirt and pulled him even closer, nearly lifting him off the ground. His words were slow and measured. "They're in big trouble. They broke into a business, they stole property and they've been doing damage all over town. You can either step up to the plate and be a father to these two, or I'll lock their skinny little asses up and turn them over to the county juvenile authorities tomorrow." He let go and Chris dropped back. "Quit making excuses and take care of business."

Tom strode off toward the bakery, leaving Chris to follow.

Twelve

The first blow came in the form of a headline. Bones Found on Novelist's Property Likely Those of Long-Missing Husband. The newspaper was from San Jose and the byline belonged to one Paul Faraday. The word *likely* was true license; the number of years the bones had lain under the flower bush had not yet been determined.

But the article was a potentially damaging account of how Myrna Claypool's husband, a man whose very roots appeared untraceable, disappeared without a trace and that Myrna never bothered to go looking for him. The article alleged that she killed him and buried him in pieces around her garden. And proceeded to spend years killing him off in her books.

The newspaper article had been faxed to Tom who had walked down to the clinic with it. From there, June spotted Elmer's truck parked outside the café and they went immediately to Myrna's.

Myrna wasn't quite ready to be receiving. She was still in her dressing gown, her white hair flat on one side and springy on the other, a pencil behind one ear, a pen behind the other, her glasses dangling around her neck and her face all crepelike wrinkles from sleep. When she opened the door to find them standing there, she said, "Oh no, not again. Now what?"

"It's those bones, Myrna," Elmer said. "Let's put on the teakettle."

"Mercy, this is becoming very annoying," she said, but she let them in. "It's a good thing I'm a spontaneous person or I don't think I'd have the humor for this. I'm barely awake and I haven't read my paper or done my crossword or eaten my bran."

"I'm afraid this might get worse before it gets better, Auntie," June said. "This could be blown out of all proportion."

In the time it took Myrna to read the faxed article, the kettle whistled and June had found muffins to warm and add to their breakfast tea.

Myrna sipped her tea daintily. "June, I don't know who those bones belong to, but I can assure you, they do not belong to Morton."

In total frustration and impatience, Elmer demanded, "And I would like to know once and for all how you are so certain of that!"

She inhaled sharply and pursed her lips. "If you speak to me in that tone again, I'll simply ask you to leave. I've had about enough rudeness for one morning."

Pleadingly then, "Myrna, *how?*"

"Very simple, Elmer. I've been digging in that garden for forty years and I have yet to come across a skeleton of any sort, and certainly not Morton's."

June reached across the breakfast table, took one

of Myrna's skinny hands in hers and said, "I don't know what's going to happen next, but if any of this article is true, if Morton's disappearance, past life or whereabouts can't be traced, I imagine there will be an investigation. And with all the times you've killed off the philandering husband..."

"Now, June, I'm a writer. It's what I do. I once wrote of a murdering doctor, but you and Elmer haven't been under suspicion. The fact is, I haven't the first idea where Morton's got to. And I'm not sure he philandered, either. You always think that when a husband wanders off, but I don't suppose that's the only reason they leave. After all, Morton was sweet. And somewhat dull, if you know what I mean."

"Do you mean to say he simply didn't come home, you never bothered to look for him, and that's that?"

Myrna stiffened slightly, and with a bent finger she toyed with the doily beneath her teacup. She was so tiny and frail that to imagine her chopping up a dead body was impossible, to say the least. But it also made the whole idea intriguing.

"It was not quite so simple as that...but then again, perhaps it was. Morton and I got on nicely when he was in Grace Valley. A time or two he came along when I went to a writers' conference or book signing, but only if it happened to be in the path of his sales job. As years went by, I suppose we grew apart. We weren't young when we married in any case. We were already set in our ways, middle-aged, independent... You know, dear," she said, tilting her head and looking at June in a way that indicated she'd stopped just short of saying, "like you."

Elmer cleared his throat. "Go on, Myrna."

"You've heard all this before! The story doesn't change! I was only vaguely aware that Morton hadn't been very attentive, probably because I had such a benign interest in his attentions to start with. Nothing like the women in my books, who are so passionate and observant and *present.* My mind has always wandered, not just since I've become, well, older."

"Do you think his interests were elsewhere?" June asked as delicately as possible.

"That would explain it one way," Myrna said. "As far as his having no record or history, what rubbish. He worked for the Sandfield Office Supplier of California. When I realized he'd been gone a bit longer than usual, I called his home office in Sacramento and they said they'd be happy to get a message to him. Of course I said no thank you, there was no message."

"Now see there?" Elmer said, slapping his knee. "There's a piece of information never before shared. Lord, Myrna, why haven't you said anything about that? It proves he wasn't dead. Why'd you keep it to yourself?"

"Well," she said, picking at the doily, "there are things a woman doesn't really like to discuss."

June, who still held Myrna's other hand, said to her father, "Think of the embarrassment, Dad, of admitting your husband has run off and abandoned you, possibly for another woman."

"Oh, that wasn't the trouble," she said. "It was, well, when I realized he hadn't been home in a while, I couldn't figure out how long it had been. I keep records of everything else, but never Morton's comings and goings. Finally, frustrated, I decided to go through his things, detectivelike. He was a traveling man. There was precious little here—four pants, two jackets, three sweaters, seven shirts, shoes. All still there, not that I thought he'd be back. It was as if he'd only visited here…and then, maybe he had. But he had claimed that little back bedroom on the third floor, the one you had as a playroom when you were a tot, Elmer. Morton used it as his library…or office, if you like. That was where he shelved his favorite books and figured his receipts after a week or two of selling. He'd take a pipe—which I wouldn't have in any other part of the house—and he'd sit in the recliner and read or listen to the radio. The view from there is marvelous, down the western slope toward Rockport. At night, there are a few lights out in the distance."

As Myrna meandered off course, June and Elmer waited impatiently. She looked at them densely, as though she couldn't remember why they were there.

"Oh!" she said. "Yes, the library. I almost never went up there. Too much trouble. Plus, it was Morton's room, and smelt of pipe smoke. So, I went to have a look, and what do you suppose? I found the newspaper he'd been reading that last evening I remembered seeing him. I was writing until dinner and he'd said he'd have a cup of coffee, read the paper,

and I should call to him when I was done. Then he'd
climbed the back stair. It was the *San Francisco
Chronicle*. His coffee cup was still there, a little
brown ring around the bottom. The paper was neatly
folded on the table beside his favorite chair.'' She
swallowed and her cheeks colored slightly. ''It was
almost a year old.''

June and Elmer were temporarily struck silent. Finally June said, ''Myrna! You didn't miss him for a
year?''

''We weren't terribly close,'' she said, lifting her
teacup to her lips and taking a delicate sip.

June and Elmer were very quiet on the way back
to town. June broke the silence as they pulled onto
Valley Drive. The café and clinic were in sight.
''When she said she lost track of him, she meant it.''

''As marriages go, they must not have had much
of one.''

''And you wouldn't have noticed that, Dad?''

Elmer cast a glance at her. ''Now, how would I? I
didn't expect Blythe and Daniel Culley to be on the
skids, either. Did you? If working in medicine all my
adult life taught me anything, it was that people have
intensely complicated private lives. Just when you
think you know what's what...''

''Leave me off at the police station, Dad,'' she
said. ''I'm going to see if Tom has found out anything
and then I'm going to go about the business of finding
Myrna a lawyer.''

"She has a lawyer, June. That Price fellow from the Bay Area."

"That's for books and finances. I think she'll need the advice of someone with a more, I don't know, criminal bent."

"You don't imagine she did anything wrong?" he asked.

"Not in the least. But someone does. Paul Faraday, for one."

Elmer pulled into the driveway of the little three-bedroom house that doubled as a police station. "I should go with you..."

"Do me a favor, Dad. Go home and get on the phone. See what you can find out about Sandfield Office Supplier of California."

"You know, Morton was just a tish older than Myrna, and she's eighty-four," Elmer said. "Can you imagine him still being alive?"

"I'm trying to imagine him working as a traveling salesman in his late sixties," June replied. "Dad, we should have looked into this a long time ago. In letting it go, we might have left Aunt Myrna vulnerable."

If the first blow was the newspaper article, the second came from the forensic anthropologist in Sacramento. Tom had taken the bones to the county coroner who'd shipped them to a specialist. No one was in any kind of hurry until the publication of Paul Faraday's scathing scandal piece, and then, in hopes of warding off further inquiry, Tom had called Sacramento. The pathologist had confirmed that the bones could be approximately twenty years old and came from a male in late life.

"His sixties?" June asked in a desperate whisper, though the only other person in the police station was one of the Wydell brothers who had gotten drunk, beaten up his cousin and was sleeping it off in a back bedroom–holding cell.

Tom nodded yes to the question. "But none of this is official. The doctor needs more time. Maybe weeks more."

"I'm going to walk over to Birdie's and talk to her about a lawyer for Myrna. I think Faraday's got it in for her."

A pained expression came across Tom's features. "I've had a call from the prosecutor's office. They want the county sheriff's office to look into this."

"Look into it *how?*" June demanded, panicked.

"They'd like to search the house and grounds," Tom said, almost wincing.

"Oh, Tom, I don't know what that would do to Myrna! She's too old for this!"

"Don't get yourself all shook up," he said. "First of all, no one around here is tougher than Myrna, and with all the friends she has, she'll have lots of support. Second, she hasn't thrown anything away in better than forty years. I was able to convince the prosecutor's office that we'd keep an eye on her, be sure she's not getting rid of evidence, at least until there's more conclusive information about those bones. In the meantime, I'm going to ask her very politely if she'll let me have a look around."

June got a faraway look. "His clothes are still hanging in the closet he used. I wouldn't be surprised if the newspaper he was reading the last evening she saw him is still folded on the table by his chair in that third-floor study—the only place she'd let him take his pipe."

Tom frowned. "Don't the Barstow twins cook and clean for Myrna?" he asked, perplexed.

"Sort of. They're all just a bunch of eccentric old women who barely keep the dust off the mantel, but they do for each other pretty well. Without Myrna, the Barstows would starve to death, and without the Barstows, Myrna would be in far worse shape than she is. That house is huge. It's like a castle, filled to the brim with junk. When she goes, I think Dad and I will just light a match to it."

"That's good then," he said. "It's all still the way it was when he left."

John walked down to the Flower Shoppe very slowly, his hands plunged into his pockets. He paused in thought outside the door, and looked inside. Justine was not in view; she must be in the back, designing, he decided. When he finally entered, the bell tinkled his arrival, but he was alone in the shop. He leisurely looked at the displays of Justine's floral arrangements, both dried and fresh. Having grown up around flowers, she was an artistic genius when working with them. If her business were in a larger city, likely she'd have grown and expanded.

"Well, Dr. Stone," she greeted, coming from the

back. She wore a stained bib apron, and was wiping her hands on a towel. She rubbed at fingers that were stained brown, red and green. "As long as Mrs. Stone stays annoyed with you, I can save for my retirement! Haven't you two made up yet?"

"There are days I think we have," he said. He shrugged lamely. "And days no amount of floral art can help."

She laughed at him. "If you men would give more flowers on occasions when your wives are happy, you'd save money. What do you feel like today?"

"I feel like talking," he said.

By her expression, she knew at once why he was there. Her eyes first registered shock, then her gaze was downcast, possibly in shame in being caught.

"I gave Dr. Worth a call. He says you've stopped the chemo."

"Well...I..."

"He said you only had one treatment. Justine, why didn't you talk to me about this? Why didn't you talk to June?"

Her head snapped up. "Because I knew what you would say! You would say I had to have chemo. You'd say there was no discussion! Why discuss something that has no discussion?"

"It's a time bomb. A killer. Ovarian cancer is the worst. And you won't even know it's getting you until it's too late."

"I want a baby!"

He shook his head sadly. "Your odds are so bad, I'd almost go with hopeless."

"Of conceiving? Hah! Well, I've got news for you. I'm—"

"Of surviving," he said somberly.

"But the baby…?"

He shook his head. "A baby takes nine months, Justine. Seven at the very least. Ovarian cancer doesn't need that much time."

She bit her lower lip and looked away from him. She was pale; there were dark rings under her eyes. She wore a ball cap with her brown ponytail sticking out the back, probably because she hadn't fixed her hair. Probably because she didn't have much energy.

Tears gathered in her eyes and she looked back at him. "I just want a chance to be normal. To have a baby and be normal."

"You're not abnormal. You've got a disease. We thought we had a good chance, but every day you ignore treatment, that chance slips farther away. Please, Justine. Come to the clinic. Let's at least see what we have. Let's at least confirm the pregnancy."

"I don't want to get in your clutches," she said pathetically. "You'll get rid of the baby."

"Don't be crazy. No one does anything to you that you don't agree to, you know that."

"You'll talk me into it! I know how you doctors work! You take over a person's body and that's it. You—"

John was suddenly smiling, but there was sadness in his smile. He thought, she must be pregnant. She's gone over the edge emotionally. "You'll do what you want to do, Justine. Let me help as much as I can."

"I don't know. I don't know." She reached into her pocket and pulled out a tissue, blowing her nose loudly.

"You must be scared to death," he suggested.

"Hah. You can't imagine."

"How's Sam dealing with this?"

"Not well." With a hiccup of emotion that was halfway between a laugh and a cry, she said, "I think he's pissed."

John chuckled humorlessly. "Yeah, I can understand that. You can't really blame him, can you? He loves you, after all."

"Some way to show love, being all cranky and pissy."

"You held out on him," John argued, shrugging.

"No, I never. He knew I wanted a baby. All along."

"After getting through chemo successfully. After being healthy and strong and ready."

"He's seventy! He doesn't have all that much time!"

John was quiet for a moment, speechless at the irony. Very probably Sam had more time than Justine. Acting against medical advice as she had, she was virtually committing suicide. And if she truly was pregnant, she'd be taking the baby with her. He wondered how Sam would get through that.

"This is going to be rough for Sam," John said. "He's so devoted to you. Just look at him. When you married him, he dropped twenty-five years, but lately he's got it back and gained some. If you aren't going to worry about yourself and the baby, could you at least consider Sam? Justine, this is just plain cruel!''

She sobbed softly into her tissue. John walked around the corner and took her into his arms. He comforted by instinct, holding her while she got his shoulder all wet. And then he thought, what's the matter with me? I don't screw up with female patients! I know what to say and when to say it. I'm good with them and they feel safe and protected and respected. How could I have erred so badly with my own wife?

When Justine's tears abated, he pulled back from her and asked, ''Will you come to the clinic?''

She nodded in defeat. ''When?''

''Whenever you like. Just call Jessie. She'll fix it so you don't have to wait.''

Trembling, she leaned toward him and kissed his cheek. ''Thanks, John.''

''Hey, you'd do the same for a friend. Anybody would.''

''You'll see,'' she said, her smile tremulous. ''I'm going to live.''

The bus dropped Johnny Toopeek at the crossroads about a half mile from his house. Most days he was with his sister, Tanya, but she had a baby-sitting job after school this particular day. The other Toopeek children were in junior high and elementary school, and since Ursula taught middle school, Jenn and Sonja got rides. Bobby, or Baby as they often called him to make him absolutely crazed with anger, was in the first grade.

So Johnny, alone, cut across the hill behind his house. At the top of the hill he encountered the twins, Brent and Brad. They were not in a friendly mood. "Hey, Tonto," Brent said. "You cop us out to your Chief-daddy?"

"What?" Johnny asked, perplexed.

"We're busted," Brad said, sauntering forward toward Johnny. "Since it was, like, the middle of the night, we figured you for the deal. You told the big Indian cop, huh, Redman." It was not a question.

Johnny shook his head, a humorless chuckle escaping him. "Get real," he said, attempting to shoulder through them.

Brent pushed the shoulder back. "Not so fast. You gonna own up to it, snitch?"

"Me?" Johnny asked, again dumbfounded. "Don't be stupid."

Brad shoved forward beside his twin, backing Johnny down the path. "How'd he know?"

Now Johnny's mirth was for real. Could these two really be so dense? "He's a *cop,*" he said in disbelief. "It's his job to know. He doesn't need his kids to tell him anything. Jeez." Again he tried to get by them and again they held him back. Johnny was thicker than the twins and probably stronger, but he was shorter. And, of course, there were two of them. "Don't start anything. It won't go the way you want it to."

"Oh yeah? How's it gonna go, Tonto?"

"Let me give you some free advice, asshole," Johnny said. "There are lots of Indians around here.

Native Americans. And none of us likes to be called names. Okay?''

"What are you gonna do about it? Tell the big Tonto?''

Johnny knew they wanted him to throw the first punch so bad they could taste it, and there was no way he'd do that. He backed up slowly, mindful of the turns in the path, the rocks underfoot. But he simply smiled at them.

"You coming through or not?'' Brad said, still facing him down, forcing him backward.

"I'd say *not*,'' Brent said, walking. "The Injun's chicken.''

Johnny realized that being a twin must be a kind of adrenaline-producing thing. He was in football practice with these two, and though they were swift and dextrous, they weren't hard hitters. They were just starting to develop some good muscles, but they were still a good two, maybe three, years and a bunch of testosterone away from manly. They were spindly. They both were going for quarterback slots, and they couldn't take a hit.

Stupid. He almost laughed out loud.

"I think you ratted us out,'' Brad said. "And you should learn a lesson.''

He wouldn't respond, though it was tempting. But provoking them was almost as bad as throwing the first punch, and it was important to Johnny that his response be clean. Lily white. He would only do what he absolutely *had* to do...and he couldn't wait.

Brent gave a hard shove. "You gonna admit it, Redman?"

"We have to beat it out of you?"

Oh, he couldn't help himself. He spread his hands wide as if helpless, but the half smile on his lips was cynical.

Brad caved first, drawing back a fist and slamming it into Johnny's jaw, causing him to reel backward and do a backward somersault on the path. He hadn't given the twin enough credit—that was a darn good hit. Johnny's jaw was temporarily numb and there was the unmistakable metallic taste of blood in his mouth. Plus, Brent was on him before he could get to his feet. These two weren't going to tag team; they were going to pound him together.

They got in a few more licks than Johnny had intended, mostly because he couldn't get up with the two of them on him. But then he rolled and rolled fast, grabbing the hair of one and the shirtfront of the other, sending them off him in separate directions. His vision was a little blurred, which meant he'd taken one in the eye, so he was through screwing with these two assholes. The closest was Brent and he pummeled his face one-two-three-four before Brad grabbed him from behind and locked his arms down. Johnny bent at the waist and threw Brad over his shoulders, flipping him right into Brent. Both of them landed with a loud thump and multiple groans. Johnny pulled Brad to his feet, spun him around, punched him right in the nose and sent him sailing again into his brother. He was going to regret that one, he realized, shaking his hand. He hoped to God he hadn't broken it because he didn't want to miss any football.

It took almost no time at all to leave a couple of bruised and bloody idiots on the trail. Johnny was feeling some pain, but he was hardly out of breath.

"I don't snitch," he said to the twins. "And I also don't do the shit you do. And don't come at me again or you'll really be sorry. You got that, Whiteman?"

He didn't wait for an answer. He went home.

His grandmother had raised four sons, so the look on her face was one of disgusted acceptance of his weakness. Then she brought an ice bag and poultice to the room he shared with Bobby. The other kids all did their homework at the big oak table in the dining room, but Johnny thought it smarter to stay in his room until his grandma could soften up his mom and dad.

He heard his father come home, and it seemed only seconds before the door to his room opened. Tom leaned in the frame, looking tall and formidable. The uniform and gun still had an effect, even if you were used to them.

"What happened?" he asked.

"I fell off my bike," Johnny said.

Tom's eyebrows immediately rose in surprise; that was a good one. He glanced at Johnny's red and swollen hand. "Fall on the hand?" he asked.

Johnny nodded, feeling stupid. Right or wrong, his dad would grudgingly admire him for not snitching. They had these talks all the time, about when it was absolutely necessary, when someone could really get

hurt. There hadn't occurred such a time that one of
the Toopeek kids held back in a dangerous situation,
and Johnny prayed that day would never come. Having a police chief for a dad could be a real drag.

Tom sort of smiled. "How's the bike look?" He
wanted to know.

Johnny almost smiled back, but held it in check.
"It took a few pretty bad dings, Dad. Sorry."

"Hey, don't beat yourself up," Tom said. "Let's
eat. Maybe we'll have June look at that hand, if the
swelling doesn't go down."

"You mad?"

"You do something wrong?"

"No, Dad. Honest."

"Then I'm not mad. Honest."

Thirteen

The day held a feeling of futility for June. She hadn't connected with either Birdie or Judge, so getting some sort of legal advice for Myrna hadn't been resolved. She was going to have to be patient with regard to the age and origin of the bones found on Hudson land, although the suspense was killing her. And Elmer had found that the Sandfield Office Supplier had gone out of business fifteen years ago. Whether there were any remaining employee records was going to take a while to uncover. Morton seemed to be missing more each moment. Myrna seemed to be getting deeper into trouble by the second.

June was discouraged.

In an effort to salvage something of the day, she did an impetuous, perhaps dangerous, thing. She went out to Shell Mountain in search of Jurea. And she didn't tell anyone that that's where she was going because anyone she told—John, Tom, Elmer—would have advised her against it and attempted to talk her out of going.

The shanty sat back in the trees and a curl of smoke wound upward from the chimney. Well, that was a good sign. There was human activity; hopefully a cook fire. Clarence's truck was there, but that didn't mean he was at home. The entire forest was his backyard.

"Hello?" she called. Though she approached the shack slowly, she was encouraged by the lack of hostile action from within. Better still, Jurea opened the door before she even had a chance to knock.

"I figured you'd be coming. You or Chief Toopeek or maybe that Charlie MacNeil from the VA. But someone would come," she said.

June smiled with awe. "I just can't get over the change, Jurea. Your face, it's so remarkable."

"Ain't it, though?" she replied, laying a palm against her new cheek. "Don't have much feeling here. I have a little mirror, and whenever I see it, I can't believe it all over again." She stood aside, opening the door wider so June could enter. "Are you coming in?"

"I'd like to. Is Clarence at home?"

"Oh, he's never very far away. I can offer you some coffee. It's not the best, but it's hot."

June went in and sat at the table. Jurea poured a cup from the pot on their woodstove, and once it was in front of June, she turned up the oil lamp, illuminating the room.

A change had come over the little hovel. June looked around in appreciation, noting that Jurea had brought back to the woods some items to make the place more comfortable. There were a couple of quilts folded at the foot of two cots, cups, plates, utensils and pots. There were also candles, towels and store-bought supplies like soap, sugar, flour, coffee, lard, salt and pepper.

June knew that Jurea didn't drive and had only one way to get back and forth to Grace Valley. ''I visited your children,'' June said, and Jurea's eyes brightened, perhaps with tears. ''They're doing very well. They love going to school.''

''They understand about this,'' she said. ''They want me to see about their daddy.''

''But you can't leave them alone for long. It will appear you've abandoned them.''

Jurea looked shocked. ''But isn't Clinton of an age to live away from his parents?''

''Yes, I think so, but just barely. And Wanda isn't. She's only fourteen. The county could decide to put her in a foster home. Jurea, it would be good if you went back to them…continued with the doctor.''

''I can't leave Clarence, Doc. You know he wouldn't leave me.''

''But he did,'' June said pleadingly. ''He ran right out of the hospital and fled for his life.''

''He was only afraid. That's how our life has been. When we're afraid, we at least have each other.''

''I know. I'm sympathetic to that. But now there's more at stake.''

''No more'n usual. This plastic surgery is wonderful, and I'm grateful, but it ain't more important than Clarence's peace of mind.''

''That's not what I mean, Jurea. Try to understand. The kids are in school now and an education is the single thing that can change their lives, assure them a place to live and food to eat so they aren't forced to forage the forest. It's important that they continue going.''

"And so, *are* they?''

"Yes, but leaving them there alone and coming out here to the mountain makes it easier for Clarence to choose this, to withdraw again and live with his fears, away from people. Maybe, just maybe, if you hadn't come back here to be with him, he'd miss you and the children enough to try the town again. To take his medicine again.''

Jurea frowned. "You don't mean to say this could be my fault?''

June shrugged. "You've made this choice a little easier for him. And I know you know, it's better that he see the doctor, take his medicine and try living among people. For his own sake and that of the children.''

Jurea lowered her gaze. "He's nowhere near ready to talk about that.''

June took a sip of her coffee—delicious coffee, made with the water of a mountain stream. Then she stood. "You know Clarence better than anyone. You should start to let him know what's good for you, too. Meanwhile, can I get you a ride into town to see the kids? And someone to bring you back?''

"Maybe so,'' she said uncertainly. "Not tonight, though. I'll have to warm Clarence up to the idea.''

"Of course. In a couple of days?''

"That would be nice,'' she said, almost smiling.

"I'll be on my way then. Please give Clarence my regards and tell him we miss him."

"That'll make him feel good," she said. "He don't admit it, but I think he misses some of his new friends."

It occurred to June to brag a little about how the people in town were looking after Clinton and Wanda without being asked. George was cashing the checks, though he had to know it wasn't Clarence endorsing them. The kids were getting all the extra help they needed with schoolwork, and June wasn't the first, nor would she be the last, to drop by and check on them. Instead, she just said, "Everyone and everything is waiting there for the two of you. Don't make us all wait too long, Jurea."

In the very darkest part of a moonless night, June heard a sound. She lay very still, tensely waiting, not even drawing a breath. Sadie got up and wandered out of the bedroom to investigate. June could hear the soft jingling of her tags, but the collie didn't whine or growl. In just another moment he was there, leaning over her. He still had his beard.

"I'm going to have to start locking my doors," she said.

"I locked it for you. Move over." He sat down on the bed beside her.

"Am I dreaming you?" she whispered.

He kissed her and in an instant she knew that it was *not* with Jim that she had uncertainty and with Chris history, but very much the opposite. With Jim she had a history that she could trust and with Chris she had only the uncertainty of a jaded past.

She put her arms around Jim's neck, holding him close, kissing him deeply. A tear of sheer gladness coursed down her temple into her hair and her heart beat wildly.

"Are you here for good?" she asked, still whispering. It was as if she spoke loudly, she might cause him to bolt.

"No. Only for tonight."

She slugged him in the chest. "Then why did you bother?" she wanted to know.

"I had a sense that you needed me, if only for a little while."

Her protest caught in her throat. "Okay. I did. I do. But it's so damn hard when you leave again."

"Tell me about it," he said. "It's not going to be very much longer. A few months at the very most, but I'm thinking way less. The people I'm dealing with are stupid and impatient."

That almost made her laugh. "What funny good news."

"You think it's funny, but it's not. It *is* excellent news, though. I'm tired of dealing with smart guys. They wear me out. It takes too much mental energy. These idiots are going to be ready for jail in no time." He brushed back her hair. "I hate it when I leave, too."

"But you're right, I really needed you. Grace Valley is full of crazy people and I'm leading the pack."

"Is that so?" he asked. He stood and took off his shoes, then his shirt, then his pants. She pulled back the coverlet and made room. As though he'd been doing it every night for the past twenty years, he slipped in beside her. She snuggled into the crook of his arm and played with the hair on his chest while he inhaled the smell of her hair.

"I've been more unstable and neurotic than usual. It's probably your fault somehow."

"Probably." He kissed the top of her head. "Tell me about your aunt."

"In a minute. First I want to know something. Do we have the kind of relationship where we tell each other deeply personal things?"

That took him a moment. Then, hesitatingly, "I, ah, don't really know."

"My old high-school flame came back to Grace Valley," she said. "Should I tell you about it?"

"Again, I don't really know. Is this something you have to unburden yourself of?"

"He's a divorced single father now," she said, ignoring his question. "He's been hell-bent we should try again, though I haven't encouraged him at all." Jim rose up on an elbow, looking down at her while she talked. "You can certainly look fierce with that beard. It's a little scary."

"Go on," he said, urging her to continue.

"Okay. I've never had much in mind for him outside of a slow death. However, I did let him kiss me."

Jim frowned darkly. "Did you sleep with him?"

"Of course not! I never even let him get to first

base. But when he kissed me, I just let him. I'm not sure why."

"Hmm. I guess you're entitled to be curious."

It was her turn to frown. That was awfully understanding. "Have you been kissing people since you've been away?"

He began to laugh. "If you could see the people I've been hanging out with, you wouldn't even have to ask."

"You don't want to go messing with some Colombian drug lord's mistress, Jim. I hear they're short-tempered and jealous."

"These are backwoods mountain men with matted beards and ropes for belts. It's like Dogpatch, except they're making a small fortune growing cannabis. The big question is, where's the money going? I suspect the sheriff."

"Where is this happening?"

"Never mind. Tell me about the boyfriend."

"Are you angry with me for letting him kiss me?" she asked. "Because if that sort of thing upsets you, I won't bare my soul in the future."

He sighed. "June, I have a better idea. Don't kiss any old boyfriends in the future."

"Ah...you plan on sticking it out with me." She snuggled against him and he lay back down on the pillow. "I wish you knew how hard it is to not tell anyone I have someone. People can't understand why I'm not tempted by Chris. Or by the new preacher who came into town, who is attractive and single."

"You haven't kissed *him,* have you?"

"Oh no, and I don't see any danger of that. I'm not attracted to him. He has, however, asked if I'm single."

"Are you trying to scare me?" he asked.

"No," she said, snuggling closer. "I'm trying to *hurry* you."

The night was deep and soft, and they talked in hushed tones of things both complex and banal. She told him about Aunt Myrna and the bones, about Chris and his explanation of why he had broken her heart. He told her about the acting job he was doing undercover, pretending to be an IRS agent, a revenuer in search of illegal stills, when he was really after the marijuana patches the locals thought he was too dumb to recognize. But he wouldn't say where, and when she asked him how he had managed to get to her he would only say, "I have connections." When she asked if he had traveled all the way from the Ozarks he had said no, but it felt like it. Then he promised that as soon as it was over, he would tell her the whole thing.

Somewhere in the midst of all this talk they made love, slowly and carefully, savoring each touch and kiss because it would have to last. How long, neither of them knew. Too soon it was dawn.

"It wasn't much," he said, "but it's all I have. How long do you think this one night will keep you from kissing other men?"

"Forever," she said. "Because I love you."

"That's the first time you've admitted that. I knew, but I'm glad you finally said the words."

"What do you mean, you knew? How could you know? How could you be sure?"

"I'm sure of the way you feel, June. You're very convincing."

"Hmmph."

"And I love you, too."

She watched him leave by the back door, walk across the porch and backyard and enter the trees at the edge of her property. There was an overgrown path that let out onto an old logging road about a hundred yards through the trees. When he'd been working undercover in her mountains, he had parked his truck back there and snuck in to her late at night. This time he would take the hidden truck to the airport.

She wouldn't let herself cry because that would be ungrateful. To weep because it was temporarily over would ruin the miracle of his appearance, of what they had had together. She took a deep breath as he vanished from sight and told herself to be strong, to be worthy of a man like him.

And she smiled.

Early that same morning, two sheriff's deputies drove their sedan up to Myrna Claypool's house. They were followed by an unobtrusive white van that pulled a medium-size trailer. Behind the van were two more officers in a CA Highway Patrol SUV.

There was no sign of life around Hudson House. The officers were all out of their vehicles, standing around in the drive. Finally the first two walked up to the door and rapped harshly. "Mrs. Claypool?" one called out. "Sheriff's deputies. Please open the door." Still there was nothing. "Should we kick it in?" he wanted to know.

"She's eighty-four and lives alone. Give her some time. When you're eighty-four it might take you a minute or two to get to the door."

"We wouldn't want her hiding evidence."

"Shit, Stan. She's had twenty years to hide evidence. Just knock again."

He did so, then said, "What if she's armed?"

"You want to break the door down and wrestle this ninety-pound little old lady to the ground, huh, Stan?"

The men from the van started unloading equipment—shovels, crime scene tape, tarps, lights. They wore white jumpsuits, boots and gloves. The Highway Patrol officers stayed in their SUV as back-up, standard procedure when serving a warrant.

The deputy pounded on the door a third time and the sound of movement within caused him to step back, out of the way of a potential shotgun blast. The heavy door slowly opened.

"Mrs. Myrna Claypool? We have a search warrant for your house and grounds."

"Oh my," she said. "You will be careful, won't you? Most of my things are antiques."

Fourteen

After Jim's departure, June couldn't go back to bed. To go there alone was out of the question. She lifted the pillow he had used and took it with her to the chair in the corner of the room. She sat there, breathing in the scent of him, hoping it would last a good long time. She was thinking of not washing the pillow slip until his return.

She decided to take this opportunity of being up extra early to drive by Culley Stables. It might have been on account of the night she'd spent with Jim, which had left her feeling sentimental toward all couples. Or perhaps the fact that relationships suddenly felt so fragile, so vulnerable. Or maybe it was just that she had not looked in on Daniel and Blythe Culley since their troubles began. Whatever the reason, she felt drawn to them.

Daniel was recovering from angioplasty, but she knew he'd be up before dawn. Men like Daniel, whose livelihood lay with the land and animals, worked long hard days, never rested much, never took time off, never pampered themselves. It was a doctor's bane to know that, no matter how crucial bedrest might be to a patient, these old farmers, ranchers and the like could not be kept still for long.

But when she drove up to the house, she was startled by the lack of activity. There were lights on in the house, but Daniel's truck was gone and the stable was still dark. No dogs came running to greet her. The porch light didn't automatically flash on at the sound of a vehicle. Maybe she had misjudged. Maybe this was the single patient who would stay down and rest a while.

"Gee, Sadie, maybe we ought not—"

But then the light did come on, and slowly the door opened. There stood Blythe in her overalls, squinting into the darkness.

"Well, Sadie, looks like we might get a cup of coffee after all." Sadie made a sound of agreement and began to wiggle in happiness. June killed her engine and got out of the truck. "Hey, Blythe," she called. Blythe didn't return the greeting, but just stood in the doorway. Funny, June thought, she'd never before been unfriendly. Then again, she'd been through a lot, first losing her husband to another woman, then almost losing him to a heart attack. June climbed the steps to the porch. "I thought I'd run by on my way to the clinic and see how Daniel's doing after his procedure. And how you're doing."

"I'm doing the same, I reckon," she said with that lilting Kentucky cadence. "If you have a mind to check on Daniel, you won't be finding him here."

June was brought up short, though when she thought about it, she shouldn't have been. Sarah had been with him at the hospital, not Blythe. "Where is he, Blythe?"

"Oh, I think you know."

The angry lines almost cracked Blythe's usually cheerful face. She was pale and drawn, her eyes flat, her hair stringy. It appeared she hadn't been sleeping much.

June whiffed the air. Aha! She might not have slept, but she'd gotten up and put the coffee on like always. "Can I talk you out of a cup of coffee?" June asked. It wasn't that she craved the coffee so much, but this woman was in trouble. Patient or not, you don't walk away from a neighbor in trouble.

"I haven't got time to dawdle. There's a lot that needs doing today." But she held the door open so that June could come in.

June told Sadie to stay on the porch and stepped into the house. What she saw stunned her. Moving boxes were scattered around the living room and dining room and Blythe appeared to be packing household goods into them. The dining table was covered with earthenware and glassware; the living-room couch was covered with stacks of linens.

"Blythe, what's going on?"

"I'd appreciate it if you'd keep this between us, June. Daniel has himself a new partner and I've made up my mind to move on."

"Move? But where?"

"I haven't quite decided that, but maybe south. Maybe back to Kentucky. And to tell the truth, I always wanted to see Florida."

"What does Daniel say?"

Blythe smiled, but it was a mean smile. "You don't reckon I need to get his permission, do you? He seems to have made up his own mind about what he wants."

Blythe walked into the kitchen and June followed. There was more order in there; only a couple of boxes, already closed and labeled, sat in the corner. Blythe pulled a cup off the wall rack and poured. June took a seat at the kitchen table.

"Sit down with me, will you, Blythe? And tell me about it?"

Blythe put the cup of coffee in front of June, then fetched her own from the counter. She didn't sit down as invited, but merely turned toward June, leaning against the sink, holding her cup with two hands. "There isn't anything to tell, June. Daniel found himself a woman he feels at home with." The anger seemed to melt from her eyes and was replaced by sadness. "I don't even have bad will for Sarah." She shrugged. "I liked her once."

"Blythe, I know this is very painful, but you must remember, divorce isn't unknown in this valley. You aren't the first person to suffer through it and you won't be the last. But this is your *home*. Your livelihood! You don't have to give that up, too. You and Daniel can work out some arrangement..."

Blythe looked away impatiently. She sighed heavily, as if to say, "What do you know about it?" Then she looked back and said, "What do I want with all the talk?" she asked. "The humiliation of it."

June reached toward Blythe, but the other woman drew back. "That's just it, Blythe," June said. "We might hear a little chatter about Daniel and Sarah, but it won't last long. And no one's going to hold it against you. You're the underdog here. You'll get sympathy and understanding!"

Blythe made a derisive sound. "You're right, that sounds so much more appealing."

"Oh, Blythe, don't run away…"

Blythe merely looked down into her coffee cup. June held her tongue, knowing she shouldn't harangue her. Maybe she could find someone who Blythe might listen to.

"I'm just thinking of it being a fresh start, is all," Blythe said. "If Daniel can start over, I can start over."

Something occurred to June. "I didn't see anyone around the stable," she said.

"Since Daniel fell ill, we're just boarding, not training or breeding. I let all but two hands go and had most of the stock returned or sent to another stable. When Daniel's better and wants to work again, he can do what he wants."

She's giving up everything, June thought. Giving up and slinking away, ashamed that she lost her man. It was so painful to see. What would become of her now?

"Are you planning to leave soon?"

"I'd like to go right away, but there's always one more detail. As soon as I can get everything organized. I might want to kill him, but I'm not going to leave him a mess that he'd just have *her* clean up.''

June studied that statement. On the surface, it sounded angry. But underneath, Blythe was saying that she wanted to go, yet didn't want to go. Which would be perfectly normal.

''I guess I'll be going then,'' June said. ''If there's any way I can help you with this, will you call me at least?''

''There isn't anything to be done, June. I thank you for caring, but there's no need to say anything about this, either.''

''Do you imagine you can sneak away without anyone knowing?''

With a hurt tone, she said, ''That doesn't seem to be necessary. These things I'm packing are mine. I'm not taking anything of Daniel's, so don't feel you have to warn him. I may have it all stored till I put down roots somewhere.''

June just nodded. She made to leave and then turned, opened her arms and clumsily hugged Blythe. Blythe hugged back, even more awkwardly. Then June left with a heavy heart.

It didn't take her long to make her decision. First of all, Blythe wasn't a patient, she was a friend. Not a close friend, not a confidante, but someone June had known for twenty years. And she hadn't made any promises to keep any secrets. Blythe had worked beside Daniel for decades, building a stable worth considerable money, and she was packing up her glasses and towels and running away. Giving up the battle to save herself embarrassment. June just couldn't let her go.

She drove straight to Sarah Kelleher's house where, indeed, she saw Daniel's truck parked outside.

Tom was usually the first one into the office in the morning, unless some police business called him before morning even arrived. He would routinely listen to any messages left on the answering machine during the night, look at the headlines on the five newspapers that were delivered to the police department, check the schedule to see when Ricky and Lee would be working, look over his appointments, then head down to George's for his complimentary coffee and the first gossip of the day.

This morning he found Chris Forrest waiting for him at the door. By his posture and expression, this wasn't a friendly visit. "Morning, Chris," he said.

"Tom," Chris returned with a nod. "Got a minute?"

"Got several. Come on in." He picked up his newspapers from the front step and piled them on top of the leather folder full of reports he carried from home. Paperwork traveled with him daily, from home to office to home.

He opened up the door and preceded Chris into the office. He let Chris follow him down the hall where he put his papers and folders on his desk. Then he turned to his old friend who he understood was no longer a good friend of his. "What's up?"

"Our boys. They've got some issues."

Tom's left eyebrow lifted into a questioning arc. "That so? Like?"

"Like, they've been fighting."

"How do you know this?"

"What do you mean, how do I know?" Chris shot back, anger in his voice. "My guys have black eyes and bloody noses. They're bruised up pretty good. They were real reluctant to snitch, but they said Johnny and a bunch of Indian friends jumped them!"

"What?" Tom asked, a smile breaking across his face in spite of himself.

"You heard me. That pack he hangs with."

Tom laughed outright. "Give me a break," he said. "Johnny doesn't run with any pack of Indians. Or, as we PC people like to refer to them, Native Americans. Their tribal names will work, also."

Chris plunged his hands into his pockets, a sour expression on his face. "When we were kids, you were an Indian."

"When we were kids, you weren't such an asshole."

"You saying my boys lied?"

"Oh, yeah."

"They wouldn't lie about that. It was hard enough for me to get them to tell. Why would they make up a story?"

"Because they jumped Johnny and he fought his way out of it. Because there was one of him and two of them and they *still* lost. Because they're in trouble a lot, Chris. They're vandals and sometimes thieves, but they can't fight. Can't fight worth a damn."

''That's ridiculous.''

''No, it's not. It's true and you know it.''

''That's just what Johnny wanted you to—''

''Johnny didn't tell me how it was. He wouldn't, even under pressure. But I've been wise to this trouble for a while now. And I watch real closely. Here's one little thing I know. Johnny's a lot stronger and tougher than the twins. He came home the other day looking like he'd run into that pack of Indians you're talking about. Now I ask you, genius, if Johnny and some pack jumped the twins, would Johnny have a mark on him?''

''Why would the twins jump Johnny?''

''Think about it, Chris. Where's your head?''

''What are you talking about?'' he asked again, genuinely stumped.

''Johnny and the twins started out friends, right? Johnny was pretty excited about them coming to town. Then cars started getting egged on the highway. A bunch of kids were running from the scene but I caught one—and he turned out to be mine. He wouldn't tell me who he was with, but he was done with the twins. They don't hang together anymore, Chris. They haven't for quite a while. Did you even know that?''

''Well, I—I guess I haven't seen Johnny in—''

''A few weeks,'' Tom reinforced. ''At least. Then I caught them stealing eggs from the bakery the other night. I suppose they think I'm too dumb to have figured things out, that the only way I could've known is if Johnny ratted them out.''

Chris frowned and shook his head as if shaking loose the cobwebs. "You build up this whole scenario without any evidence? Of any kind?"

Tom was incredulous. He looked skyward, his mouth open slightly, and shook his head. Then he looked back at Chris. "Yeah, Chris, without any evidence at all. Right up until I saw their hands in the refrigerator, pulling out the eggs."

"But...what I mean is..."

The phone began to ring, distracting Chris. "Gimme a second," Tom said. He lifted the phone. "Tom Toopeek," he said. He never called himself Chief or answered "Police department." The way he saw it, he was as much a neighbor as an officer of the law.

A dark and angry look crossed his features. "When did they get there?" he asked. He listened carefully. "You just sit tight and stay out of their way. I'll be right there. Are you okay?" He listened. "Good. I'm on my way."

He hung up the phone and told Chris he would have to finish their conversation later. There was an emergency. He ran down the hall, causing Chris to move pretty fast behind him and out the door so Tom could lock up. Leaving Chris on the stoop, Tom jumped in his Range Rover and, with lights and siren going, wasted no time getting to Myrna Claypool's house. He wasn't worried about her safety just yet. But he was thoroughly pissed.

June found Daniel and Sarah having a cozy little breakfast on her patio. He was wearing a sweater that looked to be handmade, and there was a throw over his legs, but underneath all this was jeans, boots and a cowboyish-looking plaid shirt. Underneath her fussings he was still a rancher and stable owner. But he sure did look comfortable in her care.

First she asked, "How are you feeling, Daniel?"

"I'm feeling almost normal," he said. He lifted his cup to his lips, sipped, put it down and said, "Decaf." He pointed to the remnants of eggs on his plate and said, "Egg-beaters. No fat, no cholesterol."

She nodded, though something told her that if Blythe had provided these things, he'd be complaining about this treatment. He'd demand his bacon and butter and would've given that lap throw to the dog. But this wasn't really anyone's fault. Sarah's house was like a nest, while the house he shared with Blythe had always been functional. Practical. "Very good, Daniel," she said. "Diet is the first line of defense."

"Coffee?" Sarah asked.

The idea suddenly made her queasy. She'd slept very little, if at all, and had already had a stronger than strong cup at Blythe's.

"Tea?" Sarah asked, noticing the grimace. "Something to settle your stomach?"

June's hand went to her stomach. "Too much black coffee before breakfast," she said.

"The water's hot," Sarah said, heading for the kitchen.

June sat down across from Daniel. "I went out to

the stables, Daniel. I guess I thought I'd find you there.''

"I haven't been out there nights in a real long time, June. Maybe a year.''

"I didn't know.'' Which would explain why Blythe didn't expect Daniel to have any idea she was packing.

"Doubt anyone would notice. I was never late for work in the morning. Never left the stable wanting for attention.''

"But what about Blythe, Daniel?''

"Didn't leave her wanting, neither.''

The situation was starting to take on the ring of a harem, yet these people—all three of them—were the sweetest, kindest, most apparently moral and upstanding she knew. Daniel and Blythe seemed not only devoted to each other, but almost prudish. And Sarah was so nurturing, it seemed impossible she could allow Blythe to feel this hurt. June realized that this situation was so confusing for her because she would have fully expected either Sarah or Daniel to turn away from temptation and do the right thing. Instead they seemed to blame Blythe for her own discomfort. June pressed a hand against her queasy stomach.

Sarah put a cup of tea in front of her and said, "Now, Daniel, June doesn't understand. She thinks you're making sinful suggestions. He only means he always has and always will take good care of Blythe. She should never worry about her future. Or her retirement.'' Sarah touched the saucer. "This is a special blend, June. It'll settle your stomach.''

June took a hopeful sip.

"I came right out here after talking to Blythe. She asked me not to say anything to you, but I can't keep a secret that I'm afraid might hurt someone. She's packing. She's planning to leave Grace Valley."

Sarah gasped.

Suddenly June's eyes filled with tears. "What did the two of you expect?" she asked, her voice taking on a desperate tone. "She's devastated! Humiliated!"

Daniel's fist came down on the patio table. "Damn stubborn, pigheaded woman! She promised me over thirty years ago that it would never come to this. We were partners, best friends. We shared everything! I always wanted what's best for her and she for me and now she's gonna bring all we worked for to ruin! Damn pigheaded woman!"

Sarah covered his ham-fist with her round soft hand, but she looked at June. "We'll take care of this right away, June. This surely has to stop."

"Blythe is going to be so upset that I came to you," she said, then sniffed. Sarah gave her a tissue, which she used, but she thought, What the devil is the matter with me? Why the hell am I crying? She felt sorry for Blythe, true, but she was hardly overcome. They weren't even close friends!

"We're going to make sure she isn't upset with you, June. You're not to worry. Now, how is your stomach? Has the tea worked?"

She let herself concentrate for a moment and realized she had not a hint of nausea. It was magic! "Yes," she said. "Yes, it has." And at that moment her pager began to vibrate. Tom's cell phone number showed in the window. Without asking, she went the short distance into Sarah's kitchen and dialed.

"Your aunt Myrna has been served with a search warrant by the county sheriff's department. I'm on my way there now. You'd better come."

June couldn't get very close to Myrna's house because of the crime scene van and police cars. When she got out of her truck and started up the driveway toward the house, she heard a very rare sound—Tom Toopeek shouting.

"What the hell do you mean you weren't *obligated* to bring the warrant to my attention! Is that the way you do business now? Since when do we sneak around each other like that? This is my town, my neighbor, my—"

"And it's my county, god dammit! I had a warrant to serve and a crime scene to investigate and couldn't have you tipping off the—" the deputy shouted back.

"Tipping off the eighty-four-year-old woman? In case she wanted to move the body? Are you guys stupid or just plain mean?" Tom was poking a finger into a deputy's chest, the deputy reddening more with each poke. "If that old woman has any problems—health or emotional—because of the indelicate way you've handled an idiotic and asinine—"

The deputy swatted Tom's hand out of the way. "Listen, Tonto, you'd better keep your grimy little hands—"

Pushed to the limit already, Tom grabbed him by

the front of the shirt and had nearly lifted him off the ground, ready to do some serious damage, when the man's partner came to the rescue. "Hey, hey, hey!" he shouted, putting his arms between the two of them. June jumped in as well, pulling at Tom, shouting, "Tom! Stop it!"

Tom came under control faster than Stan. The latter, a little overweight and wheezy, had trouble calming down.

"Stan, Chief Toopeek is right. We should have informed his office of the warrant, had him meet us here to talk to the old lady. He's right to be offended. Now back off."

Stan jabbed a finger in Tom's direction. "You put your hands on me! Don't you ever put your hands on me!"

"I apologize," Tom said. "Don't call me names."

"He's sorry," the other deputy said. "He can be stupid, but he's a good cop."

"Don't tell him I'm stupid," Stan ground out between clenched teeth, giving his partner a shove.

"Incredibly stupid," the man clarified. "Go sit in the car before I help him clean your clock." Stan seemed to quiver with anger. "Go," his partner said. He reluctantly turned away.

June left the men to sort things out while she ran into the house to find her aunt. There was no one in the living room, but she could hear sounds coming from upstairs. As she passed the parlor she looked out the back window and saw that yellow crime scene tape had been stretched across the backyard, strung between trees. Two men were out back digging.

"Myrna?" she called, but no one answered. She checked the kitchen where the teakettle whistled, but no one was there. She took the kettle off the fire. She could hear typing and was driven to the study.

Myrna sat at her word processor in her robe and slippers, her springy white hair flat on one side and puffy on the other, a pencil behind each ear, her glasses on her nose, her fingers going a mile a minute on the keyboard. "Myrna?" June asked.

"Come in, darling. Have they completely destroyed the house yet?"

"I haven't even looked. Oh, Myrna, I'm so sorry about this!"

She looked completely perplexed. "Sorry? June, darling, why are you apologizing? You didn't call for the warrant, did you?"

"No, no, I'm just sorry this is happening. And I don't understand why—"

"I'll tell you why. Because the bones that were found under the flower bush are approximately twenty years old, from a male the approximate age Morton was the last time I saw him." She frowned angrily, an expression Myrna almost never wore. "That seems highly unlikely to me."

"Because...?" June led, waiting.

"Because if a piece of someone were buried twenty years ago in my garden, don't you think I'd know about it? I had much more time for my garden twenty years ago than I've had lately." There was a crash from upstairs. "Louts," she said, glancing at the ceiling. A worried look crossed her features. "If they make much of a mess, it's going to take more than the Barstows to tidy up. They've never really been that domestic, you know."

June reached out and held her aunt's hand. She was so dear, so generous. She had employed the sixty-something bickersome twins for years, despite the fact that they had very few domestic talents. How she loved Myrna. Who could possibly suspect her of a crime. If not for those books...

"What are you writing, Auntie?"

"I've never been this close to a house search before, so I thought I'd get as much material out of it as possible. What I've always thought is true—I feel completely violated." The sound of something heavy being dragged across the floor of the bedroom upstairs caused them both to look at the ceiling. Myrna sighed heavily. "Believe it or not, I know where everything is in this cluttered old house." She looked again at June, her eyes quite sad. "June, darling, I think you'd better call me a lawyer."

Fifteen

June wanted to stay with her aunt Myrna, but she reluctantly turned that assignment over to Elmer. She not only had patients, but other promises to keep. Fortunately, the most important items on her list could be delegated, which she did from her cell phone as she drove. First she called Birdie and told her what was happening at Hudson House. Birdie promised to get the name of a good lawyer from Judge. Next, Charlie MacNeil offered to provide transportation for Jurea Mull so that she could visit with her children. And it was imperative that June find the time to visit Charlotte, who was barely able to get from bed to chair without help from Bud. But not today, she decided. She was coming down with a bug. Possibly the flu. Either that or she'd gotten a bad bean...

When she got into town she stopped at Sam Cussler's gas station. The Gone Fishing sign was on the door, so she pumped her own, cleaned her windows and slipped her I.O.U. for the cost of the gas into Sam's mail slot. When she drove on toward the clinic, she slowed down as she passed the Flower Shoppe. When she realized what she'd seen, she slammed on the brakes and backed up. There was a sign on the door of Justine's place of business that read Closed Until Further Notice. "Oh no," she said aloud and headed toward their home.

Justine and Sam lived in the house that had been Sam's for better than fifty years. There were a couple of cars parked out front, in addition to Sam's old truck. Instinct told June to take her medical bag with her.

Justine had four sisters and one of them wordlessly opened the door for June. She looked down at the floor. June could sense the doom in the house and, without being directed, went to the bedroom. There was Justine, pale as the sheets against which she lay, Sam sitting beside her, holding her hand. Justine's gaze left Sam's face and found June's. She smiled weakly. "Oh, June," she whispered. "I've made a terrible mistake."

A short time later John brought the ambulance and helped June load their patient into the back. He bent over Justine and placed a kiss on her forehead. "I'll call Dr. Worth and have him meet you at Valley Hospital," he told her.

"Are you very angry with me, Dr. Stone?" she asked.

"Of course not, Justine. But there's no reason for you to be in pain. Let Dr. Worth help."

She nodded and closed her eyes.

Justine's sister got into the back of the ambulance while Sam elected to follow in his truck so that he'd have transportation. "How did you know to come?" he asked June.

She shrugged. "We've all known she's sick," she said. "And the flower shop was closed."

Sam hung his head. It was the first time in June's memory she had seen him look old. And all June could do for him now was take his young bride to the hospital.

"Her father's going to blame me for this," Sam said. "And maybe he'll be right to. I couldn't seem to change her mind."

"We all tried, Sam. John and I did, you did, I'm sure her sisters did. You must not blame yourself."

He nodded weakly and shuffled toward his pickup. June got into the ambulance, up front with John.

June had no idea why people made the choices they did. This was not the first time a patient of hers had refused to be treated for a dangerous disease, nor was it the first time that denial of the illness was more catastrophic than the illness itself. But it was the first time a woman so young had made this choice. It was very likely Justine would die. And she had been diagnosed only a few months ago.

Ovarian cancer was the worst. Without aggressive treatment, it was fatal. In fact, all too often even aggressive treatment couldn't save the patient.

Justine had brushed everyone's worry aside and thought she was choosing motherhood over chemotherapy. In the end, June believed, there would prove to be no pregnancy—only cancer.

This was by far one of the hardest parts of being a doctor—having a patient you might have saved ignore your advice. June felt strongly that the decision to fight illness was an individual's right, but it was often made more palatable when strong religious beliefs were involved, or when one was choosing quality of life over a painful treatment. Or in old age, when a patient was comfortable with passing on. But in this case June couldn't help but believe Justine had been irrational. And while that might be her right, it was damn hard to accept. She wished she could turn back the clock, maybe consider a court order.

June left Justine with the emergency room nurses, who would have her admitted. "I'll leave you in Dr. Worth's care," she said. "I'll drop by and check on you later."

Justine grabbed her arm as she would have left. "June. Don't let Sam blame himself."

The morning had been full and not especially pleasant. By the time June got to the clinic, the place was deserted. The clinic was unlocked, so they couldn't be far. "Hello?" she called down the hall. No answer.

Someone might have crossed the street to grab something from the café for an early lunch or to run a quick errand. She went to Jessie's desk to look for a note, but found none. The piece of paper she moved first right and then left, looking for a message, finally caught her attention. It was a class schedule for the community college and the name of the registrant was Jessica Wiley. Biology 101, English primer, anatomy, algebra and geology. She stared at the paper for a long time. When she looked up, Jessie was standing in the front door of the clinic holding a large plastic cup with a frothy swirl of ice milk adorning the top. She was smiling broadly.

"I got my GED and enrolled last week...just in time," she said.

"Oh Jessie, that's wonderful," June said.

"I'm not sure yet whether I can make it all the way to being a doctor, but I know that for sure I'll be a nurse."

"Of course you will."

"Because of you, and John, and Susan."

"No, Jessie. Because of *you.*"

"My dad thinks I'm totally crazy."

"But he's proud of you?"

"Sure. It's just that I don't always follow through, you know. I dropped out of high school the minute I could. And now—" She shrugged.

"And now you know what you want," June finished for her. She held open her arms and filled them with Jessie.

She would need help, June thought, embracing the young woman with emotion. Maybe help with her studies, maybe schedule adjustments to accommodate classes. Maybe help with tuition. It would be such a joy.

June relaxed her embrace. "Come on," she said, putting an arm around her and leading Jessie down the hall toward her office. "Let's talk about how I can help you."

* * *

At day's end, June drove out to the Toopeek home. Elmer would not leave Hudson House while there were still investigators around, and with the size of that house and the accumulation of possessions, it was going to take a good long time for them to get through everything. June needed to talk about things, and there were only a few places she would go with such a need. She often turned to Birdie, her godmother, but not with Chris and his sons still there and their household in turmoil. She turned to her dad with regularity, but he was needed elsewhere. Although she hadn't imposed thus far, she felt she could turn to John and Susan. But right now was not a good time, even though she believed they would set aside their quarrel to help her if she needed them.

She hadn't called ahead but knew that it would be all right. It was dinnertime and that, too, was acceptable. The lights shone throughout the house; the dining room was especially bright.

June remembered the building of this house. It had started with a small brick, mortar and wood structure that Tom's dad, Lincoln, had built himself when his kids were very small. Then, one by one, the kids left Lincoln and Philana. Tom came back after college, after serving a short time as a Sacramento police officer, and he came back with a wife. Tom and Ursula had their own home built onto the first Toopeek structure and began to fill the place with children. Now there were nine Toopeeks in that house.

As June sat in her car looking at the house, she realized that she had always felt safe in their home, even when their home had been a hogan with a dirt floor. That was the way the Toopeeks made you feel.

Philana opened the door for her. "June! How good it is that you're here. Ursula! June has come."

Ursula came out of the kitchen. "Perfect! Will you eat?"

"I will," she said. "I'm starving," she added, only now realizing.

The sun had just gone down, but the fireplace in the great room was already ablaze, setting a cozy picture. Wonderful smells of fresh bread and meaty stew filled the air. The children, from six-year-old Bobby to sixteen-year-old Tanya, were picking books up from the long dining table and putting their schoolwork, one by one, on stairs that led up to their bedrooms. Then each one took part in setting the table, the younger ones putting out place mats and napkins while the older ones handled dishes and glasses.

Fresh coffee steamed the air and June found a mug hanging on a peg on the wall. She dressed her coffee with sugar and cream, something she'd only recently discovered she liked, and tried to stay out of the way.

"My eighth-graders are more sophisticated each year, and not always in a positive way," Ursula was saying. "I had to send a darling little girl to the counselor's office today so that she could have a fashion lesson. Not only do I not wish to see her belly button, I am also disinterested in her belly-button jewelry."

"Pierces?" June asked.

"Everywhere imaginable. I'm trying to decide if it's my right to forbid tongue pierces. If I cannot understand them when they speak, am I entitled to request they remove their little baubles?''

At just that moment, as Johnny would have passed her with a stack of plates, June reached out and snagged his sleeve, forcing him to meet her eyes. The bruise around one eye had faded to purplish-yellow, but there was a cut on his lip that looked reluctant to heal. She made a face. "You get this at football practice?"

He was mute, staring at June. Ursula was stirring a pot at the stove. Without turning around, she said, "Tell the truth, please."

"I was in a fight. I didn't start it."

"I thought this was an anti-fighting family," June said.

"It is," Johnny said. "It's also an anti-dying family." He carried on with his chore.

Ursula looked over her shoulder at June and lifted an eyebrow. Clearly his mother was not happy with him. June couldn't wait to ask Tom about this altercation.

"Will Tom be home for dinner?" June asked Ursula.

"He's on his way now," she said. She pulled a fresh loaf of bread from the oven; the yeasty richness of it filled the kitchen and brought Lincoln from some other part of the house. Upon seeing June, he nodded solemnly, then took his place at the head of the long table. "I never know if Tom is only taking a dinner break or if he's home for the evening," Ursula continued. "He complains of being busy."

"That's why I'm here," June said. "I want to talk to him about the search going on at my aunt Myrna's house."

"After dinner," Ursula stressed. "I'm certain he'll make the time."

When Tom arrived, the smaller children ran to him, and from his greeting, one would never know he carried so many burdens. After lifting them one at a time, remarking on their weight and telling them to eat more vegetables, he went to his wife and kissed her. Next he examined Johnny's face, made a disapproving frown that was clearly fake. Then he kissed his daughter's cheek and thanked her for helping with the food and the younger children. Then came his parents—first his mother and then his father. Each was greeted formally, then affectionately. All this was done before he even acknowledged June.

"You're a long way from home," he said, smiling.

"I need a good meal."

He looked her up and down, judging her slimness. "Desperately so, it appears. How was your day?"

"Terrible. Yours?"

"Equal."

She reached for the mug tree and selected a large one. "Coffee?"

"Please," he answered. He took his filled mug to the end of the table opposite his father. Once he sat, the children fell into their places like dominoes. June knew exactly where she was expected to sit and took her place. Lincoln led a prayer of thanks, broke bread and passed it, and the table conversation turned immediately to what each child had accomplished in school and at home.

This was the Toopeek family hour. There were occasions when this child or that had a job or activity and a plate had to be saved, but it was rare. The family hour was important to all of them. It was like June and Elmer's Tuesday-night meat loaf, when they made a point of sharing their lives. Or the Hudson Sunday dinner.

I have always been made welcome at this table as if a member of this family, June thought humbly.

When dinner was done, the children did the cleanup and some of them reclaimed the table for more homework while the younger ones were excused to TV, baths and bed.

The adults took second cups of coffee into the great room to sit by the fire.

"I'm worried about my aunt, Tom," June said. "What's going to happen?"

"The better question is, what *has* happened," he replied. "Since reading the newspaper story written by our bird-watcher, Mr. Paul Faraday, it's very clear that he spent days, possibly weeks, looking for any remains that might've been hidden on Myrna's property. He didn't 'stumble' upon bones—he searched for them. When the forensic anthropologist I sent them to didn't act quickly enough, Mr. Faraday went to the county district attorney and made a convincing argument against Myrna. All this, I believe, because he happens to be a true-crime writer and newspaper stringer on the side. He probably couldn't identify any bird other than a chicken.''

June's mouth hung open while Tom shared all this. ''He wants a story. A book.''

''Based on a famous writer's murder of her husband. That is what I believe.''

''But Myrna doesn't know anything about those old bones, Tom. Dad and I asked her pointedly. She doesn't know what became of Morton. He wandered off. We're trying to get information from the company he worked for, but they went out of business years ago.''

''I'm afraid my bad news doesn't stop there,'' Tom said. ''Do you remember the name Marge Glaser?''

''That sounds familiar…''

''The assistant district attorney who prosecuted Leah Craven for murder in the death of Gus Craven.''

''Yes,'' June said. ''That's right. That case went before Judge Forrest and Leah was acquitted.''

Tom nodded solemnly. ''I don't think Marge will ever get over that. When Paul Faraday wanted some action, he went to Marge. Marge got the search warrant from another judge. She knew better than to go to Judge Forrest.''

''Judge Forrest would never have given a search warrant to my aunt Myrna's—''

''June, your aunt Myrna would have invited them in and had the Barstows bake a pie for them. If Marge Glaser had called me, I'd have asked the sheriff's department for assistance and gone to Myrna's myself to explain. The way they're all trying to keep us out of it—from the ADA to the deputies—is an insult.''

''Might they arrest her?'' June asked in a fearful whisper.

''I'm afraid that's a possibility.''

A few days passed tensely as the crime investigators made a terrible mess of Myrna's house and grounds. The Barstows were driven nearly mad with rage over the amount of tidying up they'd be expected to do. Myrna declared she wasn't going to do a thing to the grounds until certain they were done digging and tearing things up.

Myrna settled on John Cutler as her attorney, a disheveled young man who had actually represented Leah Craven in her murder trial. Whether Myrna did that because she liked Cutler or to further annoy Marge Glaser was uncertain. Myrna could have afforded the best criminal attorney in California; Cutler was not only young, the bulk of his experience had been gained in the public defender's office. This worried June terribly.

''Relax, June. It's not as though I'm actually going to need him,'' Myrna had said. ''This has all gotten out of control.''

Myrna seemed to be holding up well. In fact, she was probably the most stable of them all. June was upset, Elmer was angry and the Barstows were in such a fit they weren't even bickering with each other. But Myrna merely frowned her displeasure, took copious notes and made comments like, "Aren't they going to feel ridiculous in the end."

In the midst of this, evidence that the harvest festival was nearly upon them began to show around town. As June arrived at the clinic one early morning, she saw the portable walls of a few booths that belonged to businesses of Grace Valley stacked up in the parking lot that separated the Presbyterian church from the café. Behind those two buildings was a large grassy yard that led to Windle River. Volunteers on ladders were stringing paper lanterns between the trees. Picnic tables moved from a rest stop on the outskirts of town sat on Rob Gilmore's flatbed truck. During this weekend the property behind the café would become a park where people could eat their corn dogs and chicken wings and barbecue. A portable stage would be set up in the church parking lot and there would be bands—local and visiting—and dancing.

June went to the café for her coffee, but took it outside to watch the lights and decorations go up. Where had the time gone? It seemed like just yesterday it was the Fourth of July and the children of Grace Valley were marching ahead of the brand-new ambulance Myrna had bought the town. Just yesterday she'd lain in the arms of her lover. Just yesterday Justine was marrying Sam, getting well, while Jurea's family had moved into town and she was having restorative surgery. Things were sane. Had all that really been over three months ago?

A sound caused her to turn and see Harry Shipton

on his hands and knees. He groaned and pushed himself upright, grass stains on the knees of his khaki pants. She rushed over to him. "Harry! Are you all right?"

"I should wear knee pads," he complained, brushing at his pants. "I've been looking for an excuse to bump into you, June. But I'd planned to do it much more gracefully."

She brushed at one knee while he brushed at the other. "Did you trip on something?"

"My feet," he said. "You're a doctor, you should know. Aren't your feet supposed to help with walking? Mine seem to do just the opposite."

They were awfully large, she noticed. But he was very tall and needed a firm base.

"As I said, I've been hoping to see you. I heard about this terrible business with your aunt. Is there any way I can help?"

"The only thing I can think of is your specialty, Harry. Prayer."

"How is she holding up?"

"Better than the rest of us, I'm afraid. Even though she's this frail, elderly, tiny thing, she's also a tough old bird. She doesn't let this get to her beyond annoying her. She says they're going to feel ridiculous in the end."

"Good for her! I know from experience. They shouldn't play poker with her. Do you think she'd like it if I dropped in on her?"

"Oh, Harry, that would be so nice of you! I think most of her friends are keeping a distance right now—

what with all those investigators around. You should see the yard! And I'm afraid they're far from finished.''

"Isn't there a point at which they have to concede there's nothing to be found?"

"I'm not sure. I'm just grateful that Myrna isn't in a worse state over it. My dad tried to get her to leave Hudson House, but she won't hear of it, so he's been staying there with her. Meanwhile, it's time for the fair.''

"The best town celebration within five hundred miles, I hear. Since you're taken, maybe your aunt Myrna would be my date."

June was shocked momentarily speechless. "Taken?" she asked weakly.

"Spoken for," he clarified.

She put a hand on his arm. "Forgive my stupidity, Harry, but what are you talking about?"

"You and Chris Forrest. I do have that right, don't I?"

She laughed in some embarrassment. "No, Harry, that's old news. Chris and I dated in high school, and don't make me tell you how long ago that was. Even though he's back and a divorced single father, I have absolutely no interest. The old men in town have been giving me the business about it."

"But I got it from him," Harry said. "Chris said you two were seeing each other."

"No way! He *said* that?"

Harry rubbed his chin. "Now, let me see... I don't want to get this wrong. What *exactly* did he say?

Something like the best part about coming home was having you on his arm again, just like the old days.''

June growled and her eyes became narrow slits. ''Why, that presumptuous—''

''Uh-oh. I hope I haven't started something...''

''It's a good thing you did, Harry, if he's going around telling people we're dating, when nothing could be more inaccurate. I'm going to hunt him down and give him a piece of my mind, before he ruins my reputation!''

Harry put his hands in his pockets and rocked back on his heels. He grinned and seemed to actually get a bit taller. ''Well, then, if you're not actually seeing him, do you suppose we might—''

''Oh, Harry, I'm sorry. Can you keep a secret? I'm completely unavailable. I am spoken for, as it turns out. Just not by Chris.''

''Oh. Well, then, who is the lucky man?''

''That's the secret, Harry. Not only can't I tell you who, you must not tell a soul that I have a special man in my life. Not a *soul*. I'm counting on your pastoral discretion here.''

He made a face. ''Sometimes it sucks being a pastor.''

Sixteen

The Thursday-night Graceful Quilters were in for a shock. They were expecting to finish their heirloom quilt just in time for the fair, but instead they would be entertaining a guest.

Sarah Kelleher had contacted Birdie and asked if she could speak to the quilters. She wanted help with a problem she was having with Blythe, though Blythe was about as far from being a fabric and needle type as one could be. Blythe was more the pick-and-shovel type and had worked beside Daniel from the beginning. Still...

"There are a few little enclaves in town that seem to anchor Grace Valley," Sarah explained to Birdie. "This group is one. Judge Forrest's poker table is another. The Presbyterian Women's League is another. I just want to talk to someone who will help me keep Blythe from moving away. And I'm in a terrible hurry."

Birdie was not one to take credit for such influence, but neither was she naive enough to suggest it didn't exist. Calling the quilting group an enclave was a kindness. It was more of a clique, made up of the police chief's wife, as well as his mother, the town doctor, a superior court judge's wife, a county social worker who knew where every legal button was and how to push them, and little Jessie Wiley, who some believed would study medicine and perhaps be the next town doctor one day. Yes, they could be a formidable group. But how in the world were they to convince a person to stay in Grace Valley, if leaving was what she wanted to do?

"When they hear the story, they'll want to help," Sarah assured her.

"I can't predict the outcome," Birdie said. "But these women are my friends and they'll listen to you politely. That much I can promise."

So Sarah went home and made the most delicious fudge cake imaginable as her offering. She was already waiting with Birdie when the first of the group, Philana and Ursula Toopeek, arrived. To say they were surprised would be an understatement. Philana said hello and stared shyly at her hands. Ursula, whose standard for marriage was high, lifted her chin and glared. "Save your anger, Mrs. Toopeek," Sarah said sweetly. "When I tell the story, you'll find no reason for it. And I've brought a delicious cake."

June came next. She was confused by Sarah's presence. It had only been a few days since she'd visited the woman's home with news that Blythe was packing. "Sarah, what are you doing here? Is Daniel all right?"

This made Sarah smile, for she knew she could

count on the town doctor to put judgments aside and show concern where concern was due. "Better every day, June. He's anxious to get back to work."

"Not too fast," the doctor warned.

Jessie was just behind June. Jessie's own mother had died when she was young and she'd been raised as the only child of an eccentric artist father. When she came to quilting, it was like coming to all her surrogate mothers. Jessie didn't really know Sarah, though she'd seen her at town meetings and events. But she knew *of* her because she was a part of the art world and acquainted with Jessie's father. "Sarah," she greeted in thinly veiled disbelief. "Have you joined the quilting circle?"

"Unfortunately, no, Jessie. I've just come for a visit. How is your father doing?"

"He's madly painting, so the answer must be 'good.'"

"Of course."

The last to arrive was Corsica Rios. She came in in a whirlwind, straight from her job in Social Services, toting her huge case-purse, chattering about just experiencing the longest day she'd had in months. She said a cheery hello to every quilter until her eyes fell on Sarah. Then her expression turned dark and unwelcoming.

"Is the coffee ready, Birdie?" Sarah asked somewhat nervously.

"It is."

"May I have a cup? For courage? Ladies, I've

come to ask your help. We can't let Blythe leave Grace Valley. Although Daniel's putting an angry face on his feelings, he'd be lost without her."

The cups were stacked by the electric pot and Sarah helped herself. The voice behind her must have been that of Corsica. "You hadn't considered that *before?*" Sarah's back stiffened in discomfort. She had been through an awful lot for Daniel and Blythe. It was a good thing she had a forgiving nature.

She turned back to the uneasy group. "Can we sit in a circle, like you do for quilting? And I'll tell you the whole story, the whole truth about it even though to do so breaks a solemn promise I made."

"Get your coffee or tea, everyone," Birdie said. "I promised Sarah you'd listen, but I didn't promise anything beyond that."

So the story began.

About two years earlier, Sarah had sought out Blythe's help in training two saddle horses she wanted to keep on her property for her grandchildren. Sarah had known nothing about horses and needed a full education in order to feed and care for them. But she'd never been shy about taking on some huge project. Inexperience was no excuse!

Blythe helped her some, Daniel helped her some, and she found herself attracted to Daniel. But so what? She never let it show. He was a married man.

Still, he kept coming around, long after Sarah was doing fine on her own. Finally she had to confront the situation head-on. "I told him, I can't have this,

Daniel. You're a married man and I have strong feelings about that.''

Someone in the quilting circle groaned. Sarah wasn't sure who but she narrowed down the culprit to Ursula or Corsica. She let it slide.

''He only said, 'It's not the way you think it is.' I fully expected him to tell me his wife didn't understand him or some other nonsense, but before he would tell me a word he asked a question. If he were not a married man, could I be persuaded to keep his company? An odd thing to ask, isn't it? He'd lived in Grace Valley with his wife for over thirty years! I answered that if he were a single man I might consider a date, a dinner or two, but I couldn't promise anything. I've been divorced for years. I've been quite satisfied with my life, independent of a spouse.'' She smiled and for a moment the women could see the light she had from within, the beauty and gentleness that Daniel might have been drawn to. ''I had never been lonely. I had never wanted another husband. But Daniel was persistent. And he told me that he and Blythe were not married, nor had they ever been. They are brother and sister.''

June actually gasped. Jessie's mouth dropped open in shocked disbelief. Corsica made a sound of distaste, Philana reached for Ursula's hand and Birdie said, ''That can't be!''

''Oh, but it's true. They haven't lived their adult lives incestuously, believe me. But as business partners and best friends. At first it was a huge relief for

Blythe to have someone in on the secret, but as you can see, it has now become a terrible burden for her. Let me begin at the beginning so you can understand.

"When Blythe and Daniel were just children back in Kentucky, their father died and their mother remarried a man who handled horses. He was a hard man in the best of times—abusive and cold. Then their mother died. Blythe was only fifteen and Daniel seventeen. They were turned into free labor by their cruel and greedy stepfather. There were many beatings and fights. Many nights Blythe cried herself to sleep and Daniel lay aching from the last thrashing. On a particularly terrible night, the fighting escalated until the kids actually fought back. Daniel hit his stepfather over the head with an iron skillet and the man fell, still. They couldn't find a pulse.

"Well, they ran. They changed their names, worked odd jobs and hitched rides across the United States. It was the '60s and there were a lot of young people on the road. They were drawn to the Golden Gate because of the racing and their experience with horses, but they were afraid to be around too many people. They thought it very likely they were being hunted for the murder of their stepfather. By the time they got to Grace Valley they were nineteen and twenty-one. Someone mistook them, quite innocently, for a young married couple. It only made sense for them to continue the charade. If the authorities were looking for a brother and sister, they wouldn't suspect a young man and his wife.

"A good twenty years later Daniel went to a lawyer about his past. Taking advantage of the confidence of legal counsel, he told the lawyer everything. The lawyer did some simple checking and learned that the mean old stepfather had gotten no more than a nasty bump on the head and never spent a nickel looking for his stepchildren. He was glad to be rid of them. He'd since remarried, died of natural causes and left the stables that had originated with Blythe and Daniel's father to his widow and her family.

"Daniel was so relieved, he wanted to come clean to the town, to their friends, immediately. But Blythe was too afraid. She thought the lie would be judged harshly rather than understood. She thought they'd be hated and run off. Well," Sarah said, "until Daniel and I met, there was really no reason to insist. Besides," she added apologetically, "I don't know if you've ever noticed, Daniel can be passive."

For the first time, one of the listeners spoke. "If I'd known he waited till his fifties to court a woman it might have become obvious," Birdie said. The relief of laughter followed.

"For a year, Daniel and I courted secretly. The three of us spent a good deal of time together. I believe Blythe was happy. We were like sisters. Then we started to pressure her to agree to telling the truth and panic overcame her. The past year has been a nightmare for all of us."

"What the devil does she think will happen?" Corsica wanted to know.

"I believe she thinks she'll be tarred and feathered," Sarah said. "And, please understand, I don't think her fears are unreasonable. People are going to snicker, point, talk behind their hands. We know how small towns are, and we're ready to stand together against whatever painful gossip erupts. But Blythe just can't face it. Once you've kept a secret for almost forty years, it's hard to let it go."

"Are you sure it isn't that she wishes you would go away so she could have her old life back?" Corsica asked.

"By now there's no question of that," Sarah said. "I'm bringing her such terrible discomfort. And when she finds out I've told the secret, she's going to be so angry with me. But we can't let her go. Don't you see? After all Daniel and Blythe have been through together, I can't let them become separated now."

"Have you considered just breaking it off with Daniel and letting them have their secret?" June asked.

"I've offered that. Though it would hurt, I could do it. I've been married, had children, have grandchildren. I've had a husband, and while it didn't work out to be forever, we had some good years. But Daniel is fifty-five and all he's done his whole life is work and protect his sister. He wants to have a little something for himself before his life is over." She shook her head. "She's more comfortable with people thinking Daniel cheated on her than with the truth, that's how afraid she is. And that's where I need your help.''

"You think we can convince her the town won't treat her meanly if she and Daniel open up, tell the story?'' Corsica asked. ''Because this is a town like all towns and—''

"I don't think anyone knows how people will act,'' Sarah said. ''But maybe you can tell her that you know the truth, and that you understand.'' She looked at each quilter. ''You do understand, don't you?''

June was thinking that, for the first time, she finally *did* understand.

June had a piece of business with Chris Forrest that she wasn't about to let anyone in on, especially Birdie. She could have hung around after quilting to talk to him, but talking to him wasn't really what she had in mind. Besides, she'd prefer to do this in daylight.

She asked John to cover her appointments while she did rounds at Valley Hospital in Rockport. After rounds she took a side trip to Bob Hanson's insurance office. Her timing was good; she was there at lunch time. But Chris had already walked down the street to a Rockport pub for a sandwich.

She'd been rehearsing what she'd say—''Did you tell the new preacher that we were a couple, you slimeball?'' Or maybe, ''Who do you think you are, telling people you had me on your arm again?''—but nothing seemed to carry the force she was looking for. She could only hope that something magnificent would pop to her lips when she saw him.

And then she saw him.

She was driving her truck toward the pub and he was out front. There were benches on either side of the pub's double doors and an attractive woman in her early thirties sat on one. She wore business attire—skirt, hose, heels. Her shapely legs were crossed and her coppery hair bounced in thick tendrils on her shoulders as she laughed in amusement at whatever entertaining thing Chris was saying to her.

His back was to the street. He had raised one foot to the bench and was leaning on the raised knee so that he hovered over her. It looked as though he was telling her secret, intimate, playful stories. He leaned closer and closer to her face, smiling, whispering. She chuckled again and gazed up at him with adoration. She gently caressed the calf of his raised leg and he twisted one of the coppery tresses around his finger.

He hadn't changed a bit since high school.

It all came flooding back to June, how he had always been this big flirt who wanted to have his cake and eat it too. He'd wanted June as his official girlfriend, but he'd wanted others on the side. That's right, *others*. It hadn't been just Nancy, though it had been mostly Nancy. Indeed, Nancy had done her the biggest favor by winning him!

The louse. He had the temerity to tell people he was happy to be back and wanted another chance with June, yet he was clearly courting this pretty young woman. He was a *joke!* And he needed a taste of his own medicine.

Talk about closure. It certainly wouldn't take much more than this.

She stopped at the curb, but the couple on the bench were oblivious. She rolled down the window on the passenger side, then leaned on the horn in a huge, long blast that caused them to jump. The woman grabbed her heart and Chris whirled around in surprise.

"How can you do this to me?" June cried out. "After telling Pastor Shipton we're a couple?"

Chris looked completely perplexed. His mouth opened and closed a couple of times in a silent stammer. His hands moved in futile gestures that said nothing. He lumbered unsteadily toward her truck and, placing his hands on the door at the opened window, leaned down. "June," he began.

"How many times in one life do you plan to break my heart? How many women will you cheat with, you oaf?" she yelled. He looked stunned, and that made it all the harder to keep a straight face. She might have felt a little bit bad about the way the attractive young women went pale, her eyes as huge as saucers. Of course, she thought she was the only one.

"June…" he attempted.

"Don't you *ever* speak my name again, you… you…*monster!*"

"Hey, June-bug, I was just—"

She pressed the heel of her hand against the horn

for another long, loud blast, causing him to jump back
from the truck and put his hands over his ears. "Bye
now," she said, and drove away. She laughed all the
way back to Grace Valley.

Birdie had stayed up late working on the festival
quilt because there was only one week in which to
finish, so she was tired and perhaps a little cranky.
Then she was up early, as usual, on Friday morning.
Judge was in a foul spirit over this Myrna Claypool
thing, Chris had showered and left the house as
quickly as possible, and she was stuck with the noise
and mess of her grandsons. And their insolence. She
was just about at the end of her tether.

The Graceful Quilters had decided, unanimously,
not to converge on Blythe. Birdie would go to her
first, Corsica and Ursula would be backup if Birdie
failed to make headway, and June was to be the last
line of defense. Philana and Jessie were excused—
Philana for her shyness and Jessie for her inexperience.

Birdie said a quick prayer for patience as she drove
her big yellow sedan up the road toward Culley
Stables. No one answered the door, which wasn't
much of a surprise. Birdie went out to the stable closest to the house. She heard a scraping sound and
called out, "Blythe?"

Shovel in hand, Blythe stepped out of the shadows.
"Mrs. Forrest?" she said in surprised confusion.

"I'm sorry not to have called first, Blythe. I must talk to you. Do you have a minute?"

"What is it?" she asked, worried. Birdie Forrest was about the last person Blythe ever expected to see in her stable. "Is anything wrong?" Would Birdie be sent to the stables to inform her of Daniel's death? Surely not.

"I think everything is going to be fine, Blythe, if we can just talk a minute. I've had such a rugged week. Could we go to your porch? I'm done in. And Lord knows, I don't want to go back home and face those little delinquents my son is raising...or rather, sticking me with." She lifted a hand to her forehead and tried to push her silver curls into shape. "They're going to be the death of me, Blythe."

"Well, mercy, come on then. I'll get you some lemonade."

"Would you? That would help so much." They walked together toward the house. "It seems unusually quiet around here, Blythe. Where are all the hands?"

"We're not real busy right now. Only doing some boarding. No training or breeding. We're down to just a couple of hands."

Birdie looped her arm through Blythe's. "Is that because Daniel isn't here?"

They made an odd-looking couple, Birdie in her wool plaid skirt, sweater and brown lace-up shoes and Blythe in jeans, flannel shirt and cowboy hat. Plus, Birdie had almost twenty years on Blythe. But they walked along like girlfriends, and when Birdie asked about Daniel, Blythe dropped her gaze and looked down. "He's had a heart problem, you know," Blythe answered.

"Indeed. From what I understand, you've had a heart problem, too. The three of you have."

"It sounds like you're here on a mission. You should save your breath," she said.

"Whatever you want in the end, Blythe. But can I please have that lemonade? I'm completely exhausted. And you know that thing you did to Daniel with the buckshot? If I had any skill at all, I'd nail those two sassy, disrespectful grandsons of mine in the same place."

"They must have gotten the best of you," Blythe said.

"Not yet, but they shall soon." Birdie sank into a porch chair. "You're kind to indulge me, Blythe. I promise to return the favor someday."

"Sure," Blythe said tiredly, going for the drink she'd promised.

Birdie could tell it was hard for Blythe to patiently sit with a glass of lemonade and listen to an old woman say her piece, but to her credit she didn't squirm or wiggle.

"So. I hear you're planning to run away before it gets out that you and Daniel are brother and sister and have only pretended to be husband and wife for convenience' sake."

A huff of chagrined laughter blew out of Blythe

and she shook her head. "Well, hell. There isn't much more to it than that."

"Oh, but there is. First, you were frightened children when the assumption was made. Frightened children on the run. Second, how would your life have been different if you'd admitted to being siblings from the start?" Blythe frowned in confusion. Birdie pressed on with a shrug. "Seems to me you would still have built this house and stables, still have worked as partners, side by side. You'd still have been successful. He'd still have fallen for Sarah. I can only think of one difference in all this."

"Which is?"

"You wouldn't be threatening to run now."

"Mrs. Forrest, it's nice of you to go to all this trouble to try to convince me to stay, but I don't think the rest of the town is going to be as understanding. I don't think—"

"I don't think they care near as much as you think they do, Blythe. And if you go, you'll never find out if you could have just as easily stayed in your own home, with your own business, in your own family."

"There will be talk. Maybe vicious talk."

"It's so unlike you to scare easily," Birdie said. "Even less like you to be ungrateful and self-pitying."

A little fire crept into Blythe's usually warm eyes. "Ungrateful? Self-pitying? How can you accuse me of things like that when you know what I've gone through? When you know how humiliating this has—''

''Let me tell you something, dear girl,'' Birdie said, not for one second thinking it strange to call a woman in her fifties a girl. ''When I was just a girl, I buried my mother. I was ten and had to take over the house. Then my father went soon after, leaving us impoverished and living on the mercy of neighbors. Then I lost two brothers in the war. Nine years ago my very best friend's heart gave out while I held her hand. I have a friend whose wife is dying of cancer, a husband who's trying to keep an old friend from going to jail for a murder she never in a million years would have committed, and my son has saddled me with two thieving, lying, incorrigible brats in the winter of my life. And you're worried about *talk?*''

Blythe's eyes clouded with unwanted tears. ''Horrible talk,'' she said in a breath.

''Well, lift your chin, girl! I'm here to tell you that, in addition to a family who loves you, you have friends in town who will stand up for you! And if you need more than that to get by, then you need more than anyone can give!''

It took her a second to respond. ''But, Mrs. Forrest—'' she said through a hiccup of emotion.

''Yes, I know. You're hurt and embarrassed. Perfectly understandable. Now it's time for you to be brave, Blythe. Daniel deserves his chance at happiness, too, you know. And Sarah is a good woman who loves you. You can have the best of all worlds if you'll just summon some inner strength.''

Blythe looked into her lap. ''It might be I just can't.''

Birdie reached for the hands folded into Blythe's lap and gave them a strong squeeze. ''But of course you can, dear. You're much stronger than all this.'' Birdie stood. ''If you go in spite of all the people who are pledging their support and begging you to stay…well, there's no help for you.''

When Birdie got home, the house was blessedly quiet. By the clock she had another half hour before those hellions burst upon her. She'd done her part for Blythe and more than her part for her son. She lay a cool cloth on her forehead and reclined on the sofa. Within seconds, she was deeply asleep.

It was the sound of whispering that woke her. She remained still and listened raptly. ''She keeps it in here,'' one of them said.

''It's not here!'' said the other.

''Dig around a little. That's where I saw her put it.''

''Okay, okay…''

''Under the tea bags maybe…''

''Got it!''

''Hurry. Let's go!''

The shuffle of footsteps, the squeak of the screen door, then quiet.

Birdie slowly rose from the sofa, pain dragging

down her spirit. Did they not know how this hurt her? How ashamed she was of them? How could they steal from her, their own grandmother? And for what? Were they driven by some drug-crazed addiction, or just out for a good time in any naughty way they could find?

She went to her kitchen canisters and opened the smallest one. She lifted out a half-dozen tea bags and pulled out a small fold of bills—her Christmas money. She clipped her coupons, scrimped by making soup out of chicken wings, and put by a few dollars every week. She'd spent a nice chunk on Judge's birthday last summer and had, since then, saved eighty-four dollars. She unfolded the bills and counted...fourteen.

She went to the phone and called the police department. Deputy Lee Stafford answered. "Hello, Lee, it's Birdie Forrest. I'd like to report a theft."

Seventeen

"You're crazy, right?" Chris shouted at his mother.

Birdie sat at the kitchen table and gently massaged her temples. "I *was* a little crazy," she said. "I'm not now."

"You've had my children locked up!" he yelled. "What were you thinking?"

"Relax, Christopher. They're in Tom Toopeek's police station. It's not the federal penitentiary."

"It's jail!"

"They stole seventy dollars from me, Chris. I heard them sneak in the house and prowl around, whispering and searching for it. Aren't you even a little worried about where this is all leading?"

"I'll give you the goddamn seventy dollars!"

Her hand came out like a shot and slapped his face. The minute she'd done it, she wished to recall the act, but it was too late. It was like he was fourteen himself, and she wouldn't take that kind of talk from him. And how dare he defend thieves. How dare he try to make this her fault.

He stared daggers at her, his cheek reddening, then he turned and stomped out of the house.

Where have I gone wrong? she asked herself. She would not have allowed Chris to get into the kind of trouble these boys did. She and Judge were disciplinarians, perhaps too much so. She had always worried they were too strict, but Chris turned out all right. He didn't have a fancy job, but he made a decent living. And except for his divorce, he'd had a good adult life. Divorce wasn't the worst thing. It happened to good people.

But these boys! Stealing their grandmother's pin money! What was he thinking, to want her to just let it go?

Well, she wouldn't.

Chris was back, stomping through the house to his room. He began throwing his things in a duffel bag. She followed him and stood in the doorway, watching.

"So, now you're going to punish me by packing up and running away. Just like a boy."

"Mother, don't start with me. I've been through enough and I don't want to argue with you. The house isn't quite ready, but it's close, and we can stay there now. It'll be like camping. I think the boys are just plain too much for you."

"They definitely are. And they're apparently too much for you, too!" And with that, Birdie went to her bedroom and slammed the door.

Birdie sat on her bed for a long time while the sounds from without indicated that Chris was packing to leave. On the one hand, she hated to see him go. It made her feel as though she'd failed him. On the other, he couldn't go soon enough. She was exhausted with trying to do a good job, to make things right. And the fact that he'd have quite a lot to do to organize his sons' messy room enough to pack almost made her smile in sinister delight.

He never should have run off and married Nancy. He had complained about his wife and his marriage on and off since the beginning. In remembering, Birdie thought he'd been miserable more often than happy. Nancy, he said, had a temper. She spent frivolously, though he worked hard to provide. She spoiled the boys, then expected them to behave as if disciplined. She—

Now wait, Birdie thought. *Nancy* spoiled the boys and didn't discipline them? That may have been, but clearly, Chris was no disciplinarian. He was in such denial about their behavior, even his best friend catching them red-handed as they stole couldn't get his attention. Those twins hadn't even been grounded after all the trouble they'd been in.

Nancy had called a few times to talk to her sons and the boys had called her a few times, but Birdie hadn't talked to Nancy in over a year. She had not been surprised by the divorce and, in typical motherly fashion, had gone along with the notion that her son, her good-natured and always upbeat son, had been a victim of a poor matrimonial choice.

She could still hear him out there, probably in the boys' room now, gathering up belongings. Unintimidated by the fact that he was still in the house, she picked up the phone and dialed. Nancy answered on the second ring.

"Hello, Nancy, it's Birdie Forrest. How are you, dear?"

A moment of silence answered her, and Birdie thought, fervently, Don't hang up, please don't hang up even though it's what I might do if I were in this situation.

"Well, Birdie. What a surprise. I guess I'm all right, under the circumstances. And you?"

"I'm not very well, dear. That is, I'm not ill, but awfully disappointed in my son. I felt an urgent need to talk with you. It's about the twins."

A huff of laughter came first. Then, "Quite a handful, aren't they, Birdie?"

"To say the very least...."

"Maybe you can understand my ultimatum then. I honestly couldn't take another second without a little support. I was getting nowhere. They need an intervention—and fast. Or they're going to end up in *jail!*"

Birdie was overwhelmed by confusion. "Jail?"

"They're pretty well known in our neighborhood by now, and the police have returned them to us with warnings a few times. I can't put all the blame on Chris, I'm sure I've made many a mistake mothering them...but every time they get in trouble, Chris wants to brush it off as if it's just boys being boys, as if it's nothing. Now, I didn't know Chris very well when he was fourteen, but I knew him all through high school, and he didn't steal and vandalize and cheat in school and sass the teachers. Birdie, they're at a very important crossroads, and if something isn't done, I fear for their future.''

''But Nancy, they're not doing very well here. And Chris—''

''Don't let him off the hook, Birdie. It's time for him to take some responsibility for his sons. He'll be forced to take some action. That's why I told him the only way I'd agree to a trial separation is if he'd take the boys with him.''

''Trial separation,'' Birdie repeated softly.

''I won't lie to you I miss them terribly...though I don't know why I should. These past couple of months have been the first migraine-free ones I've had in fourteen years. But they can't come back here until they're changed. The juvenile services officer was very clear—anymore truancy, petty theft or vandalism and they're going to be locked up. Perhaps moved to foster care.'' Nancy sighed. ''I apologize for what you must be going through, Birdie. It seemed the only way.''

''Trial separation,'' she said again. He had lied. They were not divorced. ''Nancy? What do you think is in the future for your marriage? Do you hope to reconcile with Chris?''

''I love Chris very much. I've loved him since I was a girl. And I would like to grow old with him, but I'm not sure that will happen, Birdie. It's true, we were having a real hard time. Lots of fighting...and lots of it over what to do with the boys. Chris was ready to walk. If he'd had his way, he'd just leave us to work things out as best we can while he moved on to his next life, found himself a new wife. One with fewer complications, I suppose. I thought the best thing I could do for my sons and my husband is to stop helping them. They're going to have to take responsibility, once and for all. Does that sound cruel?''

Birdie was suddenly ashamed of herself. Once Chris and Nancy had married, Birdie accepted the marriage, accepted her daughter-in-law, but not without a small grudge that she hoped was her secret. All these years Birdie had had an impression of Nancy stalking Chris, trying to tear him away from June's loving arms. And now she knew that this simply was not true. Chris had made victims of both these women—June, by leaving her, and Nancy, by wedding her.

All these years, Birdie had resented the fact that Nancy had taken him away from her, from Grace Valley. She often thought about how perfect life would have been had Chris stayed in their town and married June, who Birdie and Judge loved as much as if she were their own. Birdie thought the children would have been better behaved with a mother like June. Hah! It was a father like Chris that appeared to be their problem. All these years, though she'd tried to hide her true feelings and make Nancy feel like a cherished daughter-in-law, she knew she had held back a part of herself. And if Nancy were honest, she would admit to feeling it.

Oh, Birdie had amends to make. But that would have to wait. ''Nancy, you mustn't blame yourself. I know you did your best. I'm calling to give you some bad news and you might be very upset with me.''

''What is it?'' she asked, panic in her voice.

''It's the boys, Nancy. I caught them stealing from me and I called the police. It's the second time they've been caught stealing. The first time went practically unnoticed, so this time, despite very vocal protests from Chris, I'm pressing charges. They're in Tom Toopeek's office jail.'' There was complete silence on the other end of the line. ''They're completely safe,'' Birdie went on. ''There aren't any other inmates or prisoners or whatever they'd be called. But I'm unwilling to ignore this—this blatant disregard for the rules.''

''Birdie,'' Nancy said. ''You go, girl.''

Friday afternoon, just as the last patient was leaving the clinic, Jessie received a call from Valley Hospital. She listened quietly, made a few notes on a tablet, then put the caller on hold. When she turned around to look for someone to take the call, all three of her co-workers happened to be present. ''June? John? I don't know who wants to take this call—it's Dr. Worth. It's about Justine. She's very bad. She's dying.''

Everyone knew how really bad it was the day she went into the hospital. The cancer she'd been diagnosed with months earlier had spread. Justine's immune system had been under attack and weakened long before she collapsed. And, of course, there was no pregnancy.

When all the test results were complete and the extent of the disease confirmed, Justine, Sam, her sisters and her father had made the decision—she did not want to prolong the pain. There was a Do Not Resuscitate order in place on her medical chart.

John took the call at Jessie's desk, learned the facts and repeated them to June. "It's really just a matter of saying goodbye," he said.

"Does Dr. Worth say how long?" June asked.

"A few days, a few weeks," he said with a shrug. "She's in very bad shape."

"Well then," June said. "I'll go tonight and—"

"This is just stupid!" Jessie snapped. "Why was she so stupid? I don't know if I can be a doctor if people are going to waste good medicine and sign a damn death certificate!"

John dropped an arm about her shoulders and gave her a squeeze. "There are several things you need to think about right now," he said patiently. "One is, Justine might not have made it even with treatment. Another thing is, there are often no symptoms until ovarian cancer is advanced, so undetected and untreated, she might not have had even the last few months. But finally, Jessie, what you have to know is that each patient is allowed the dignity to decide for herself, for himself, what kind of life they want to have, be it short or long, be it filled with the struggle to survive or the peace of letting go. We're only here to help, not to remove choice."

"First, do no harm," June said.

Jessie let a tear drop. "Well, it really sucks."

"Doesn't it just," John said, hugging her.

Pretty soon Susan and June joined their hug and the four of them stood embraced in the center of the office for a long time.

Miles away in Rockport, near the ocean, on the third floor of the hospital, Justine's family took turns sitting vigil at her side. Sam left her rarely, though her father and sisters pleaded with him to take breaks. Justine drifted in and out of consciousness, due to the weakness of her body and the high doses of morphine used to dull the pain.

On that Friday evening, June, John and Elmer all dropped by, patted her hand, wished her well and embraced those who would mourn her. On Saturday a few people from Grace Valley stopped by, reminding Sam and the family that they were not really alone. And although the doctor would not have guessed it would happen so soon, she passed on Sunday, just a few days after being admitted to the hospital. Some would find it shockingly fast, others would give thanks that she did not suffer long.

Justine had requested that her ashes be scattered from the rocky coast out over the Pacific Ocean, something that could be done whenever the family could find a gathering place and put together their few words. Sam told the sisters to come and collect whatever of Justine's they wanted. The door would be unlocked.

Sam had not done too much fishing since marrying Justine. In the first place, he had only been trying to help her get over a broken heart by being compli-

mentary and friendly. And, oddly enough, she took to
him. In the second place, he could see they were good
together, so there was no point in knocking good fortune. He knew when they married that they were both
on borrowed time—he was seventy and her cancer
had been diagnosed before they were wed. He thought
it more likely they could cure her cancer than his age,
so this loss came hard. Harder still because he felt
she'd been robbed more than he; she was just a girl.

He fetched his pail and pole from his gas station
and drove his old truck out to his favorite stream.
He'd rather fish at dawn than at dusk, but he could
think of nothing better than fishing to help him deal
with the ache in his heart. He was there less than an
hour when he heard rustling behind him. Through the
trees they came—Lincoln Toopeek, Elmer Hudson,
Burt Crandall, Judge Forrest, George Fuller and Harry
Shipton. Each one gave Sam a nod, put down his pail
and baited a hook. They lined up along the river, three
on each side of Sam, their lines in, and fished. In a
little while there was more rustling, and Standard
Roberts walked up behind them. There was some
shifting at the edge of the river as they made room
for Stan next to Sam. Stan clapped a hand on Sam's
shoulder, Sam clapped a hand on Stan's back.

They fished a while, and in the way that men fish,
they took great comfort in the fact that they were
friends and they were never intended to bear any pain
alone. When the sun was nearly down, Harry Shipton
said, ''May each fish thank God for the time he has

given them to swim in the river." And all the men said, "Amen."

Jurea Mull was not an educated woman. In fact, her husband had taught her to read, a pastime that had become a passion for her. She lived for the used books, magazines and newspapers Clarence would scrounge and bring to their little shanty in the woods. And when they had moved to town and Jurea learned of the library in Rockport, not far from the hospital where she'd had her surgery, she was giddy with excitement. Imagine, a place where you could borrow the books for free and keep them for up to four weeks in your own home!

But she had gone back to the woods with Clarence after only two brief visits to that library in Rockport.

Jurea wasn't educated, nor would she consider herself clever, but she did have good sense and sound instincts. It took her a little while, but she knew that what June had told her was true—as long as she coddled Clarence, he would stay back in the woods. And it would be better for their whole family, including Clarence, if they lived together in town and Clarence tried the medicine and therapy again.

Charlie MacNeil thought he was coming to the forest to pick up Jurea and take her for a visit with her children in town, but Jurea was packing up the few articles of clothing she owned, waiting for Clarence. If he didn't come back, she would attempt to write him a note.

But he came. He walked in with his rifle balanced

over his shoulder, a couple of rabbits strung together and dangling lifelessly from a rope. He had trapped them; he was an excellent trapper.

"I'm glad you're back, Clarence," she said. "I'm going back to town. Much as I want to stay and help you figure things out, I need to go back."

He nodded curtly and tossed his rabbits on the ground in front of the woodstove. He pulled a crude bowl from the shelf to hold the innards, drew his hunting knife from his belt and got ready to clean them on a board on the dirt floor.

"Clarence, I think you should try and show a little courage and come back to town. For the sake of your kids, who need you."

"They'll get over that soon enough."

"No, I don't think so. Just like I still feel the need to see my family though I haven't lived with 'em in twenty years, your kids will always feel the need to have you. They won't be with us much longer, Clarence. They're growing up. I just can't have them spend their lives hiding in the forest."

He turned around and looked her in the eye. "You go on, Jurea. You go on and have a better life. I don't need you here." He turned back to his rabbits and kneeling, began to gut and skin them.

His words had stung, but she knew he didn't mean them the way they sounded. He needed her, but he could exist without her help.

"Well, I need you, Clarence. I hope you decide to come back to town. Come back and go to the VA clinic and get you some new medicine and have a good life with us again. If it's easier for you, I'll promise not to have no more operations on my face."

Clarence, on his knees, slowly turned toward her, looked up at her and asked, "You would do that?"

"I would do just about anything to help, except keep our family apart. If I didn't think it would hurt the kids real bad to live back here, I'd bring 'em back. But you should see 'em, Clarence. They're so happy going to school. They're learning real fast and making some friends. I mean, Clarence, *you* got to go to school when you was a boy. It wasn't a town and family and friends that made you sick, it was a war. The kids deserve our best, not our worst, fears."

Charlie MacNeil had arrived and gave the horn on his car a toot. Jurea opened the door, waved to him that she'd heard, then went to her husband. She bent at the waist so that she might kiss him on the cheek, but he turned away from her and she was left to kiss the top of his head. She picked up her bundle and made to leave.

"I hope you get over hurting, Clarence. I hope you come back to town because that's where I'll be."

Tears smarted in her eyes as she left the shack in the woods, knowing she would never return to it, hoping Clarence wouldn't die there alone.

On Monday morning, Harry Shipton phoned both John Stone and Mike Dickson, one at a time, but had almost identical conversations with each of them. "I understand you've been in trouble with the missus for weeks now."

"More like months," John said.

"My wife *and* mother," said Mike.

"With any hope of patching it up anytime soon?" Harry asked. He was told by each that, however hard they tried, however apologetic, the women had been offended enough to carry a grudge. "That's a shame," Harry said. "Well, how far are you willing to go to get back in the good graces of your wives…because I have an idea of something you can do, something we can all do together for the town and the women who have been insulted."

Of course both John and Mike said they'd do anything. Harry was going to have some fun.

Every time Myrna Claypool looked out the window of her study into the yard around Hudson House, it irked her more. She was no longer the gardener she had once been and she was too old and frail—something she hated to admit—to put that mess to rights again. It was not as though she couldn't afford to have a professional landscaping crew come in from one of the larger towns and make the grounds more beautiful than ever. It was the idea that this could be done to her without conscience, without substantial probable cause.

Someone was going to pay for this, but she wasn't quite sure who it would be.

Her attorney, John Cutler, was positioned in the sunroom, using the coffee table as a desk. He used his cell phone while Myrna used her house phone. They were working on separate research projects, either of which could bring this mystery to a close. Myrna was trying to find out what Paul Faraday really had to do with the discovery of the bones, and Cutler was trying to get information on what had become of Morton Claypool.

Myrna peeked into the sunroom to steal a look at Cutler. His name was John, but she addressed him as Cutler because she liked the sound of it. He had corrected her a couple of times, then let her be. He was a rumpled mess, and June thought they should hire an older, more experienced lawyer, but after having a brief conversation with him on the phone, Myrna knew he was exactly what she wanted. He was a little socially inept but very bright. And most important, he was perfectly willing to do things her way. At her age, after all the years of independence—virtually from the age of fourteen—it wasn't likely she was going to be ordered around by anyone.

Cutler scribbled something on a yellow pad and simultaneously looked up to see Myrna peeking in. He lifted his eyebrows and inclined his head in a gesture that meant she should enter. "Thank you, thank you very much," he said into the phone. "Mrs. Claypool, we have something important. Your husband took retirement from Sandfield Office Supplier. He was sixty-two and his retirement income from them was very modest, but he continued to pay into his social security for five years after the last time you saw him."

"Well, that old dog. I always suspected another woman. Where was the old coot?"

"That's a problem. He had his check sent to a post office box."

"So I wouldn't find him, I suppose." She tapped her pen idly on the rim of her glasses. "I should have thought of social security. He's either dead or collecting it now."

"There's the problem. They don't have records of either." At her alarmed look, he said, "Now, that doesn't mean anything, Mrs. Claypool. He could have stopped paying in because he had no further income. His pension with the office supplier dried up when they went bankrupt. The pension fund, like the rest of the company, was mismanaged."

"Oh my! I wonder, did they let Morton run the place for a while?" she asked facetiously.

Cutler ignored her sarcasm. "He stopped paying into social security. He didn't file for receipt of social security, which could have been because he didn't need it. Not everyone collects, you know."

"Now, why in the world would Morton stop paying in and fail to collect, unless he was dead?" she wanted to know.

Cutler shrugged. "He could have married a rich woman. He could have left the country. In fact, he could have died out of the country and been unidentified. There are a million possible explanations. I just want to be sure we can prove he wasn't buried out there," he said, giving his head a jerk toward the window.

"My dear Cutler, if he were out there, don't you suppose he'd have been found by now?"

He grinned, then asked, "How are you doing on your detective work?"

"Not nearly as well, I'm afraid. Mr. Paul Faraday is a true-crime writer and stringer for the San Jose paper. I gather from some of his interviews that he fancies himself a screenwriter as well, but hasn't had any success. Obviously he's targeted me for a story, but I can't understand why."

"Your books, Mrs. Claypool. I'm afraid you might have set yourself up for this investigation."

"Oh, so everyone says. But then answer me this, Cutler. The ADA, Ms. Glaser, she's a bright woman, isn't she?"

He nodded. "Some say she's brilliant."

"Why does she go along with this—this warrant, this collection of evidence, based on Mr. Faraday's flimsy and concocted story?"

"She must believe he's on to something. The bones were found to be those of a male, approximate age of sixty, dead twenty years. That fits a certain bill."

"Then there's only one explanation," she said. "Mr. Faraday didn't get them here."

Eighteen

Though the people in the clinic had every reason to feel the weight of grief after what had happened to Justine, June was ready to move forward with optimism. She had a quiet and serene acceptance of her life, her future. She watched from the café as Rob Gilmore used a rented cherry picker to string colored lights up Valley Drive, and saw with some melancholy Sam and Standard Roberts erecting Justine's booth in front of her flower shop. The dried wreaths and arrangements she had spent late summer making would be sold after all.

There was something about the fall that seemed to wash the land clean; the sunlight filtered through colored leaves was like a kaleidoscope on the ground and streets. The air was snappy and made one think of soups and hot bread. The chopping of wood for winter fireplaces had commenced. It made one want to nest.

"I need to see you after your last patient, if you have some time," June said to John.

"I've had my last," he said. "I'm leaving in about a half hour."

"My office," she said, leading the way. She sat behind her desk, feeling awkward.

"What's up?" he asked, entering behind her.

"Close the door, please."

He hesitated, then did so.

"This is a medical matter, John," June said, folding her hands on top of her desk.

By the solemn look on her face, John was made more than a little uncomfortable. "Am I sick?" he wanted to know.

She rolled her eyes. "John, I've been fighting a case of the flu for about two months now," she said.

"Hmm," he answered. "Fatigue, nausea, aching...? We should start with some blood work. It could be a simple case of iron deficiency. With your diet, I'm frankly surprised you haven't been anemic before—"

"I don't know when my last period was," she said. "But I've been alternately crying and biting people's heads off for a good six weeks."

"Oh," he said, then had the good sense to shut up.

"I'm thirty-seven...almost thirty-eight, I didn't think I'd ever have a child, and now I find myself a geriatric pregnancy. I need a good OB-GYN and you're the best I know."

"Well, then," he said. "I'd be honored. Go ahead to exam one and I'll get Susan."

"I'm not ready to share this with Jessie," June said.

"You can have your chart, lock it in your file cabinet if you like. But before we make any diagnosis, we examine. Besides, we're done for the day. I'll go ahead and send Jessie home.''

A short time later, June assumed the position. She wasn't sure what she was feeling, excitement or dread. It certainly wouldn't be dread at having a pregnancy, but at having one accidentally and being left to hope the gentleman wouldn't be too upset. In her entire experience with Jim, she'd never seen him upset about anything. Of course, she had to wonder when he'd return, and what she'd tell people if she began to show before she had a partner.

"It's not Chris Forrest," she said suddenly, forcefully.

Susan, who'd been at the counter compiling her chart information, looked over with a curious frown. John peeked over the sheet that covered June's knees. He lifted his eyebrows; he had not been about to ask. "Obviously," he said.

"It's not," she said more sanely.

John pulled out the speculum and stood over her. He palpated her uterus. He did this thoughtfully, she decided, his eyes rolling to the ceiling. Then he looked at her. "That last period, whenever it was, could it have been a lighter than usual one?"

She shook her head. "Can't even remember. I pay no attention."

"You don't keep track? At all?"

"Periods have never been a problem," she said.

"So uneventful that you don't even know you're having them?"

"Well, I..."

He snapped off his gloves and said, "Congratulations. You're definitely pregnant."

"Whew. I thought so. Damn. Talk about a surprise."

"Oh, your surprises are just beginning. We'll need an ultrasound, but it looks a little more advanced than you're prepared for. I don't think you're going to be able to keep this quiet for long, June."

She sat up, bracing on her elbows. "Well, how long?"

"You might be able to keep it to yourself till the harvest festival this weekend. You're about four months. Haven't you felt anything?"

"Like...?"

"Fluttering?"

"Oh Jesus! I can't be that far along!"

"Can't you figure it out? By when you had... contact." He didn't want to say relations because, for all John knew, this could be a donor baby.

"Maybe...but... Oh, I don't know!" June fell back onto the exam table and felt the emotion begin to well up inside her. As often as it had happened lately, she was beginning to recognize the phenomenon very well. Tears spilled over and splashed down her cheeks. She pulled a trembling hand to a nose that was beginning to redden. John reached out to help her sit up and Susan aided from behind, pushing gently on her back. She sat on the edge of the examining table with a bare bottom and a paper sheet covering her and wept. "I'm not too old, am I?"

"Certainly not! You're in excellent health, despite your crappy diet, and you're as fit as a racehorse."

"Racehorse?" she choked. "That's nice, John."

"Just be glad he didn't say broodmare," Susan interjected, getting herself a glare from John. "Well..." She shrugged.

"By the way, I don't mean to make so many assumptions," John said. "Of course you have options."

"Don't be ridiculous! I'm thrilled," she said, but tears ran down her cheeks. She wished she could tell them that she cried because there was no one to share her excitement with, and she didn't know when there would be. In fact, though she didn't think it likely, it was possible she could get all the way to the delivery alone.

And there was also the chance that when she told Jim, he'd be less than pleased and would leave her to have a family on her own. Would he? He could. But would he?

Susan was hugging her, telling her she'd be a wonderful mother. John was asking if there was anything he could do for her. She said yes—prenatal vitamins and a night off.

June and Sadie went home. She couldn't remember the last time she'd gone home from the clinic at a reasonable hour to spend an evening relaxing by herself. The best she could do was rush home at six on Tuesdays for meat loaf with her dad, but she always felt as if she was on the run. On this night, this very special night, she wanted to celebrate what she'd done. She was having a baby. She would love to have spent this time with family—her dad, her aunt, maybe the Toopeeks—but there was no way she could keep her news inside if she did. And she needed a little time to figure out how she was going to tell them…and tell them *soon*.

She warmed herself some chicken noodle soup, remembering not so very long ago when she'd come home to find Jim, injured from his flight from the bad guys. She'd warmed soup for him that night, but he'd fallen asleep before he could eat it, so she had put it on a tray and, while she watched him sleep, she had eaten his soup.

Until he was home from this assignment—home *free*—she wouldn't tell him about the baby. She'd keep it under wraps until she could get an ultrasound and learn exactly when this baby would come. Then she would have to tell those closest to her. But she would not tell Jim until he was safely home. It was the only kind and sane thing to do. She couldn't have him upset or worried while undercover.

The early-October night was crisp and shivery, so she built a nice cozy fire. She drank tea, reclined on the sofa and smoothed her shirt over a belly that had seemed to grow since John examined her at four o'clock. She waited patiently for movement, but it didn't come. She talked to the baby. "If I can take Sadie with me everywhere, I can take you. I don't know what kind of work your daddy is going to do—maybe he'll be one of those stay-at-homes… No, I don't see him as a stay-at-home. Frankly I'll be happy if he stays *around*." But there were plenty of excellent people in Grace Valley for child care, including Elmer.

The phone rang and she thought it might be Elmer or Myrna, or even John or Susan checking on her. In fact, she found herself wishing for the latter so she could talk a little about having a baby. If it's Elmer, she told herself, take all traces of motherhood out of your voice!

But it was not Elmer.

"Hi, gorgeous. I miss the hell out of you."

Him.

"I want to be with you more every day," he said.

"Jim!" she said, breathless. "I'm pregnant!"

The Forrest twins were not happy in their new digs. Their new house was barely habitable and their dad was completely inept at those homey little touches. Oh, he was a good enough carpenter and handyman, but life had gotten real rugged since moving out of their grandmother's house. While they were relieved to be free of Grandma Birdie's nagging, life was more comfortable than this in the jail.

Chris had picked up a couple of cots, blankets and some kitchenware at the army surplus in Rockport and borrowed a card table and chairs from Bob Hanson. When they asked what they were supposed to do for a TV and stereo, he told them to read. He was in a badass mood.

"You're uncomfortable?" he asked them. "Live with it. If you hadn't been so damn ungrateful and insolent at your grandparents' house, you might still be sleeping in a soft bed and eating a hot meal!''

"Hey man, she had us *arrested!*" Brad protested.

"You stole from her!" Chris yelled back.

"We did not!" Brent insisted.

"Yes, you did," Chris accused. "You know you did."

"Hey, Dad, she was just hallucinating. It's probably that blood pressure medicine she takes or something!" the other twin claimed.

"She doesn't take medicine, but you're going to take yours. I want you home after school. I want all your clothes folded up in neat little piles. I want the trash hauled out to the end of the drive—it only gets picked up once a week. I want your homework done so you can help me tonight. As soon as I get the baseboards finished, I get carpeting, so you'll have to help. And I'll bring dinner home."

"You don't believe us, do you?" Brent wanted to know.

"No. I don't believe you. You've been lying to me for a long time and I'm done being your patsy." And with that, he left for work.

Brent and Brad were steamed. They'd spent a whole night in that poor excuse for a jail before their dad could convince his old pal, Chief Toopeek, to let them out. And all this over a few bucks that their grandparents didn't need anyway.

School sucked, too. They weren't sure if someone was talking trash about them, someone like Johnny Toopeek, or what, but there were fewer people interested in hanging with them than before. They were potential football stars, but the girls hung around the varsity guys, the goody-goodys, and the only people they had to eat lunch with were losers who smoked under the bleachers and were just about flunking out.

They didn't even talk about it long. Most of their decisions, like stealing eggs or taking Grandma Birdie's cookie-jar money, they came to impetuously.

"Who's she think she is? God?"

"Grandma God?"

"What's a couple bucks? Ought to show her real stealing."

"Take the jewels. Or the car."

"Yeah, the car. That big old Plymouth."

"Think she'd miss it?"

"She hardly drives it. She walks everyplace in town she can."

"I could drive that big old Plymouth," Brad said.

"Yeah, but you couldn't steal it. You don't know how to hot-wire nothing."

"Don't need to hot-wire nothing. I know where the key is—on the peg right inside the back door."

And that's exactly how petty thieves and vandals became car thieves. They got such a rush out of planning to steal their grandmother's car, to show her, to get even with her, that they never even discussed what they were going to do besides drive it. They didn't talk at all about the possible consequences, such as, if you could spend a night in jail for stealing seventy dollars, what could happen to you if you stole a *car?*

Football practice lasted till five and there were two

buses for kids who stayed after for sports. One dropped kids in town, the other dropped them on the west side, which was where the twins should be going. Instead of taking the school bus to their new but unfurnished house, they jumped on their old bus, as if they were going to their grandparents' home. They walked casually to the Forrest house, book bags slung over their shoulders. The sun was setting earlier and earlier as fall deepened, and dusk would soon be falling.

Brent stood in the driveway holding both book bags. Brad sashayed up to the back porch and peeked in. Birdie was in the kitchen, chopping something, getting dinner ready. The news was on in the living room and it was turned up loud to be heard in the kitchen. She moved back and forth, from the kitchen counter to the living room, to catch a little piece of the news. On one of her trips to the TV, Brad slipped a hand through a barely opened screen door and lifted the car key off its hook. He then sashayed confidently back to the yellow Plymouth.

The twins exchanged grins. This was too easy. They looked around; there was no one on the street. Birdie was in the kitchen, in the back of the house, and wouldn't even hear the engine start. Brad got behind the wheel and Brent threw their bags into the back seat. He started the car, put it in Reverse and hit the gas. The car jerked into high speed and they blew the garbage cans all over the street.

"Way to go, dipshit!" Brent said.

"It wasn't my fault, man!"

"Who's driving, dickhead?"

They looked behind them. They had hit the cans so hard they'd flown down the street and emptied in the process. There was trash everywhere and the cans lay on their sides, badly dented.

In that moment they became acutely aware of how little time and energy they'd spent on planning for contingencies.

"Let's go then, dumb-ass!" Brent ordered.

And Brad, who had never actually driven a car before, spun out and laid rubber all the way out of town. West. Toward home. Though they had no idea what they were going to do.

Johnny Toopeek got home a little after five. His mom wasn't home yet and his grandma had dinner started. Tanya was baby-sitting and would be home by six, three Toopeek kids were at the table doing their homework and the house was quiet and smelled good. Johnny kissed his grandma's cheek.

"I don't have homework, Grandma. Can I fish for half an hour or so? Till dinner?"

"Your mama likes you to study something," she said, but she had a real soft spot for Johnny. He was handsome and sweet and doted on her.

"I'll study something after dinner. I might catch you a breakfast trout or something, huh?"

She patted his cheek. "Not very long, Johnny."

"Okay," he said.

He passed his grandpa on his way out to the shed. Lincoln was sitting on the back patio, whittling. "I'm going fishing for half an hour, Grandpa. Wanna come?''

"No, Johnny, you go. Unless you need me to help you pull it in.''

"Hah!'' He took his bike, his pole and his tackle box. He rode down the driveway to the road that led to their house, then down that road half a mile to Highway 482 and along 482 another half mile. He left his bike leaning against a tree. The terrain was steep, but he'd traversed it a million times. The river at the bottom of this ravine was deep and fish were plentiful, especially when the weather was cool, like now. Before he reached the bottom of the ravine, he could see his breath.

He'd only fished ten minutes when he got one. It wasn't big, but his grandma would act as if it was a whale and would fry it up for him. He strung it and let it float in the stream. Another ten minutes brought another fish, this one just a little bigger. The sun was going down. Another ten minutes passed and it occurred to him that to be late for dinner would be stupid, especially since he probably shouldn't be fishing at all. His mother was not as easy on him as his grandma was. If she'd been home, he would not be fishing and he knew it.

Just as he would have started up the slope to fetch his bike, he heard the roaring engine of a racing car in the distance. He was frozen, listening. It came closer. It sounded as though someone was careening down 482 out of control. He could hear gravel flying, tires squealing and maybe even screaming. It was growing dark, and as he looked up toward the road all he could see was the darkness of tree trunks. Then suddenly the lights of a vehicle strafed the trees and exploded through them like a bomb. Johnny dived to the right as a vehicle crashed through the trees to his left. He rolled against the rocks of the stream; his pole flew from his hand. When he came to his feet he began to run away. Behind him he had the sense that the car was still plummeting into the ravine.

The trees were thick and the car slowly came to rest wedged between them. Johnny saw that it was on its side, the underbelly facing him, the front end suspended in the air, held there by thick branches. The hood was lying halfway up the ravine, the front bumper had torn off and lay up in some tree branches. It was smoking; the smell of spilt gasoline was pungent in the air.

"Hey Injun," a hoarse voice beckoned. Johnny looked around but didn't see anyone. "Help me down, wouldja?" He ran toward the car. "Up here," the voice croaked.

He looked up. Dangling from the branches about ten feet off the ground was one of the Forrest twins. "Holy Jesus," he said.

"Get me down, Toopeek," Brad begged, his voice little more than a gasp.

"I'll go get my dad," Johnny said, starting up the hill. But then he stopped and ran back. What if the branches broke and hurled the twin to the ground. "Okay, I'll get you down. You alone? Brad with you?"

"I'm Brad," he said. "Brent. Brent's here. In the car." He winced. Every word tore out of him as though his chest was on fire.

"Okay, you first," Johnny said.

The tree leaned downhill and Brad was captured by two branches that formed a V, hooking him under the armpits and hanging him out over the ravine. Johnny shimmied up the tree behind him. When he got even with Brad's armpits, he locked his legs around the trunk and leaned around. "Where's it hurt, man?" he asked Brad.

"Heh. Everywhere."

"Okay, I don't think this is gonna feel good. Help me if you can, just don't buck against me, okay? I'm gonna pull you backward."

He wove his arms under Brad's armpits, locked his hands together in front of his chest and, with a slow, powerful pull, dragged him through the V of the branches upward till he sat at the V rather than hung there. While he did that, Brad issued a low painful moan. Johnny gave his legs a little rest, then locked them tightly around the trunk again, again reached under Brad's arms and pulled him all the way out of the branches. He hung there, nothing between Brad and the ground but Johnny's arms, as Johnny slowly let himself begin to slide down the trunk one miserable inch at a time. The bark tore at his inner thighs, but he hung on until Brad's feet touched the ground. At that point he could gently lower him and climb off the tree.

Brad slumped softly to the ground and Johnny jumped down beside him. "Can you walk, man?"

"Walk? I don't think I can roll over."

He lay there, limp, as though paralyzed. Johnny didn't want to think about that, though a vision of Brad the Bad in a wheelchair, typing on a computer by holding a straw in his teeth, came instantly to mind. He pushed the image away by saying, "Let's get you up to the road so I can try to find your brother before—" He stopped as he saw a little poof of smoke ignite into a small flame on the underbelly of the car. "Okay, pal." He reached again under Brad's armpits. He counted to three, hefted him over his shoulder and began to climb out of the ravine.

Tanya Toopeek was being driven home by Mary Lou Granger, the young mother she occasionally baby-sat for. In the back seat, tucked into their car seats, were the little kids. "Look at this," Mary Lou said to Tanya, indicating skid marks and tire treads in the gravel at the shoulder, first on the right, then on the left, then again on the right.

"Looks like someone needs driving lessons," Tanya said. Then she saw the piece of metal at the side of the road and recognized it as her brother's crushed bike. "Mary Lou! Stop! That's Johnny's—" Just as they might have passed the crushed bike, they could see the mowed-down trees at the road's edge.

"Oh God," Mary Lou said. She put on her emergency flashers and pointed her high beams into the trees. About halfway down the ravine, balanced and crushed between the trees, was a big sedan, turned on its side and hanging in the trees. "Oh God," she said again.

"Johnny," Tanya whispered in prayer. She opened the door. "Keep the lights on! Let me see if I can see him down there!"

Tanya jumped out of the car and began down the ravine, screaming her brother's name. "Johnny! Johnny!"

"Tan!" he called back. "Here!" He came slowly into view, pulling himself up the hill by grabbing on to thin tree trunks and low branches, Brad hanging limply over his shoulder.

Tanya rushed to him and helped pull him the rest of the way up. "Are you hurt? Did the car hit you?" While she questioned him, she helped him lower Brad to the ground in front of the car, in the headlights. In the distance they could hear the sound of a siren.

"I was fishing," he said, breathless. "It came through the trees like a rocket."

"Look, Johnny," she said, pointing to his bike. "You know what I thought."

But he didn't have time to think. Though out of breath and nearly out of strength, he ran to the car window. "Mrs. Granger, pull up about three feet. I gotta go back down there and I need the headlights." He stepped away and marshaled her forward, then gave her the stop gesture. "Stay with Brad, Tan. Brent is still down there somewhere and I saw the car spark."

"No!" she screamed. "No, don't go! What if it explodes?" But he was already on his way, sliding down the hill as fast as he dared. "Johnny!" she screamed at his back.

Even with the help of the high beams, it was too dark to see clearly in the ravine. If the car hadn't been turned sideways, it would have been too far off the ground for Johnny to look inside. He went nearly underneath to the front of the car and checked inside. "Brent?" he called again and again, but there was no answer. He could see into the front seat easily, since the windshield was gone, but the back seat was dark.

Remembering where he had found Brad, he looked up and called Brent's name. Nothing. He went past the car, lower into the ravine, down toward the stream. He had to assume the twin was unconscious and couldn't answer, so it was up to Johnny to just look carefully. Behind him the car made a loud popping sound and erupted in flames.

Back up on the road, Tom Toopeek pulled up next to Mary Lou Granger, lights flashing. He jumped out of the Range Rover, shock drawing his features down when he recognized his daughter standing next to an injured Forrest boy.

"Daddy, Johnny's down there looking for the other one, and the car has caught *fire!*"

He didn't waste time. He grabbed the fire extinguisher from his SUV, the flashlight from the door, and headed down. "Tanya, call the fire truck and ambulance. Use the radio. Hurry." Then he was skidding down the hill toward the fire, trying to keep from sliding down on his face. Within seconds he was standing at the undercarriage of the Plymouth, spraying extinguisher fluid onto the fire. He kept spraying as he went around the car to the front and drenched the exposed engine.

When the fire appeared to be out, he shone the flashlight into the trees. "Johnny?" he called.

"Dad! Over here!"

Tom slid the rest of the way down the ravine to the stream, shining the light again.

"Over here!"

Down the river about thirty feet, and on the other side, Johnny knelt next to Brent. He held a hand firmly over a head wound that had been gushing blood. Tom dropped to his knees at the water's edge and put the light on Brent's face. He squinted painfully in the light, but then opened his eyes.

"Don't move him, Johnny," Tom said. "The ambulance is coming."

Brent looked up at Johnny. "Am I gonna die?" he asked weakly.

"Naw," Johnny said. "You'll make it. Brad's up on the road already. He's gonna be okay." Johnny wasn't sure there was any truth in what he said, but what the heck.

"I think I'm gonna die," he said.

"You're not gonna die," Johnny insisted. "But you're gonna be grounded forever."

Nineteen

"**Y**ou're *what?*" Jim asked June. "I think we have a bad connection."

"Oh dammit, I swore I wasn't going to tell you until you were out of that assignment and home free. I'm such a wimp. I just found out about an hour ago."

"Did you say pregnant?" he asked.

"I did. Are you upset?"

"Upset? Are you upset?"

"Me? No! I'm kind of excited. But that doesn't mean you have to be. I mean, I didn't exactly do this on purpose."

"And you did warn me," he said, "that you're a little sloppy about birth control."

"Oh, Jim, I'm sorry. I mean, I'm sorry for you. You didn't have anything to say about it and that's not fair. Will you ever—" She stopped suddenly. "Wait a sec," she said. "Uh-oh, this is not good. My pager is going and John knows I need a night off since he just confirmed I'm pregnant."

She looked at the pager and it was flashing the police department number with a 911 added. At just that moment, her call waiting beeped. "Jim, hold on, please." She picked up. "Yes?"

"June, we got the Forrest twins in a car accident on 482 about a mile shy of the Toopeek house—both critical," John said. "I'm taking the ambulance over and the fire truck is en route. If you can, I need you."

"I can," she said. "On my way." She clicked over to Jim. "Jim, I've got a car accident out on the highway with critical injuries. Listen, try to call me later if you can. If not, just remember that…that…"

"That what, June?" he demanded.

"That everything is going to be fine. And you be *careful!*"

She hung up. What was she going to do? Whisper sweet nothings to her lover when two kids were bleeding out on the highway? She slipped into her shoes, grabbed her bag and truck keys and said, "You have to stay, Sadie. Be a good girl!" And out the door she went.

The first thing John thought when he arrived at the scene was how much he wished he had Susan with him. She could anticipate his needs in an emergency. Her years as a surgical nurse had fine-tuned her into an assistant who knew what the doctor needed almost before the doctor did. And that was why not only he, but *medicine,* needed her so much. John had a flash of shame at having ever discouraged her.

The ambulance made three vehicles at the scene, all pointed into the ravine, their headlights shining on the surreal image of a scarred yellow Plymouth suspended in the trees, halfway down the hill. Two women, Mary Lou and Tanya, kneeled over a boy on

the road and John went to him first. He listened to
his heart, palpated his abdomen, shone his penlight in
his eyes. "Where's the other one?" he asked Tanya.

"My dad and Johnny found him down at the bottom of the ravine by the stream. He was thrown from
the car. This one, Brad, was hanging in a tree."

"Jesus," John muttered. "How'd you get out of
the tree, Brad? You fall out?"

"Johnny," he said weakly. Then he winced in pain
as John pressed on his abdomen.

"Johnny climbed the tree and got him out, then
carried him up here because the car started to burn,"
Tanya said. "My dad got here and put out the fire.
They haven't moved Brent."

"We're going to need medevac transport, Tanya.
Where's the nearest landing site?"

"I don't know," she said. "I'll call the deputy on
Dad's radio, then turn up the spotlight on the Range
Rover so they can see the accident site. They'll let
you know where they can land and you can transport
the boys to that site. Maybe our house. It's just up
the road a half mile, and we have a big clearing."

John smiled at the girl. "You sound like someone
who was raised by a police chief."

"Yeah, it sort of rubs off, doesn't it," she said, and
jogged the short distance to Tom's Range Rover.
"Ricky, come in, Ricky."

"Right here, Tan," a voice crackled.

"Dr. Stone says he needs a medevac helicopter out
here. I'll turn the Range Rover's spotlight to the sky

so they can make out the accident site. Tell them to
let us know where they can land and pick up.''

"Ten-four. I'm on my way."

She then jogged to the ambulance where John was
getting the stretcher out of the back. "I can help you
get this down into the ravine, if you want," she said.
He paused and looked at her doubtfully. She reached
behind her head, pulled her long silky black hair up
and tied it in its own knot. "I'm stronger than I look,
Dr. Stone. Plus, I've been in and out of that ravine
since I was a little kid."

John rummaged around in the back of the ambulance for rope, backboard, neck brace, portable oxygen tank—all of which he stacked on the stretcher.
As he pulled the stretcher out of the ambulance, the
wheels popped out and supported it as a gurney.
"We'll collapse the stretcher and slide it down," he
said. "You can show me the way and carry the flashlight." He transferred his medical bag into a canvas
pack that he put on his back. "Do you know the condition of the other boy?"

"No. Dad only yelled up that he was going to wait
for a stretcher."

John rolled the gurney down the rough asphalt toward the ravine's edge. "He's alive then," John said.
"Show me the best way, Tanya."

"Follow me," she said.

As he passed by Brad and Mary Lou, John said,
"When June gets here, tell her to tend this boy. We'll
cover the other one."

Tanya led him down the ravine slowly, showing

him where to brace a foot against a rock or tree trunk, where to grab a branch or shrub. John collapsed the gurney. He let it rest against the small of his back, keeping it in place with one hand, then the other, using whichever hand was free to assist his descent. Most of the way down he was on his butt, bouncing along the sharp edges of broken sticks and rocky crags.

John had been in many emergencies over the years, but they had always involved working in the clean indoor environs of the emergency room or operating room. Never had he strapped a medical bag to his back and shimmied down a steep hill, a stretcher precariously balanced behind him.

Through the thick trees in the distance he could see a moving light. Tanya paused to move her flashlight from right to left to right to left. "There they are," she said. "It's not so far. You okay?"

Citified John's butt hurt like the devil. The strain on his legs from holding the stretcher back so they wouldn't all go tumbling to the bottom was excruciating. "Fine," he said. "Let's go."

Tom Toopeek was waiting for them at the bottom. He seemed to pop up out of nowhere, because he'd left his flashlight with Johnny. "Right over here, Doc," he said, grabbing the front end of the stretcher to lead the way. "Watch your step. We're crossing the stream down here. It's shallow but slippery. Tanya, help him with his footing."

She held on to John's end of the stretcher with him. "Follow my steps, Dr. Stone," she said.

Of course he had the wrong kind of shoes. He should have known by now. His introduction to this little town had had him mucking through about two feet of mud to get to Julianna Dickson's house where he delivered her fifth child at home. Julianna had a reputation for not being able to make it to the hospital. Not long after that, he and June had performed an emergency Caesarean section in the treatment room at the clinic without the benefit of a general anesthetic. June had told of car wrecks on isolated stretches of freeway, on mountain passes. Now here was a ravine wreck. John had never seen June in a dress, and she always wore boots. She couldn't take the chance that she'd be called out to some logging site or farm for an emergency, have to climb a hill or slide down an embankment and end up with her skirt over her head.

He was going to get some smarter clothes and shoes, he thought as he slipped on a slimy rock and fell to one knee in the icy stream. He bit back a yelp of pain as his knee made contact with a rock.

Finally at his destination, he knelt beside Brent Forrest. "Can you tell me where the pain is worst?" he asked, directing Johnny's flashlight as he looked over the boy.

"My knees and legs," he said. "And my head."

John put the neck brace on him first, then pulled bandage scissors out of the bag and cut Brent's pant legs open from ankle to thigh. Both legs were broken. They bent oddly, but were not compound fractures— a blessing. "We have fractures. I'm going to start an

IV, Brent, so I can give you some morphine. Then we're going to splint your legs and get you out of here." He gently palpated Brent's abdomen and the boy's painful reaction indicated internal bleeding, just like his brother.

"Is Brad okay?"

"He's okay," John said. He moved the flashlight again so it shone on the boy's arm. He had the IV started quickly and the morphine administered immediately. He instructed Tanya to hold the bag of Ringers.

The boy's pupils reacted and his eyelids fluttered. "Wouldja tell...tell my mom...I'm sorry?"

"You can tell her yourself, kiddo."

"She's not...here."

"Oh, I'm sure she's going to be visiting. Listen, this morphine's going to make you sleepy, but I want you to keep talking to me, okay? Tell me...who was driving?"

"Brad... He...um...took the keys off the peg."

"Where were you guys going?"

"Dunno. Just away."

"No seat belts, huh?"

"I didn't get the trash out," he said.

"That's okay...just this once," John said. He had the right leg in an air splint, and when it inflated, Brent cried out. "Yeah, son, it's tough. We gotta do that to get you out of here." He applied the second splint and Brent yelped, then dissolved into tears.

"Okay, we're going to roll you to the right, slip the backboard under you and roll you back. Then we'll transfer you to the stretcher. Tom, at the feet. Johnny, keep that light steady. On three. One, two, three," he counted, and they rolled him. When he was on his side, John pushed the backboard under and they let him roll slowly back. "Tanya, hang on to the bag and keep the line from tangling. Tom, let's lift him onto the stretcher."

Once Brent was transferred, John secured him with the straps. "Brent? Brent?" he said. The boy didn't respond. John checked his carotid pulse, pulled back his eyelids and shone his penlight into first the right eye, then the left.

"He's lost consciousness. Let's get him up the hill."

"We got him, Doc," Tom said. "Our chances of not falling back down the hill are better than yours. You and Tanya light the way."

Johnny and Tom worked together like professionals. They carried the heavy stretcher up the hill sideways. There were a couple of times they had to lift the stretcher high over a shrub or move around a tree trunk, exchanging places like a do-si-do.

When June came upon the accident site, she found the back doors to the ambulance standing open and the stretcher and backboard both gone, as well as the oxygen and medication bag. She hefted her own bag from her truck to the convergence of Tom's SUV, Mary Lou's car and the ambulance front, where she found Brad.

She looked past the boy into the ravine to see

Birdie's Plymouth halfway down the hill. The front end appeared to hang in the trees. "Dear God," she said.

"John and Tanya have gone down into the ravine to help Tom and Johnny Toopeek bring the other twin up," Mary Lou told her. "He says for you to tend this one. They've called for the medevac." Mary Lou stood. "I have to check on the kids. They're in the car." June crouched beside Brad. "Are you in a lot of pain?" she asked him.

"I feel like I was shot out of a canon," he replied.

"Looks like you were," she said. "Let's get an IV started and give you something for the pain. Which one are you?" she asked.

"Brad. Hey, is my brother alive?"

"He must be. I don't think the chief would stay down there with him if he weren't. Does your grandma know you took the car?"

"She should. We were trying to sneak it out of the driveway, but I smashed up the trash cans. It sounded like an explosion." He winced in pain. "We're going to go to jail forever for this."

"Why'd you take her car?" June asked as the IV started.

"I don't know. We were pissed at her for something. I don't know. We're *stupid*. If my brother dies..."

"Your grandma and grandpa were in a car accident on this same stretch of highway, but on the other side of the valley. Not very long ago."

"They were?"

"They were." Mary Lou came back and June handed off the IV bag to her. "Hold this up here for me. Kids okay?"

"They've eaten an entire bag of Oreos and are working on graham crackers. They're in a sugar zone."

"As long as they stay in the car," June said. She heard the sound of running footfalls behind her and looked over her shoulder to see Ursula crash through the cars and almost fall over June.

"My God," Ursula said. She looked down at Brad. "Whose car is that?" she asked.

"The twins apparently stole their grandmother's car," Mary Lou explained. "Half your family is down in the ravine with the other twin. Tanya, Tom and Johnny."

In the distance, they could hear the sound of the approaching helicopter.

"Ursula, I have a cell phone in my truck," June said. "Call Birdie and Judge. See if someone can find Chris. These boys are going to have to be transported to Ukiah. They may as well get on the road and start driving. If they can find something to drive."

As the chopper sounds grew louder, Tom and Johnny rose out of the ravine carrying the stretcher. Behind them were Tanya and John, toting the rest of the emergency gear. The helicopter drew in slowly, the spotlight shining down on the accident site, then the craft retreated down the road about a thousand feet to a spot where trees and wires didn't interfere.

There were flashing lights down there, indicating Ricky Rios had blocked the road for the landing.

"If you guys aren't done in, you can start toward the chopper," John shouted to the Toopeek men. "Can't put the wheels down, though. We want to keep from jostling him. Tanya and I can load Brad on the backboard and start down."

"Done," Tom shouted above the whacking of chopper blades.

"Is he dead?" Brad asked. "Is my brother dead?"

"No, son, but he's hurt badly and we have to get both of you to the hospital." John and Tanya crouched beside Brad, rolled him and put the board under him. "June can't lift," John explained in a shout. "I'm treating her for back strain!"

"It's okay, I can do it," Tanya yelled back.

June realized she wouldn't have even thought twice about it, that's how far from her senses her personal issues were during an emergency. She took the IV bag from Mary Lou and walked beside the backboard toward the waiting chopper. Members of the medevac crew were running toward them, silhouetted in the spotlight from the helicopter.

Beside June, Brad was crying, "Mama! Mama!"

When Chris drove up to his house, it was dark. There were no trash cans at the curb and he began to seethe. Damn brats couldn't do the smallest thing to help out. When it was his wife or mother complaining about the laziness of the twins, Chris blew them off, but when he needed a little help and the boys ignored him, the truth began to sink in.

He carried the take-out burgers, fries and shakes into the kitchen, flicked on the light with his elbow and shouted. "Brad! Brent!" No answer. He stomped toward the bedrooms they occupied and saw that their clothes and shoes, as usual, were strewn all over the room. Back in the kitchen, he put the food on the counter and pulled his cell phone out of his pocket. He had run out of juice before leaving the office and had left his auto attachment at home that morning. He plugged the cell into the wall and dialed his mother's house. If they had gone back there after all they'd done to wear out their welcome, he'd tan their hides. But the phone rang and rang. No answer.

He went out to the car to get his briefcase for phone numbers. As much as he hated to, he was going to have to call the Toopeeks. They were only a couple of miles away, and although the twins had complained of a falling-out with Johnny, chances were they'd patched things up. The boys were hurting for snacks, music and TV. They could probably swallow their pride and make amends if the Toopeeks would extend some hospitality.

He wanted to slap them senseless.

"Mrs. Toopeek, this is Chris Forrest," he said to a voice he thought belonged to Tom's mother. "I was wondering…"

"Oh, Mr. Christopher, I'm so sorry for the accident! Are your boys going to be all right?"

"Accident? What accident?" he asked, his blood

running cold. His stomach gave a sudden lurch and he knew, beyond any doubt, that the worst had happened.

"Not too far from here, they drove off the road."

"They *drove?*"

"Mrs. Birdie's car. They drove off the road. My Lincoln walked down there on 482 to see. The helicopter took them to the hospital."

Stay calm, he told himself. "Mrs. Toopeek, what hospital?"

"We don't know that, Mr. Christopher, but you can call the police. Tom and Ricky were both there."

He didn't even bother to say goodbye, but punched in the number for the police department. In a recorded message that moved too slowly, the caller was asked to either leave a message or, in the case of an emergency, dial the number of the police chief's pager. Which he did.

His cell phone rang almost immediately. "What the hell happened?" he shouted into the phone.

"The boys decided to take your mother's car for a spin and they drove off the road into the ravine just down 482 from my house. They've been airlifted to Ukiah to the county hospital. Chris, drive carefully."

"Tom, tell me the truth. Are they all right?"

There was a pause, a deep breath. "No. But they're alive."

Mary Lou Granger took her kids home, Ursula drove Tanya and Johnny up to the Toopeek house, and Ricky Rios closed 482 at the crossroads both north and south so the scene of the accident would remain relatively undisturbed until daylight.

June, John and Tom stood at the highway's edge in the stillness of a dark and cold night. Tom walked a few paces down the road and picked up the deformed handlebars of his son's destroyed bike. "It's hard to believe the accident could have been even worse," he said. "They gonna make it?" he asked anyone who would hazard a guess.

"They have a pretty good chance," John said. "But it wouldn't hurt to pray." He kicked a pebble in the dirt. "I'm going to take the ambulance back to the clinic and clean it up and restock. Then I'm going home to hug my little girl."

"I'll follow you and help," June said. "Then I'm going to bed."

"You feel okay? Did I hear something about a back problem in the middle of all this?" Tom asked.

"It's a small thing," she shrugged. "I just can't afford to let it get worse."

"Understandable. The road is closed, so let's shut this place down. Thank you, everyone. Thank you very much."

Tom walked to his Range Rover with the mangled handlebars still in his hand.

Chris really didn't know how he couldn't have known it would get this bad. It should have been obvious the first time they waxed someone's window, egged someone's car. No matter how many times they denied a wrongful act, he knew they were lying.

Every time they talked to their mother as though she
were a lowly servant in their house, he knew he
should step in. But he hadn't. He wanted them to
grow up and turn into nice men who respected their
parents and others.

And that was the respect he showed his wife, parents and others—he let his incorrigible children abuse
every rule they came into contact with and never corrected their actions. In the end, he may have assisted
them in their own deaths.

They were both in surgery. They had been in surgery for a long time. Brent had two broken legs and
a skull fracture, and Brad had a fractured pelvis and
a broken collarbone. Both had internal injuries. The
surgeons had warned that they might find even more
once they were in there, operating.

Chris had sent his parents home. They would have
stayed through the night, but at their ages, and with
the trauma of it being his mother's car that was stolen,
he didn't want the situation made even worse by having them exhausted and sick. The emergency physician had given them mild sedatives to take once they
were at home, in bed. Chris promised that when he
did leave the hospital, he would go to their house and
fill them in.

Possibly the hardest call he'd ever had to make in
his life was the one to Nancy. There was a time, he
supposed, when she thought herself the winner, to
have snagged him, married him. She had certainly
gotten over that. She must now hate him. To hear her
softly sobbing into the phone as she tried to ask all

the right questions tore his heart out. Worse than that, she took the blame. "This is my fault. I should have found help for parenting them a long, long time ago." That just made him sick. She had begged him to be a more involved parent.

He lifted his head at the sound of footfalls approaching, at first hopeful that he might see medical personnel bearing news. But it was Tom and Johnny Toopeek. Johnny was almost as large as his father, broad-shouldered and flat-bellied. He also wore the long ponytail, hat and boots.

Chris stood, but hung his head. His shame could not be more complete.

"They gonna make it?" Johnny wanted to know.

"They're pretty beat up...lots of broken bones... lots of internal injuries."

"I was there, you know."

Chris lifted his head finally, questions in his eyes.

"I was fishing down in the ravine when the car exploded through the trees. It's still there, Mr. Forrest, hanging in those trees like it fell out of the sky."

"They're not going to pull it out till morning," Tom said. "We'll get photos for the accident report and you can have copies for the insurance. Is there anything I can do to help you now?"

"There's nothing. I sent my parents home and called Nancy. She'll be here on the earliest flight tomorrow. Now we just wait to see if they pull through."

"Will you call if there's anything we can do?"

Chris nodded. "Thank you, Tom. I have a lot of

amends to make, and you're way up on the list. You tried to tell me.''

"This is not a time for regrets or amends, but for prayer. My father has made a fire for your boys. The whole family prays.''

"Thank you.''

They stood awkwardly for a moment. "We should go then, if there's nothing we can do,'' Tom said. He put an arm around his son's shoulders.

"Dad, I'd like to wait here with Mr. Forrest, if that's okay with him.''

Chris and Tom both looked surprised.

"It's okay, Johnny…but…I don't know why you'd even want to. Didn't the boys make life pretty tough for you? Didn't they jump you, beat on you?''

Johnny shrugged. "This kind of changes everything, don't you think?''

Chris put a hand on the boy's shoulder and gave it a squeeze. "Yeah. Everything.''

The Forrest twins each had their spleens removed. Brad was in traction for his fractured pelvis and in a great deal of pain. Brent had multiple fractures in his legs but he had escaped any brain damage resulting from his skull fracture. Both boys were going to be in physical therapy for a long, long time. There was no question, they were lucky to be alive.

At ten in the morning, Chris stood with his wife and a small group of townsfolk looking at the amazing and terrifying visage of a yellow Plymouth hanging in the trees over a deep ravine.

"I wish we could leave it there," Tom told Chris. "I'd like to show my boys and every junior-high and high-school kid who comes through Grace Valley."

"Take some good pictures," Chris said. "And show it to their parents."

Twenty

Tuesday at the clinic had been long and dreary for June for a number of reasons. There was the accident the night before, an event that was exhausting both physically and emotionally. June winced each time she saw John Stone take a painful step. His rear end and thighs were painfully bruised and he was popping ibuprofen as if they were Chiclets. If there was one positive aspect, it was that Susan was being nicer than usual to him.

Then there was the fact that, of course, Jim was unable to call her back. Well, she hadn't really thought he'd be able to. His calls were spaced by days, if not weeks, at the best of times. But there was this nagging at the back of her pregnant mind that perhaps he would never call again. She wouldn't know how to find him if he did that. If this idea of a baby was not of his choosing, he could easily disappear into thin air.

With that issue clouding her thoughts, she was getting mentally ready for the mother of all meat-loaf nights with Elmer.

The sounds of reunion issued from the front of the

clinic and June followed the voices to find Charlotte Burnham embracing Jessie.

"Well, look who's up and about," June said, next to give her a welcoming hug. "Getting your daily exercise walk?"

"Something like that," the gruff old nurse said. "I'm bored out of my skull."

"But how are you feeling?"

"Old, useless and in dire need of a dye job," she said, touching her hair, more gray than June had ever seen it.

Maybe it was the hair, or the fact that she didn't blow in with the usual cloud of cigarette smoke, but Charlotte looked different. She seemed softer somehow, perhaps more vulnerable.

"Jessica, I happened into your father at the farmers' market. He says you're going back to school."

"Mostly nights," she said, nodding. "I got my GED and I'm going to study sciences. If it turns out I like it as much as I think I will, I'm going to go into some kind of medicine. Nursing, physician's assistant, maybe even medical school. We'll see."

"Well, that's why I'm here," Charlotte said. "I can't work as a nurse anymore—don't have the stamina for it. And I'll be damned if I can sit around the house with Bud all day. He's about to drive me crazy. So maybe you need someone to spell you now and then? For classes or for study?" She smiled at Jessie. "I was sure proud to hear you're going to finish school."

Jessie was speechless. While they had worked together, Charlotte and Jessie were constantly on each other's nerves. And what was this? Charlotte actually offering to *help?* "Are you sure?" Jessie asked.

"Oh, I'm sure. Do you have any idea how awful daytime TV is?"

June laughed and gave her old nurse a playful punch in the arm. "I wouldn't mind having you boss us around in here now and then. If Jessie needs you, that is."

"I just can't believe it," Jessie said.

"Can't believe what? That I'd be *nice?*"

"No, no, not that. Well, yes, that, too. But what I meant is, I can't believe how perfectly things seem to be working out for me."

"Me too," Charlotte said.

June opened a bottle of good cabernet and let it breathe. She went the extra mile and whipped the potatoes. Instead of putting plates on the kitchen breakfast bar, she appointed the dining table. She sliced a late-season beefsteak tomato, sprinkled it with wine vinegar and basil, and steamed fresh asparagus. And sitting near the oven to capture its warmth was one of Burt Crandall's very best apple pies.

Ever since John told her she was farther along than she thought, she had been famished and couldn't button her pants. She had seen this happen to women before. They would enter the clinic their slim selves and upon learning they were already four months pregnant, they would blossom. Stomach muscles appeared to be controlled by the mentality of pregnancy.

Elmer knew immediately that this was no ordinary meat-loaf night. If not the pie and the breathing wine, the look on June's face would have tipped him off. "What's wrong?" he wanted to know.

"Nothing's wrong. Have a glass of wine."

"Gladly." He lifted the lid on the stove and saw that the potatoes had been whipped. He glanced into the dining room and saw plates on a crispy white tablecloth. He reached for the glass of wine she was handing him. "You're softening me up for something."

"That's right. And if you don't take this well, I don't know what I'm going to do."

"Well, spit it out," he said. "Have you ever known me to be unreasonable?"

"Have a little wine, please." He took a sip. "It seems I'm going to have a baby."

He dropped the glass. It shattered, splattering wine. Sadie skittered out of the way. Elmer bent down to retrieve the largest pieces. "I'm sorry," he said. "I thought you said you were going to have a baby."

June went for the paper towels and started soaking up the spill. "I knew you'd be surprised, but I thought you had better nerves than that."

"So that *is* what you said?"

"Uh-huh."

"Are you married?"

"You know I'm not married!"

"I just want to be sure I wasn't having blackouts or something. I guess you have some kind of story to tell me."

"Yes, but I'm not sure which one," she said. "Let's clean this up while I think."

Elmer swept up the glass shards while June mopped up the red splatters. When things were under control, Elmer got himself a new wineglass. "Sure am glad I didn't drop the bottle. I think I'm going to need it."

June poured for him. "Come on. Let's sit down. I'll tell you what I can about this, then we'll have a nice dinner to celebrate."

"Whatever you say."

They sat at the dining table and she told him that she'd been having a relationship with a gentleman from out of town. She'd met him when he stopped by the clinic after hours, looking for first aid for his companion. They'd been hunting and had a minor accident, which wasn't that far from the truth. She didn't expect to ever see him again, but he kept turning up because, it turned out, he was as taken with her as she with him. She hadn't told anybody about him, nor had she introduced him to anyone, because he never had much time. He was always just passing through.

"He's starting to sound like Morton Claypool. Maybe he's married," Elmer supplied.

"He's not," she said. "I...ah...had him checked out, sort of. I have connections, you know."

"So, what's his name? What's he do for a living?"

"Here's the thing, Dad. I just found out I'm pregnant. I mean, I knew it in the back of my mind, but I hadn't been paying attention, so I didn't know it officially. John just confirmed it for me yesterday. I was able to tell the gentleman the news last night, about five seconds before John rang in on the other line to tell me about the Forrest twins being in a car accident." She shrugged. "I didn't have time to talk to him about it. I don't even know if he took it as good news. Until I know the answer to that, I think I'll keep the news to myself."

"What are you going to tell people?"

"That I'm pregnant."

"And when they ask who the father is?"

"Do people ask questions like that?" she replied, aghast.

"This is Grace Valley. They want to know which nights of the week you did it. Don't act like you don't know where you live."

"Well, then, I guess I'll tell them it's none of their business."

"They'll all think it's Chris Forrest."

"No, they won't," she said with a smile. "I have to schedule an ultrasound for the details, like when I'm due, but I'm already feeling little flutters." She touched her stomach. "This baby was conceived before Chris Forrest came to town." She touched Elmer's hand. "Dad, does this make you disappointed in me?"

"Are you disappointed in you, June?"

"No, Dad. I was actually thinking about having a baby alone. I talked to the quilters about it once. You know, using an anonymous donor."

"So this man—"

"Oh, I didn't plan this at all," she said, shaking her head. "In fact, I'd just broken it to him that I was pretty sure I was infertile, and I asked him if that would make a difference in how he felt about me, about having a future with me. And he'd said he was very flexible." She smiled a melancholy smile. "We'll see."

"June, what if he abandons you?" Elmer wanted to know.

"Don't you think I'll be okay? I have you. I have Aunt Myrna. I have the Toopeeks, the Stones, Judge and Birdie. Don't you think I'll be okay?" she repeated.

"It's hard enough to be a doctor and a parent when you have a spouse."

The phone rang. "Oh, please don't let this be an emergency. I'm so tired and I think I might have made the best meat loaf yet. June Hudson," she said into the phone.

"Is it meat-loaf night?" Jim asked.

"It is! How are you?"

"Forget me. How are you? Are you telling him?"

"I just did."

"How's he taking it?"

"He dropped his wineglass. It was a terrible mess, but I think we'll be okay. How are you taking it?"

A laugh rumbled low in his throat. "Like a man. Like a man who can't wait to hold you."

June let out a sigh of relief and contentment. "Are you almost done there? There are people I want you to meet."

"Almost. I'm trying. I'm trying even harder now."

"He wants to know what your name is and what you do for a living."

"Tell him my name is Jim. And I fish."

In the end, Elmer thought it was her best meat loaf ever. And the idea of having a grandchild after this many years was welcome news too, especially now that it appeared June was not going to be abandoned by the baby's father. "He's not here yet, however," Elmer added, trying to keep perspective, trying to guard against the potential of disappointment.

One difficult thing for him was that he wasn't going to be able to tell anyone. At least not until after the ultrasound. Perhaps until June began to show, which was going to be soon. "It's damn tough on an old guy," he told her, "to have to keep a secret like this one. Especially when the shock of it would be so much fun to watch settle over the town."

"Very funny," June said.

"Think about it, June. It's going to be *fun*."

If June already felt fluttering, then this baby might have happened back when Jim escaped from the drug farms in the Trinity Alps. Or even earlier. Which meant that, not far after Christmas, she was going to be a mother for real. And that's what was going to be *fun*.

June was on call the next night, so she had dinner at the café and then went to the clinic. Her ultrasound was scheduled for the next morning; she would be getting in to the clinic late. She hoped she would be able to sleep. As she walked, her feet never touched the ground. Though she longed for Jim's arms, waiting for him had never been more luxurious, for she felt as if she kept their secret warm and safe within her. And now she knew that once he arrived, everything would be different. Three times that day she'd been asked if she was all right—once by George, once by Tom and once by Harry Shipton.

June heard the clinic door open and footsteps come lightly down the hall. Nancy Forrest tapped lightly on June's opened office door. "June?" she said, asking to come in.

Any other time in her life, June might have resented the intrusion. She might have looked at Nancy, seen that she was still looking young, very attractive and fit and hated her for it. But on this night she felt nothing negative toward her lifelong rival. Rather, she leaped to her feet and rushed to embrace her. "Nancy," she said, giving her a welcoming hug. "I've been checking with the Ukiah hospital. I'm told the boys can expect a full recovery."

"Yes," she said, "though not a quick one. It's thanks to you and Dr. Stone that they're alive."

"We did our part, but we owe Johnny Toopeek the real credit." Nancy frowned. "You don't know?" Nancy shook her head. "Johnny was fishing in that stream when the car came crashing through. The first thing he did was climb a tree to pull Brad out of it. He was dangling ten feet off the ground, hooked onto the branches. Had Johnny left him there, he might've fallen the rest of the way down that rocky ravine. He carried him to safety. Then he ran back into the ravine because the car was on fire. He searched for and found Brent and held his hand over a gushing head wound until help arrived."

"I had no idea," Nancy said weakly. "Every time I hear the story, it just keeps getting worse!"

"Did you see the car before they pulled it out of the trees?"

"I did," she said with a shudder. Her hand automatically went to her chest as if the mere thought made her heart stop beating for a moment. "I've never seen anything so terrifying."

For the very first time, June's heart jumped at the thought of raising a child. From her years as the town's doctor she'd learned one indisputable fact about being a parent—there were lots of people who did their best and one or more of their kids, despite all efforts to the contrary, turned out bad. By the same token, there were gems in this town who had nearly raised themselves. Here was a job with no guarantees and no promise of benefits.

"Am I interrupting anything?" Nancy wanted to know.

"Just a little paperwork. I'm coming in late tomorrow morning so I thought I'd better look at what Jessie, the clinic receptionist, has stacked up on my desk. What to sit down a minute?"

"Thanks," she said, taking the chair in front of June's desk. "I spent the afternoon with Birdie, and after comparing notes, I thought I'd better talk to you. You might have gotten some misinformation."

"Oh?"

"It's about our divorce...."

"Oh, Nancy, I was so sorry to hear about it. Really."

"Well, that's just it. We're not divorced. We're barely separated."

Stunned speechless, June found herself leaning across her desk, staring.

"Chris wanted a separation. He thought he'd get himself an apartment. Our home was too stressful, he said. By now I'm sure you've figured out that most of the stress was due to teenage twins who were constantly in trouble. So, he thought the answer might lie with him visiting them on weekends!" She shrugged. "I turned the tables on him. I told him that I thought maybe I should get a job, an apartment, and he could be responsible for the twins. I would visit *them* on weekends!"

"But...why did they come back to Grace Valley?"

"I'm sure he couldn't manage without Birdie."

"But..." she stammered again. "Has he no concept of her age? She was no match for your boys. Meaning no offense—"

"Not to worry, June," she said, holding up a hand. "It's absolutely true. In fact, Chris and I together have proven no match."

"Why did he say you were divorced? I just can't imagine why—"

"Can't you?" Nancy asked, knowing.

Sure, she thought. Some things never change. If he could get another woman interested, then he would divorce Nancy. He'd replace her. It had always been that way. For two cents she'd tell Nancy that, right after he asked June for a second chance, she'd found him twisting his fingers in the tresses of some pretty young thing right on the streets of Rockport, but "Brother" was all she said.

"Yeah." Nancy and June sat there looking at each other for a moment, a slow smile spreading across Nancy's face. "I wonder if Chris really thought he might have a chance with you if he said we were divorced. It's obvious you moved on. Who is it, June? Who's the guy?"

"What?" she asked, but her lips curved in spite of herself. When you were feeling this much in love with life, it was impossible for it not to show all over your face. "What guy?"

"Never mind," Nancy said, standing. "I've had a

long day at the hospital and I'm going early tomorrow so I can be there to meet the physical therapist. I'd better get some sleep. I'm staying with Birdie, in case you're looking for me.''

"What about Chris and the new house?"

"I don't know…"

"You going to give him a second chance?"

"I don't know," she said again, adding a shrug. "My focus right now is on my sons." Her eyes became moist. "Thanks again, June."

"Hey. It's what we do."

"Do you think…" She paused, took a breath and said, "Do you think we'll ever be friends?"

"I think we could be. Now."

Jurea and Wanda shared a mattress on the floor of one bedroom while Clinton had another bedroom to himself. With the transformation that was taking over the town in preparation for the harvest festival, neither of the kids could seem to settle down to sleep. With the weather getting colder, they liked to burn a fire every night, but the fire in this fireplace didn't fill the house with smoke the way it happened in their old shanty.

On the weekend, Clinton was going to help George Fuller in the café with dishes and cleaning up. There would be a million people in town, and even with all his employees and family, George wouldn't be able to keep up.

Wanda was going to earn a little extra money by

helping Julianna Dickson keep track of the children. After she completed the Red Cross baby-sitting course at school, she'd be able to do a little baby-sitting after school and on weekends.

Jurea, who was learning to use the gas oven, was going to help the Presbyterian women at the cake walk...and she'd provided a cake she'd made herself. Her very first.

There was only one pall on an otherwise vastly improved lifestyle for the Mulls—Clarence had chosen to remain in the forest. But in the early morning when Jurea opened the door to the brightness of dawn, she found some fresh trout from a forest stream and knew that he had been there. He was getting closer every day. And one day soon he would knock, enter and perhaps decide to stay a while.

She smiled her little lopsided smile and blew a kiss in the direction of the trees.

Twenty-One

Myrna and her attorney had been investigating and plotting and were about to stage a coup so unconventional, it probably should be filmed. Alas, that wouldn't do. It would only serve to distract the participants. But Myrna had taken copious notes and she would be writing another mystery next year, after all.

The only thing left to chance was the food to be served at this most unusual dinner party. Even with Myrna and both Barstows combining their efforts, there wasn't a decent cook among them.

"I wish you'd told me," Cutler said. "I can do a number of things with chicken breasts."

"That's very kind of you," Myrna said. "But since I had already given you so much to do, it never occurred to me to ask you to cook, too."

Once Myrna and Cutler had done their own research and investigating, Cutler personally issued invitations to this exceptional dinner party. Included were ADA Marge Glaser, Paul Faraday, Cutler and Myrna, of course, and a certain forensic anthropologist by the name of Niles Galbraith.

"This could be construed as ex-parte communication," Marge Glaser had said.

"How so?" Cutler countered. "I'll be present as Mrs. Claypool's representative."

"Mr. Faraday is a prosecution witness and you have to have a court order to depose him."

"After dinner, we won't need one," Cutler said. "Oh, speaking of dinner, I'm not sure how to approach this, but I've dined with Mrs. Claypool a couple of times and she, well, isn't what I'd call the best cook in the world."

Marge Glaser's eyebrows lifted suddenly. "She isn't planning to poison us all, is she?" she asked.

"Well, you might think so, but she's merely a terrible cook. Have a little something on your way to the party so you don't go away starving. That's all."

Paul Faraday had been much easier to convince. "Mrs. Claypool would like to have you to dinner and explain everything about the disappearance of her husband," Cutler had said. "She thinks that, since your interest provokes this confession, you should be included."

"Marvelous!" Faraday replied. "May I bring a tape recorder?"

"Oh, by all means," Cutler assured him.

As they prepared for the evening, lighting the candelabra on the formal dining-room table, Myrna said, "I do wish this weren't such a hectic week for our little dinner party. Ordinarily I'd invite my niece, my brother, my poker table. But with the festival starting in just two days, they're all much too busy. Tell me, Cutler, will you be attending the festival?"

"I wouldn't miss it. Perhaps I should escort you?"

She pinched his roundish cheek. "Cutler, if I were sixty years younger and if you could tuck your shirt in..."

As had become something of a ritual, Cutler and Myrna had their martinis at five in the sitting room with a fire blazing in the hearth. Company would arrive at six. Cutler raised his glass to Myrna and said, "I want you to know, this has been a very pleasurable murder case for me, Mrs. Claypool."

"And for me, Cutler," she replied. "Once we've had done with these legal people and our bird-watcher, you must call me Myrna."

"With pleasure. Will you call me John?"

"Cutler suits you so much better."

"Then Cutler it is."

The sound of something breaking followed by shrill bickering came from the kitchen. Cutler jumped, sloshing a bit of his martini onto the Oriental rug.

"My apologies, Cutler. It's the Barstows. That's why I always have them here one at a time. They can't be in the same room together without constantly arguing."

"Have they ever actually come to blows?"

"Several times. But with age, they do less damage. They do try your patience at times though."

"Mrs. Claypool, just once more before the guests arrive...have you any idea whatsoever what might've happened to Morton? Mr. Claypool?"

"I've often suspected another woman, but I just

can't imagine what another woman would want with Morton. He wasn't rich, handsome or humorous.''

''Yet you were fond of him.''

''Well, for a while I was. But you must remember, he read my manuscripts and offered suggestions to make them better. I found his input valuable.''

The doorbell rang and there was a rapid shuffling from inside the kitchen. Myrna and Cutler leaned forward in their chairs to view the Barstows both trying to be first to the door. They ended up stuck in the frame, wriggling to get free.

''Well, for pity's sake,'' Myrna said, disgusted. She got to her feet quickly for a woman her age and answered the door personally. The Barstows withdrew into the kitchen, grumbling. ''Mr. Faraday, I knew you'd be the first to arrive! You must be eager to hear the story.''

He bowed elaborately. ''I'm very enthusiastic. I thank you for including me.''

''It wouldn't be a celebration without you,'' she said, turning to walk back into the house, leaving him to follow.

''Celebration?'' he asked eagerly. ''What are we celebrating?''

Cutler stood, extending his hand. ''If there's one thing I've learned, we don't want to get ahead of Mrs. Claypool. John Cutler... How do you do? Martini?''

''Don't mind if I do,'' Faraday said, his teeth appearing to grow even larger in his happiness.

The doorbell rang again and there was again a shuffle in the kitchen, but this time only one Barstow appeared. She made a face as she passed the sitting room. "How grand, Endeara. You're learning to share," Myrna said with a sneer.

Endeara took a wrap from Ms. Glaser and led her to the sitting room. Marge Glaser followed slowly, distracted by the old and eccentric arrangement of furnishings and doodads. The knight's armor just inside the foyer had her attention for several seconds. Finally she made it to the room where the others waited, a rather glazed look in her eyes. Myrna and the gentlemen stood. "How do you do, Ms. Glaser," she said. "It's so nice to see you again."

"Again? Have we been introduced?"

"Not formally, but of course you're very well known around Grace Valley," Myrna said, and enjoyed the way Ms. Glaser seemed to puff up a bit. "Martini?"

"Thank you, no. Have you something a bit lighter?"

"A Chablis, perhaps?"

"Perfect," she said. She extended a hand to the men, each in turn. "Mr. Faraday. Mr. Cutler."

The doorbell rang again. "Ah, the mystery guest," Myrna said, nearly giggling. While Amelia brought the young gentleman into the sitting room, Endeara delivered the Chablis to Ms. Granger.

Cutler and Niles Galbraith shook hands, obviously renewing their acquaintance. "Drink?" Cutler asked him.

Niles carried a large accordion folder, which he put to rest beside a vacant chair before the introductions were made. He accepted the offered martini, took a generous sip and sighed in appreciation.

"Ms. Marge Glaser, Mrs. Myrna Claypool, Mr. Paul Faraday, I'd like you to meet an old friend of mine, Niles Galbraith," said Cutler. "Niles and I attended undergrad together at Stanford University. It's been at least a year since we've seen each other."

"Pleasure, Mr. Galbraith," Paul Faraday said. "And what is it you do?"

With a slight nod of his head, he said, "I'm a forensic anthropologist. I specialize in old bones."

Expectedly, both Marge and Paul frowned, but there was no need to panic. If they went to trial, naturally Mrs. Claypool and her attorney would supply expert witnesses of their own to try to rebuke the prosecution's experts. This was only premature, not unexpected.

With precision timing, the dinner bell chimed and Myrna led her party into the dining room. "Cutler," Myrna said, "you and I will share the heads of the table. Ms. Glaser, on my right, if you please. Mr. Galbraith, on my left. And Mr. Faraday, if you'll sit beside Cutler, you'll find there's plenty of room for your tape recorder. How's that now?"

"Tape recorder?" Marge asked, holding her Chablis.

"Mr. Faraday was most polite in asking," Myrna said. "I suppose he could have hidden it and tricked us all. But I encouraged him. I told him if he wanted to, he could consider this a deposition."

"Jesus," Marge muttered, taking a drink. She

looked around the ornately cluttered dining room. "This is…really…quite something, Mrs. Claypool."

"Isn't it? After those investigators were here, it took Endeara and Amelia forever to put the place to rights again. They've been even grouchier than usual."

One would think that salad could hardly be hurt by preparation, but unfortunately Endeara favored greens suspended in unflavored gelatin with a scoop of mayonnaise on top. It was during the salad that Myrna slowly told the story of how she met and married Morton.

Next came a rice soup with a bitter root added. It was Amelia's contribution and made everyone at the table grimace. Fortunately, bread and butter, hard to ruin, came at the same time. During this course, Myrna told the story of how Morton seemed to drift off without anyone, including herself, seeming to notice.

"I know that seems strange," Myrna said. "But to tell the truth, I didn't mind that he was coming to Grace Valley less and less…and I didn't rely on Morton for anything, really. Oh, it's true that once I noticed he had been gone for several months, I was hurt. After that, I wouldn't have welcomed him back unless he could come up with a story that included critical injury or imprisonment."

"Did you search for him, Mrs. Claypool?" Faraday wanted to know.

"Not at that time, I did not. I was just a little miffed, you see. And I assumed if something terrible had happened, I'd have been notified. But remember, his absences had been growing. I suspected another woman. Incidentally, I still do."

Eyebrows lifted all around the table.

The main course was delivered. A savory roast smothered in onions and mushrooms with a halo of fluffy white potatoes surrounding it. To everyone's surprise, it was delicious. It melted in the mouth. "Mrs. Claypool, this is delightful!" Cutler said.

"Ah, yes, Endeara's mystery meat. Don't ask."

Marge Glaser, a pet owner and lover, put down her fork, but the others kept eating.

During that course, Myrna explained what she had learned in her more recent research, that Morton had taken retirement from his company and received a modest pension for five years after disappearing from her life. His check was delivered to a post office box in Redding, California. There didn't seem to be anyone available to bear witness as to who had picked up that check, but the original contract for the box was signed by Morton. Myrna and Cutler had a copy of the signature and it appeared identical to other signatures in her possession. At the end of five years the company had declared bankruptcy. The pension funds had been mismanaged and were gone. At that time, Morton, who was a few years older than Myrna, would have been eligible for social security, but he didn't collect it. "For the five years he collected a pension, he paid into social security, but when the pension was gone, he didn't file to collect. We were unable to find a death certificate. Oh…and he never again filed a tax return.''

"Can you explain this?'' Ms. Glaser wanted to know.

"I have theories, but they're only theories,'' Myrna said. "He might've left the country. He might've died. He might've died years before he stopped collecting his pension checks and perhaps someone collected them feloniously. But I can assure you it wasn't me. And if you want a complete accounting of my financial affairs for the last twenty years, you are welcome to them.

"But now, with the dessert, I think it's time to talk about someone else at this table.''

Myrna and Paul Faraday met eyes, but Marge Glaser only said, "What's for dessert?'' She hadn't taken Cutler's advice. She was starving.

"Peach cobbler and coffee,'' Myrna said, smiling. "I admit to bringing some of this on myself,'' Myrna continued while the Barstows served dessert. "I've had a good time at Morton's expense in the plotting of my suspense and mystery novels. If you had known Morton, you'd know how much he'd actually *like* that! People around here have speculated for a long time. If he's missing and she keeps writing these stories about missing husbands buried in the flower garden, could she have?''

"Hardly anyone has ever taken the bait as far as you, Faraday,'' Cutler said. "Did Mr. Faraday tell you, Marge, that he writes true-crime dramas and hopes to do a story on Mrs. Claypool's murder of Mr. Claypool? Of course, he would have told you...."

"Why else would I be investigating the widow and her property," Faraday said somewhat shortly.

"Why else indeed," Myrna said, dipping into her peach cobbler. "You haven't had the greatest success with your books, have you, Paul? Pity. Seems you need something with more of a kick to it."

Marge Glaser took a bite of her cobbler and made a face. "*Bllllkkkkk.* What in the world could you do to cobbler to make it taste like it has shoe polish in it?"

"Oh dear, I hope you're not right. Though the Barstows do have very strange tastes. Well, the coffee is good, dear. If you don't like the cobbler, we'll leave it for the cats.

"As I was saying, Mr. Faraday was looking for a story with a little more kick to it, so he decided to dig up some proof that I murdered my husband and buried him on Hudson House property. But you couldn't find any bones, could you, Mr. Faraday?"

Faraday frowned. "Where is this going?"

"But," Cutler said, "Faraday has friends who teach at the college of medicine, don't you, Paul? All you had to do was find the *right* bones. You asked for the twenty-year-old bones of a sixty-something-year-old man. Right?"

"Bloody nonsense," he said, but he flicked the tape recorder off.

"Turn that back on, please," Marge asked a little

too politely. "Did you go looking for bones to plant?"

"That's absurd. Why would I do something like that?"

"Mr. Faraday was seen visiting with friends around the anatomy, physiology and anthropology departments. That's why I invited my old friend, Niles, to dinner tonight."

All eyes turned to Niles. Niles, by the way, had eaten everything but the soup. He reached into his accordion folder and pulled out a thin stack of stapled pages with letters, numbers, symbols, dashes, dots and periods. "I learned from John—or Cutler, as he's called around here—the name of the individual doing the tests for the prosecutor's office on these old bones." He handed the paper to Marge Glaser. "They're the twenty-year-old bones of a man around sixty-five, all right. Or men."

"Men?"

"The bones—four of them—come from four different bodies. While you were interested in the age, the sex and the length of time buried, it never occurred to you to ask how many different DNAs were represented. And since you don't have anything of the victim's to compare to the DNA here, I guess it wouldn't occur."

"So," Myrna said. "That's that. No body. Just a few old bones collected from the San Francisco School of Medicine by Mr. Faraday and tossed under my rhododendron. And what a mess was made of my house and yard. The Barstows are still complaining, although I did pay them overtime. If I weren't so old, Mr. Faraday, I believe I'd sue you.''

Ms. Glaser sipped her coffee and said, "Good God, what's in the coffee?''

Myrna held a napkin and slapped it onto the table. "You haven't been entirely pleasant this evening, and here I've made your job so painless.''

"She's right, Marge,'' Cutler said. "We could have saved all this for court, but frankly, we'd rather not go to court.''

"I'd like to go to court,'' Niles Galbraith said. "I love going to court. I do it all the time. I'm a professional expert witness. I get a thousand dollars an hour.''

"Well, you may get your chance,'' Marge said, standing. She walked around the table, clicked off the tape recorder, popped out the tape and tossed it up in the air, catching it in the other hand. "If we prosecute Mr. Faraday for planting artificial evidence, for obstruction of justice, for fraud. Let's see, there must be more....''

"Ms. Glaser, there's absolutely no reason you should believe this eccentric old woman over—''

"*You*, Mr. Faraday?'' She made a half bow in the direction of Myrna. "Thank you for dinner and for your most delightful company, Mrs. Claypool. Our office will be in touch.''

"Do you have groundskeepers at your office, Ms. Glaser?''

"I'm certain we do, Mrs. Claypool.''

"Do you suppose the district attorney's office

would consider loaning them to me in the spring? To clean up that horrid mess out there?''

"I'll mail you a form for restitution, how's that? And now, my coat?''

Myrna rang the dinner bell, and Ms. Glaser's coat, as well as Mr. Faraday's coat and hat, were delivered by the Barstows. Ms. Glaser stomped toward the door with Faraday stumbling behind her, babbling.

"Thank you for coming," Myrna called. "Do come again.''

The only reply was the closing of the door. Myrna, Cutler and Niles were left in the dining room.

"Now, wasn't that a pleasant evening," Myrna said.

Getting ready for the festival was almost as much fun for the town as the event itself. Thursday night saw townsfolk completing their own booths and decorations, the erection of the stage, the arranging of games and prizes. Once the Thursday preparations were complete, the town filled with strangers. Vendors who traveled from town fair to town fair would converge on Grace Valley early on Friday and begin setting up their wares—every form of art and craft imaginable. On Saturday the public would come, hundreds if not thousands. And on Sunday night, the people would drift away, the vendors would pack up and Grace Valley would go back to its old self again, with a few extra bucks for town use in the coffers.

One of the most sought-after prizes at the festival was the quilt of the town designed and sewn by Birdie

and her group. It was proudly hung in its own booth
and beside it was a clear plastic barrel. Chances were
sold for five dollars and the money would be donated
to benefit the town.

They did the town quilt every year and it was always just a little different than the one before, but it
always had the important buildings represented. This
year they had added characters. John and June stood
outside the clinic, Tom Toopeek and his SUV were
outside the police department, George Fuller was beside the café, Burt Crandall near the bakery, Sam Cussler with his fishing pole beside the garage, Harry
Shipton beside the church and a little pixie with white
springy hair in the gardens of Hudson House.

When the Thursday-night preparations were near-
ing completion, George brought out a couple of huge
vats of ice cream with bowls and spoons. George's
oldest son set up the disc player and speakers on the
stage and turned up the volume for the crowd of volunteers that had gathered behind the café and church.

John Stone was still having trouble walking without pain, his buttocks looking a lot like blueberry
marble, but he was glad to be part of the decorating
and congregating. Because it was getting late and the
volunteers were mostly middle-aged, George's son
kept the music light. John heard the music and saw
Susan helping Birdie hang the quilt. He went over to
the booth and came up behind his wife. He put his
arms around her from behind and she, remarkably,
leaned back against him.

"John, have you ever seen a more beautiful quilt?" she asked.

"Never. We'll buy a bunch of chances."

He pulled her away from Birdie's quilt, and right there, in the yard behind the café, he took her in his arms and began to slow dance with her. "John!" she said, sweetly surprised. "Are you sure you're up to this? What about your…"

"My bruised butt? Hurts like the devil," he said. "But not feeling close to you has hurt more."

"Oh, John."

"Can I tell you something?"

"Please…let's not argue about our roles anymore."

"It's not about that. It's about the accident and my trip down into the ravine. I've had lots of emergencies in my day, but nothing like that, ever. You know what my emergencies have been like—you were there for a lot of them. Scrubbed, sterile, struggling to save a life under the most advanced and pristine of conditions…and even *that* could get my adrenaline pumping for hours if not days. But this time…" He pulled her closer.

"Not advanced…not pristine…not sterile," she added.

"No. There, by the side of the road was a young boy, bleeding, possibly dying. And at the bottom of the hill, another. Their car hanging in the trees like an apparition. The nearest hospital miles and miles away. Country medicine. Do you know how it made me feel?"

"Inadequate?" she suggested.

"Yeah." He laughed. "And alive. Never more alive. When I got to that accident site, my first thought was that I wished you had come with me. You're the kind of nurse who can anticipate a doctor's needs accurately, assist perfectly, keep the pace, move the doctor along when he or she lags, reassure the patient confidently. You're the best nurse I've ever worked with. And I was so ashamed that I'd ever discouraged you in any way. Not only does the clinic need you, medicine needs you. Susan, do you think you'll ever forgive me?"

She looked up into his eyes with tears in her own. "John, do you really mean that?"

"You can't know how much I mean it. I'm just sorry that it took a near-fatal accident for me to see it. To *really* see it."

"I wondered if you'd ever again respect me and my skills in the way you did when we first met. I've hungered for that."

"I don't know what happened to me, Susan. You and June were completely right—I was so stupid!"

"June said you were stupid? I thought she was staying out of our little tiff."

"She's much nosier than she looks." He kissed the top of her head. "I know I still have amends to make, but are you going to eventually forgive me?"

"Eventually," she said, but she said it with a smile.

"And are we going to have sex again?"

"Eventually," she said. "John?"

"Hmm?" he said, holding her close, dancing with her.

"I do love you," she said.

He stopped dancing and looked down at her. "I love you," he said.

He lifted her chin and kissed her deeply. Her arms went around him, holding him closely as she moved under his lips. There was a promise in the kiss. And when they broke apart they were met by the applause of all the festival volunteers.

Susan laughed, covering her mouth in embarrassment. John bowed.

Since there was no hospital within two hundred miles where June wasn't known, it was pointless to travel far for her ultrasound. She went to Rockport's Valley Hospital and tried to relax about the whole thing.

When the technician called her into the room, June said curtly, "No one knows about this pregnancy except me, my doctor and now you." She left out Elmer and the baby's father on purpose, hoping to cow the technician into enforced silence. "Of course, Doctor" was all that was said in reply.

While she lay there, her belly jellied, she felt her heart begin to race in excitement.

"Tell me what you want to know," the technician said. "It's up to you."

"Just turn the monitor so I can see it better," she said, this time keeping the shortness out of her voice.

The image came into view, faded as the wand was moved, came into specific relief again, faded again.

"I'm looking for a due date," June said somewhat absently.

"We'll send the film to your OB, who can provide a more detailed summary, but it looks…it looks…"

"Four months," June said in an almost reverent breath. How had this baby grown so much without her knowledge? So fast? Where had her mind been.

"Looks very healthy, don't you think? And happy?"

June squinted, looking for the happiness in the image, and then saw what she hadn't been looking for, but sprang out at her just the same.

"Yes," June said. "She does look happy."

And then she cried again.

Twenty-Two

The transformation of the town began at dawn, with the first sounds of a semi-flatbed hauling a load of portable public potties. Not long after that the engines of trucks, vans, SUVs, RVs and cars were added as vendors began to arrive and set up their booths. Then came the sound of voices, laughter, hauling, hammering and the greetings of friends as artisans who traveled to weekend fairs found themselves running into acquaintances they hadn't seen in months.

June and John watched the activity from the steps of the clinic. Every year, George Fuller, Sam Cussler and Burt Crandall, who all had businesses on Valley Drive—the main drag—headed up the committee that organized the space for the vendors. June elbowed John when she noticed, with some surprise, Sam holding a clipboard in the middle of the street, directing people this way and that. She hadn't expected Sam to be up to the job; no one had. In fact, Elmer had come into town early to help, expecting his old friend to be beset with grief and therefore unavailable.

"Sam? What's he doing here?" John asked.

"What he does every year," June said. "Helping set up for the festival. He's going to have to operate the gas station this weekend if these people are to get out of town when it's over."

"You'd think he'd get a replacement," John said.

"I should have known he'd be here. This town is his family. He'd feel better being a part of it." She pointed to the booth set up just in front of the Flower Shoppe. "I think Justine's sisters are going to keep her booth open and sell the dried-flower arrangements that she worked on."

"Man," John said, scratching his chin. "People around here certainly persevere."

"Don't we?" she returned with a smile, giving him a playful swat on the rump, bringing a yelp out of him. "Sure was sweet the way you and Susan made up last night. You're the talk of the town, you know. Lovebirds."

He looked down into her eyes and a sly, crooked grin began to blossom on his face. "I'm sure that will change soon," he teased. "Someone else is going to be all the talk."

"No question about it," she said. "Let's go over our clinic hours. Inside."

"Yes'm, boss," he said, following her.

No one seemed to notice an armed man in camouflage lurking behind houses and garages, his beret pulled low, antiglare paint on his cheekbones, as he watched the gathering of vendors suspiciously.

Inside the clinic, June, John, Jessie and Susan leaned over Jessie's desk and studied the schedule. The clinic would have to remain open during the hours that the harvest festival ran. Friday was limited to emergency patients only. There were no scheduled appointments as a couple hundred visiting artisans would be getting their thumbs in the way of their hammers, tripping over their wares and stepping on their tools and twisting ankles.

"My dad and Blake Norton from Rockport are both volunteers for day shifts—Dad on Saturday and Blake on Sunday. Blake's nurse, Lisa, is going to volunteer both afternoons, but Susan, it would help if we could have you on call."

"I'll be on call, too," Jessie said. "I can help in the clinic, but I can also watch Sydney if Susan is called in."

"That's good, Jessie, thanks. This is all just as a precaution. Most of our work is going to be simple first aid, and a physician can handle it without help, just as an RN can."

"The Dicksonses have hired Wanda Mull to help watch the kids," Susan said. "I think that will include Sydney most of the time. You can hardly separate Sydney and Lindsey."

"Isn't that nice," June said. "I'm so glad people are including Wanda."

"And Clinton is going to be helping George and his son," Susan added. "And Jurea actually managed to bake a cake for the cake walk the church is putting on. It was her fourth or fifth try, but it turned out well."

When June found out that Jurea had moved back into the little house with her children, she had told Susan, who'd spread the word to some of the other

Presbyterian Women. They had reached out to Jurea, pulling her into their fold, helping her with some of the new challenges she faced. Though she'd been in town for months, she avoided using the stove; it made her nervous. Some of the women from church showed her how.

"I wonder if Clarence will ever come around," Susan said, thinking aloud.

In fact, that's exactly what Clarence was doing—coming around. He was lurking close to their house, making sure that Jurea and the children were safe. And he was growing increasingly alarmed by all the activity in the town. It looked, for all intents and purposes, like an invasion.

With the leaves wearing their jackets of copper, orange, red and burgundy, the air a clean and crisp breath of fall, the streets of the valley filled to capacity. Ricky Rios's car blocked the street at the west end while Deputy Lee Stafford's car blocked the street at the east. Within lay the wares of many, from paintings to pots, T-shirts to saddles, relishes to soy nuts. Clowns sold balloons twisted into animal shapes, artists drew caricatures and junk food of every stripe took over the diets of hundreds.

When the elder Doc Hudson arrived at the clinic to spell John, the latter said, "The bulk of my business has been dosing antacids."

To which Elmer said, "Thanks, I think I'm needing some myself."

There was a rented truck parked behind the church

with a padlock on the door. It seemed to be in the charge of Pastor Shipton, who refused to reveal the contents, until Tom Toopeek inquired on behalf of the law. Harry whispered in Tom's ear. Tom chuckled lightly and turned away to other business.

In the sunniest part of the afternoon, the pastor backed the truck up to the end of the street where it was blocked, right in the middle of the street, between the clinic and the church, and unloaded was a large container made out of some kind of strong plastic. Pastor Shipton ran a hose out to the big box, and while it filled, he set up a folding table about twenty feet away and unloaded a bucket of balls. It appeared the pastor had rented himself a dunking booth, but he wouldn't give any information to the curious crowd that began to form. And just as the pastor would have planned it, most of the onlookers were townsfolk.

June, a huge cotton candy in her fist, was drawn to the sight, as was Elmer. "What's this?" she asked.

"No one seems to know," Elmer said. "What are you eating?"

"What does it look like I'm eating?"

"Should you be eating that junk?"

"Shh. I'm a *doctor*."

Elmer sighed in frustration. "The cobbler's children have no shoes."

"Ladies and gentlemen," Harry Shipton finally shouted into a microphone, "While we're waiting for this tank to fill with icy-cold water, can I take a minute to thank the Presbyterian Women for all the hard work they've put into the festival. Ladies, are you around here?"

A couple of women came forward and gave a wave.

"How about Susan Stone? Susan?" She walked over and lifted a hand in a half wave, then tried to escape, but Harry held on to her. "Stay here a second, Susan. Julianna Dickson? Are you here?"

"She's back there!" someone yelled.

"Well, get her up here! We need her."

"Pastor, what's going on?" Susan asked.

"Just a little fun, Susan. You deserve to take your best shot."

"What?"

Julianna came through the crowd holding the baby and dragging a four-year-old. "What?" she said.

"We've had a situation in our town that's been almost impossible to ignore. Well, okay, we didn't try very hard to ignore it, but not because we're *nosey*. It's because we care so much about each other. We have a couple of guys, a couple of our best Grace Valley guys, who find the need to make amends with those they've insulted. Yes, ladies and gentlemen, we have a couple of good, well-meaning guys, some of our best, who are seriously in the doghouse."

People began to cheer and applaud.

Harry went around to the back of the tank, which was open about halfway, and stuck his hand in. "Oh boy. Cold. We're looking for *amends*, here." There were more cheers.

"Now, ladies, it has come to the attention of the

town that you two have put your husbands in the dog-house—and deservedly so. But we all think the time has come to give them a chance to make some amends, get themselves back in your good graces. Don't we, folks?'' The crowd cheered in response. ''Guys? You ready, guys?''

They came out of the side door of the church, prancing. John was wearing a short, tight, turquoise wet suit and his daughter's water wings. Mike was wearing an old-fashioned gentleman's bathing suit, circa 1900, and carrying a parasol.

They came together in front of the tank and lifted their arms high in the air, as if in victory. Then they split apart and, going back to the opened truck, lifted out a large prop and carried it to the front of the tank. They leaned the painted prop of a doghouse against the tank to the absolute delight of the crowd.

''Now,'' Harry said to the women. ''Who wants to go first?''

''Oh, let me,'' Julianna said, handing Harry the baby and giving Susan the hand of the four-year-old.

Mike took a bow and turned the tank. With John's help a plastic backdrop was raised to catch the balls.

The crowd went nuts as Julianna took her stance as a pitcher with blood lust in her eyes. Mike cautiously climbed onto the seat so it looked as though he sat inside the doghouse.

The first two balls missed and the crowd moaned miserably. But the third hit. Mike crashed into the ice-cold water, and the cheers could be heard in the next town.

Mike dragged himself out of the icy water, shivering, his lips blue, and yelled. "You keep pitching those balls till you love me again, baby!"

"Get back on your perch, Mike, darling," she yelled back.

"Don't be a pig about it, Julianna," Susan pleaded.

All in all, Mike went down five times, John three. Susan went easy on John because of the condition of his butt. But never in the history of the Grace Valley Harvest Festival had amends been so gloriously met.

Although Tom didn't attend the festival to enjoy himself, he never failed to. There was rarely any trouble. Oh, there was the odd fight that started with arguing and ended in fisticuffs, the occasional drunk who needed a place to sleep it off. But basically the festival was a chance for people to come together and do something for each other, for their town.

The Saturday-evening festivities were going to kick off with a presentation from the high-school choir, then a couple of local bands—one rock for the young set, a group with a slower tempo for romantics—would set up on the stage and provide the music for dancing. The lanterns would soon be lit, the small bonfire in the middle of the park would warm the stargazers, and then they would sleep fast and do another day of festivities.

The fall festival also proved to be a time of coming together, year after year, without that ever being the conscious plan of the committee. This year was no exception. He noticed that Daniel, Blythe and Sarah had set up pony rides just at the edge of town—their way of breaking the town into the truth, Daniel and Blythe were brother and sister. Sarah would soon join their family as a wife and sister-in-law. She was sporting a generous diamond engagement ring, while Blythe was wearing a handsome gold bracelet. Tom bet if he could get it off her, he would find some kind of sentimental engraving. But the most important fact was that all three looked content.

"Officer, is there going to be some sort of military presentation?" a woman asked.

"I don't think so, but I'm not privy to all the goings-on. Maybe the high-school color guard is here."

"Oh. No, I was thinking of some combat-type exhibition. I saw someone in fatigues."

"Could be army personnel here. We have an army post not far…"

"With his face painted?"

"Face…? Ma'am, you saw a military man in fatigues with face paint? At the festival?"

"Well, no. Back there." She pointed. "Behind that house. The garage, really."

"Hmm," Tom said, looking. "I wonder if the school's ROTC group has something going on."

He drifted away from the woman and tried to melt into the crowd, out of sight. He didn't like the feeling he was getting. He slipped around to the back of the clinic, then into the neighborhood east of the roadblock. He tried to creep around behind a couple of houses without looking as if he was creeping, but for a man Tom's size, that wasn't easily done.

It didn't take him long to spot. Clarence. He was all done up like a Ranger, complete with a branch of something in his hat and greasepaint on his face. Clarence crouched behind a bush at the side of a shed in a backyard, far enough from the crowd to keep from drawing too much attention to himself, yet frighteningly close with a gun. Fortunately for Tom, Clarence was not as good at not being seen as he probably once had been.

Tom went back around the block, quickly. He found Lee Stafford leaning against his car, talking to a neighbor. Tom drew him away and whispered in his ear. Then he went across the street to the café. There he found Clinton with a big rack of glasses to wash. "Hey, Clinton, take a break. I need you a minute."

"What's up, Chief Toopeek?" the boy asked.

"Come with me, will you? George, I need Clinton a minute. He'll be back."

"Sure thing," George said.

"Follow me, son," Tom said. Clinton tossed aside his apron and went along. Tom led the way, but didn't explain until they were well away from the people. "It's your dad, Clinton. He's acting out."

"Oh man, what's he doing?" Clinton fairly whined.

"I'm not sure. He's all done up for combat, carrying his gun. He seems to be spying on the fair. He might be thinking he's in country again."

"His PTSD might be acting up," Clinton said.

"I'd like to get him in custody with as little commotion as possible. I don't expect we can talk him out of any delusions he's having, but I'm afraid we're going to have to get him out of here and disarm him. It's got too much potential to turn bad.''

"I know, Chief. I'll go with you.''

"Has he ever had trouble recognizing you?''

"Not that I ever noticed.''

"Are you comfortable walking up to him?''

Clinton shrugged. "I lived with him for sixteen years. I reckon I can walk up to him.''

"If you can do that, I'll come around the back. Clinton, I'm going to have to cuff him. I don't want to hurt him, but I don't expect he'll come along on request.''

Clinton hung his head for a moment, then lifted it again. "I understand.''

Tom didn't really think Clarence would open fire on the crowd, but then, who knew what fragile hold he had on reality. One thing was certain—he had to get Clarence out of there, get his gun, get him taken care of.

"Maybe this is a good thing, Chief,'' Clinton said. "If he gets in enough trouble, gets himself locked up, they'll put him back on his drugs. It might set him to rights again.''

Tom clamped a hand on the boy's shoulder. Clinton was a big kid. If not for the fact that he wore a prosthetic leg, he could do some real damage for the football team. He was brave. He'd been through a lot. "I'll hope for that, Clinton. Let's go.''

Clinton walked straight down the street toward the house behind which his father crouched. Tom went through the backyards, sticking to the shadows, skirting close to houses and garages. Clinton walked up the driveway of the house while Tom, staying low, crept around the back.

"Daddy?" Clinton called. "What you doing back there, Daddy?"

"Clinton! Get down! They'll see you!"

"Who's gonna see me, Daddy?"

"The whole village has been invaded! Are you blind? I'll get you and your mama out of there in—"

He was cut off as Tom hit him from behind, knocking the rifle from his hands. They rolled onto the ground. They were much the same size and Clarence was unexpectedly strong. Tom got him facedown on the ground, a knee in his back, and managed to cuff his wrists together behind him. "Easy, Clarence, easy. You're going to be okay now."

"What the hell you doing, Injun? We got us an invasion here!"

Tom sat back on his heels, winded. "Yeah, I know. We'll take it from here. Clinton, go find Deputy Stafford. He's waiting. Tell him to bring around the car."

"Sure. Can I go with my dad?"

"'Course you can, son. We'll get in touch with the VA, have somebody come out for him right away."

Clinton crouched down and rubbed a hand along his father's greasy forehead. "It's going to be okay now, Daddy. You'll see."

June sat on the top of a picnic table and watched her friends and neighbors dance to some of the best crooning around. The band was from Westport and specialized in love songs to dance to. Apparently Nat King Cole was a personal favorite. John and Susan were back in each other's arms. The Dicksons, too, had mended their fences and danced not far away.

But there were some other fun couples worth watching. Aunt Myrna waltzed with her young attorney and they looked to be having a real time of it. Birdie and Judge cut a mean rug with something that resembled the rumba. Then there was Elmer rocking along with Jessie. And there were the two who weren't present but had been mentioned many times over the weekend—Chris and Nancy. They were at the hospital, but at least they were together.

Some couples in town had presented images that were not true, she realized. Blythe and Daniel, thought to be married for over thirty years, were not married at all. And her old beau, thought to be divorced, was barely on hiatus from his marriage. And then, she thought with a sly smile, there was herself, the spinster town doctor... Oh, there were going to be some raised eyebrows.

She pulled her sweater tighter around her, chilled even though she sat near the fire. She looked down at her dusty boots and when she looked up, he was standing there in front of her. She had to blink to clear her vision, because he had shaved. His cheek, scarred from his fall last summer, was ruddy and rough-looking. But it was the best-looking cheek she'd ever seen.

"You!" she said in a breath. "How did you...?"

"It's not important how. What's important is, I'm here to stay."

"With me?"

He reached for her hand. "Try to get rid of me." He pulled her off the picnic table and into his arms, leading her to the asphalt where everyone danced.

"I didn't expect you so soon. Do you know what this means?"

"What?"

"That I don't have to try to hold my stomach in anymore!"

Anyone who saw the way he laughed, like the jest had been the most intimate, and the way he pulled her closer, would have known everything that very moment. And they watched. The town watched. Though Jim tried to be discreet, his lips found her neck and his large hand slid over the slightly round spot on her abdomen. As if on cue, there was the slightest flutter within. He jumped back in surprise, looking down at June.

"She's been a little feisty. I might've given her too much cotton candy."

"She?"

June nodded. "What do you think of that?"

"That's perfect," he said.

It was all John and Susan could do to keep their feet moving. Elmer led Jessie to the side, stopped dancing and stared. Tom Toopeek wasn't dancing anyway, but he was leaning a hip against a picnic table on which Ursula sat. His wife had been talking when Tom suddenly quit listening, crossed his arms over his broad chest and smiled a secret smile.

"Who is that, Tom? Who is that dancing with June?"

"I can't say for certain, but I think he's going to be a new neighbor," Tom said.

"But who—"

June and Jim danced, whispered, held each other close. They were oblivious to the stares because they had each other. But the whole town watched, because she belonged to them. And they knew, though they hadn't been told.

Their doctor was deep in love.

USA TODAY Bestselling Author

ANNE STUART

For Sophie Davis, turning Stonegate Farm into a quaint country inn is
the fulfillment of a lifelong dream. She doesn't even mind that the
farm was the scene of a grisly murder twenty years earlier....

When a stranger moves in next to the farm, Sophie believes
the sense of peace she has created is threatened. Because there's
something different about John Smith. It's clear he's come to Colby,
Vermont, for a reason…and that reason has something to do
with Sophie and Stonegate Farm.

Now her dream is becoming a nightmare. Who is John Smith? Why
does his very presence make Sophie feel so completely out of control?
And why is she beginning to suspect that this mysterious stranger will
put in jeopardy everything she's dreamed of—maybe even her life?

STILL LAKE

"A master at creating chilling atmosphere."
—*Library Journal*

Available the first week of August 2002 wherever paperbacks are sold!

New York Times Bestselling Author

LINDA HOWARD

Claire Westerbrook found it hard to believe that Max Conroy
was truly interested in her. Then she discovered he wasn't—
he only wanted information about her boss. Max was studying
her company for a takeover and had decided the quickest
way to discover their secret was through her.

Now Claire wanted nothing to do with a man who could deceive her
with so little remorse. But Max wasn't leaving Houston without
acquiring everything he wanted. And that included Claire....

ALMOST FOREVER

"Without a doubt, Ms. Howard is an extraordinary talent."
—*Romantic Times*

Available the first week of August 2002
wherever paperbacks are sold!

ROBYN CARR

66839	THE WEDDING PARTY	___ $5.99 U.S.	___ $6.99 CAN.
66609	DEEP IN THE VALLEY	___ $5.99 U.S.	___ $6.99 CAN.
66545	THE HOUSE ON OLIVE STREET		
		___ $5.99 U.S.	___ $6.99 CAN.

(limited quantities available)

TOTAL AMOUNT	$_____
POSTAGE & HANDLING	$_____
($1.00 for 1 book, 50¢ for each additional)	
APPLICABLE TAXES*	$_____
TOTAL PAYABLE	$_____
(check or money order—please do not send cash)	

To order, complete this form and send it, along with a check or money order for the total above, payable to MIRA Books®, to: **In the U.S.:** 3010 Walden Avenue, P.O. Box 9077, Buffalo, NY 14269-9077; **In Canada:** P.O. Box 636, Fort Erie, Ontario, L2A 5X3.

Name:_____
Address:_____ City:_____
State/Prov.:_____ Zip/Postal Code:_____
Account Number (if applicable):_____
075 CSAS

*New York residents remit applicable sales taxes.
Canadian residents remit applicable GST and provincial taxes.

MIRA®

Visit us at www.mirabooks.com   MRC0802BL